PROVIDENCE

CRAIG WILLSE

PROVIDENCE

U

UNION
SQUARE
& CO.

UNION
SQUARE
&CO.

NEW YORK

ISBN 978-1-4549-5199-5 (paperback)
ISBN 978-1-4549-5200-8 (e-book)

For information about custom editions, special sales, and premium purchases, please contact specialsales@unionsquareandco.com.

Printed in Canada

2 4 6 8 10 9 7 5 3 1

unionsquareandco.com

Cover design by Melissa Farris
Interior design by Igor Satanovsky

Cover images: Addictive Creative/Offset by Shutterstock.com; dokudokunomi/Envato Elements (glass); Interior image: photopsist/Shutterstock.com

"For us there is only one season,
the season of sorrow."
—Oscar Wilde, *De Profundis* (1897)

PART I

CHAPTER 1

Before I completely destroyed my life, I taught English at Sawyer College in Ohio. I wasn't the world's greatest professor, but I also wasn't the worst—although it's possible I would become that. The position was an amazing opportunity, or at least that's what everyone kept telling me. When I got hired, someone from my grad program called it a "dream job," but in my wildest dreams, I'm definitely not attending mandatory trainings on "new innovations in learning outcomes assessment tools." Although to say I had bigger hopes for myself wouldn't quite be true, either. I never put a lot of time into hoping, or thinking about my own future. What I wanted—or even what I could want—did not often occur to me. I just kind of slogged forward through each day as best I could.

Of course, I was relieved when I got the job. After eight years in a PhD program, a two-year post-doc, and an increasingly desperate year of adjuncting (a sign of my desperation: I bought an LSAT study guide), I was panicking it might never happen. And then it did. The school was founded in 1850 in the town of Sawyer, smack in the middle of Ohio, by a bunch of Lutherans from Pennsylvania. Despite its location, or I guess because of it, the small school flourished, attracting the sons (and later, begrudgingly, daughters) of wealthy families who hoped the pastoral setting would inspire a seriousness of purpose. Some things had changed since then—like you no longer had to be white to attend. And the school was now secular, though a kind of Lutheran stinginess lived on in its motto:

vita studii, a life of study. But lots of things had not changed. Like many small, liberal arts colleges, Sawyer turned inward, shunning the locals and hiding behind its towering gray-green stone walls. In any given year, there were more first-year students from the Upper East Side than all of Ohio. After the last plastics factory shuttered its doors and shipped south to Mexico, townies were left with few options besides Walmart or McDonald's or—if you were lucky—cleaning up the shit and spills of Sawyer students. A life of study, indeed.

While obviously much better off, junior faculty were hardly rolling in money. After student loans, credit card debt, used car payments—there was nothing left. I tried to talk with my department chair, Susan, about when the college might lift its pay freeze. (The college president called it "a necessary tightening of belts as we ride out the aftermath of the recession"—he lived rent-free in a small mansion and made $460,000 a year.) Given the state of the academic job market, Susan thought I should consider myself lucky. "We had over three hundred applicants for your position," she told me, not for the first time. By May of that year, the monotony of it all had started to wear me down, and a simmering resentment kicked in. I'd arrive on campus already exhausted and park my sad little hatchback, hoping (after three recent stints in the shop) it would start when I returned at the end of the day. Crossing the lot, I'd pass students descending from gleaming, brand-new SUVs, shouting about plans to meet up in European towns I'd never even heard of, and I would think to myself—how did I end up here?

That summer, I stayed in Sawyer, supposedly to work on my book. I tormented myself through all of June, staring daily at the same blank Word document. By July I gave up, reasoning that I needed the constraints of a teaching schedule to motivate me. My first day back for the fall semester, I swore to god the hallways had shrunk, claustrophobic tunnels closing in around me, ricocheting with the hyped-up thrum of students as they reunited in boisterous, showy hugs—white teeth, fresh skin, clear eyes shining with anticipation of all the good things coming their way. I snaked along, hurrying past them, head down. Is this really my life? Is this everything?

And then, I met Tyler.

It was September 2012, the third week of the fall semester. A Tuesday. I had taught my morning Composition course. On my way to my next class, I stopped at the library to deal with some overdue fines. At the front desk, a work-study student played with her phone as I explained that while, yes, the books had been returned a few months late, faculty were exempt from penalties. Eventually, without a glance up, she tapped at a computer. "Okay," she said and sighed, then grabbed a book from the shelf behind her and passed it to me. "This came in for you." I had put in a request for it months ago and had forgotten all about it. I started to thank her but before I could say anything, she was back at her phone.

I checked the time—I was already late. I rushed from the library, down the steps, and across the quad, dodging a student making hazy, careless loops on a scooter. A group of boys, peacocking and shirtless, tossed a Frisbee across the grass. I made it to the building—TAFT HALL carved across the stone entrance in pious letters—and was about to sprint up the steps when the high snap of a voice stopped me. I turned to look. There, at the other side of the landing, two students stood, arguing. One was tall and broad-shouldered, high Roman forehead topped in a pile of dark curls. The other was smaller and stood rigid, legs clamped in a wide stance, as if to block any sudden movement. The morning sun caught his fairer hair, quick flashes of heat. He raised his voice again, but I couldn't make out the words. Whatever was going on, the taller one looked relaxed, almost leaning back, long ropey arms loose at his sides. I was wondering what could be such a matter of life and death to cause a scene like this when, above me, a voice called out—"Hey, Dr. Lausson, coming to class?" I looked up—a smiling student held the door for me.

The classroom was full, buzzing with conversation in my tardiness. It was a large group, or large for Sawyer—thirty students. I was still figuring out who they all were. I got set up at my desk and pulled out my copy of the day's reading—Patricia Highsmith's *The Talented Mr. Ripley*. The binding was split and a page slid out, worn from years of rereading. I tucked the page back in and raised the book. "Okay, sorry I'm late, let's get started. How is the Highsmith going?" A few heads nodded, a couple groans. The class was called *Sex and Death in American Literature*, which I thought was a fun idea, but I guess not everyone was convinced. "Let's stick with it and see what happens." Though we were reading from an earlier era—Highsmith published the novel in 1955—I told the class I wanted to deal with the book on its own terms, in its own period of history. And to try to hold off thoughts about what it meant for today. "And that includes its relationship to the movie."

Someone called out, "I could have just watched a movie?" The room laughed.

"Who said that?" A student cautiously raised a hand. "You don't know the film?" He shook his head. "Matt Damon? Jude Law?"

"Who?"

Laughs again.

"Wait. Who here knows the movie?" Not a single body stirred. "None of you?" I couldn't believe it. I, of course, had learned of the book from the movie, which came out—well, when I was their age, I guess. I could feel myself in the theater, seeing it for the first time. Terrified that everyone in the rows around me sensed the warmth spreading across my skin as I watched Jude Law lift himself from that bathtub, golden and dripping. And my cellular understanding that Matt Damon's eyes, lingering a moment too long, were my own. The students had probably seen much more than that on the internet before they even hit puberty. I sometimes forgot how much the world had changed in the fourteen or fifteen years between us.

"Well, speaking of history, now I'm feeling old." Some laughs again. "Let's pretend this didn't happen and get to the sex." A few more laughs, now some nervous. "It's okay, we can talk about sex, even if Highsmith won't." I explained that there wasn't much recent scholarship on the novel. Highsmith was considered a bit of a relic, an embarrassing reminder of a less liberated, more ambivalent time. A recent essay had declared the book "largely homophobic," which I found a shallow and obvious read. "Let's approach the text in terms of its honesty, which doesn't mean we have to like what it says. But let's try to understand it first. I want—"

The door in back swung open and two students stepped in. A young woman, loose sandy hair and a light, patrician smile. I couldn't recall her name—she hadn't joined any discussions these first few weeks. And beside her was the smaller of the two boys who'd been fighting outside. Had he been in my class and I'd never noticed? He grimaced and mouthed *sorry*. They slid together into a row in back, coffee cups in hand.

"Well," I said—I'd lost my train of thought—"let's take a look at the first chapter. Will someone read those opening paragraphs for us?" A student raised her hand. "Go ahead, Marissa."

Marissa began: "Chapter One. Tom glanced behind him and saw the man coming out of the Green Cage, heading his way. Tom walked faster. There was no doubt the man was after him . . .".

The discussion went well enough. Despite the early grumblings, the class was engaged, more so than the previous week. But I felt weirdly distracted by the late arrivals. The young woman of the pair followed along in a kind of neutral manner. And while her friend didn't participate in the conversation, he kept flipping around in his book, scribbling notes in a way that didn't seem to correspond with what was happening in the discussion; in a lull or a transition, he would be furiously writing, scanning a page, intent on something or other. Like he was having his own private experience of the story.

A group got into a debate about the pivotal moment, when the wealthy Mr. Greenleaf mistakes Tom Ripley as a friend of his wayward son, and asks Tom to travel to Europe to track him down. Marissa felt Tom's motives were not totally clear, and the ambiguity was important.

"I don't know if it's ambiguous. The entire thing is premised on deception." This was Constantine. I had talked with him last year about exhibiting patience with his peers, but the speech had done no good; if anything, he took it as confirmation of his superior intellect. "Tom isn't at all who Mr. Greenleaf thinks when he asks for his help finding . . ." He looked down at his book, turning some pages. "What's the son's name?"

From the back, someone yelled, "Dick," to laughs.

"Technically, Dickie," I said. "But yes, his name might have some meaning for us."

"Okay, going to look for Dickie," Constantine continued, ignoring some giggles. "So from the onset, the whole thing is based on lies."

At this, the mystery student looked up from his notebook and shrugged.

"Do you have some thoughts on this?" I asked.

"Oh," he said, stumbling, and I felt bad putting him on the spot.

"Or anyone else?" I asked, trying to let him off the hook I'd hung him on.

But he continued. "I guess I'm not sure the misunderstanding is all Tom's fault."

"How do you mean—and sorry, remind us your name?"

"Oh, sorry," he laughed, "I'm Tyler."

It didn't ring a bell from the roster. "Okay, Tyler, go ahead."

"But I mean, this idea of deception. Like, is Tom hiding who he really is? Or is it that Mr. Greenleaf can't see it. Or won't?"

"But Tom leads him on," Constantine said. "He lets Mr. Greenleaf think he and Dickie are really friends. And he lies about his job."

"I guess," Tyler said, and shrugged again.

"You're not convinced?" I asked.

"I don't know. I mean, alright, Tom doesn't correct Mr. Greenleaf. But I feel like the book is setting that up for us to think about. Like, is that Tom's fault—other people's assumptions?"

"That's a great question," I said. He was taking us somewhere interesting. "But, of course, these are characters, not real people. Guessing at motives in fiction only gets us so far. Let's think about

Highsmith's motives." I explained that I liked to approach a text as if everything were there on purpose. That every detail had been included by the author with intention. "This is only one way to read, and if you take Professor Safie Hartwell's class on psycho-analytical theory next term, you'll get some tools to think about everything the author *doesn't* know they're doing. But let's stick with my thought experiment for a moment. If we assume this is an intentional choice—these misconceptions based on assumptions— what might Highsmith be asking us to think about?"

"Maybe something about the truth?" Marissa said.

"Yes, I think that's right," I said. "What else?" Marissa frowned and opened her book. I could see Tyler in the back, waiting. "Go ahead, Tyler."

"I agree. I do think she's talking about the idea of truth. And lies. But not really what that means about who you are. More like who people *think* you are. In the story right away, how Mr. Green-leaf sees Tom is totally based on all these things about race and class and gender. Mr. Greenleaf sees what he wants to see, and that makes the deception or whatever. It's like, it's not Tom lying—it's the world."

The class sat quietly and I let the moment hang there. It was a beautiful reading, exactly right.

But then Constantine wanted back in. "So it's all just a metaphor? For being in the closet?"

"Hmm—" I shook my head "—Well, sure. But it must be more than that as well. I think Highsmith is flipping something for us. Rather than all secrets being a stand-in for homosexuality—" I made air quotes around the word "—I think we can ask how homosexuality is made to carry a burden of secrecy for everything else. In other words, what might be hidden inside a story that is supposedly about being gay?" I noticed the clock on the back wall—we had run over. "Okay, let's wrap there. We'll pick this up again next class."

I chatted with a few students as they filed out, and then Tyler made his way down to the front of the room, his friend remaining behind.

"Professor Lausson, I'm sorry we were late."

"It's okay, but—what's your last name?" I scanned the class list. "I'm not seeing you on here."

"Cunningham. Tyler Cunningham—oh," he laughed. "Actually, I just registered."

"Ah—I see."

"I hope that's okay. It's just—" He trailed off, looking around the classroom and chewing at his lip. "I was having a problem at the registrar's office. With my financial aid? So they just let me sign up for classes. I'm really sorry I missed the first two weeks." He looked anxious. A spattering of small pimples lined his cheekbones, giving his face a kind of flushed quality.

"Oh—it's okay," I said, surprising myself—two weeks was a lot to miss. But it wasn't his fault his parents couldn't just write out a check like most of his peers—why should he be punished? "You seem like you caught up quickly. That was good work in the discussion."

"I got all the books. And notes from Kennedy." He motioned to the back of the room at his friend—ah yes, I remembered the name now.

"Okay, great." I rummaged around in a folder and found a copy of the syllabus and passed it over. "Take a look through this and let me know if anything is unclear."

"Actually, I was wondering—could I stop by your office later? Just to make sure I'm caught up?"

Just then, Kennedy called out, voice low—"Hey, Tyler." She motioned at the door.

"Gimme a sec," Tyler said. "Sorry."

The door opened and a student stepped in. It was the tall one, from the argument outside.

"What's the holdup?" he said to Kennedy, and then noticing me—"Excuse me, professor. I didn't mean to interrupt." I had a clearer look at him now. He was quite handsome, in a kind of unnerving way—easy but assertive good looks.

"I'll be right there," Tyler said, "Go ahead."

"Sorry again," the friend said, holding the door for Kennedy. They stepped out and Tyler rolled his eyes.

"My roommate Addison. He's insanely impatient."

"I guess everything's okay now?" I asked, trying to reconcile their argument with what I'd just seen—no trace remained of the anger that had gripped Tyler just two hours ago.

"What do you mean?"

"I—" Of course he didn't realize I'd seen them. I felt stupid and mumbled, "Nothing. Just—anyhow, I've got office hours until four. In Walton."

"Okay great—wait, shit. Sorry!" He laughed, a soft and quiet *ha ha*. "I have soccer practice. But maybe I can get out early? I really want to make sure I'm caught up."

"It's fine," I said, "just come by when you're out. I'm working late anyway."

He beamed with relief. "Thanks so much."

"It's nothing." I didn't want him to worry, it's just school—but I appreciated that he cared enough to be stressed.

He seemed about to leave and then tilted his head, examining the book I'd picked up at the library. He read aloud from the cover—*In the Dark of Night*. It was a pulp paperback from the 1980s about John Wayne Gacy—the so-called "killer clown" who buried the bodies of twenty-nine murdered boys and men in his house. The cover image: a lurid face moist with hunger at the lit window of an otherwise pitch-black street. "You write about gay murders or something, right?" he asked.

"I do." *I should be* would have been more honest—it had been months since I'd gotten any writing or research done.

"I saw that on the department website. On your faculty page. I was kind of obsessed with true crime stuff when I was a kid. I guess that's a little weird." He laughed. "Anyway, sorry I'm rambling. But I'm excited about class." And then, as abruptly as he'd shifted the conversation, he took off, bounding toward the rear. He paused at the door for a moment. "See you later, Mark."

The door slammed shut behind him and I started at hearing my name. At the beginning of each semester, I told students they could call me whatever they wanted. I had a whole speech: "I don't have a preference, whatever works for you. You can call me Professor, you can call me Dr. Lausson, you can even call me Mark." But I didn't really mean it, and no one took me up on the offer. "Mark" was me outside campus—it sounded weird coming from a student. Was there an outside to this place?

The door opened again and the next class flooded in. I grabbed my things and noticed on the corner of the desk—he'd left the syllabus behind.

At the start of office hours, two students from my Comp course stopped by. They were the sort of young women who dominated my classes: neat blonde hair in low ponytails, dressed in formless sweatshirts and sweatpants stamped with the Sawyer logo. I understood the uniform as a defense against attention. (It worked; I sometimes couldn't tell these students apart.) One of them sat without saying a word, shoulders stooped, hands clasped at her phone like she might misplace it. I couldn't tell why she'd come except maybe the other had asked. Her friend was worked up about an assignment due at the end of the week. I had told them to write something about themselves, anything. "It's just two pages," I said, "to get us going." "What if I don't have two pages?" I wasn't sure how to calm the fear that your life couldn't yield a few hundred words. "Don't overthink it," I told her, but she didn't look convinced.

The rest of the afternoon no other students showed and I frittered away the time—checking email but not replying to anything, straightening my bookshelves. It's not like I had nothing to do. I had gotten yet another email from Susan about my overdue first-year self-assessment. I was also past deadline on two article revisions and I had to finish an application for conference funding. The semester had just started, how was I already so far behind? I stared out my window at the students crossing below, the last classes of the day letting out. I plucked at some dry leaves from the plant on the windowsill, a gift from Stephen—shit, Stephen. I'd completely forgotten.

I grabbed my phone—there was a text from him.

That movie is showing at 7:45. Pick you up 6:30?

I checked the time. Just past six. Fuck.

Hey sorry can we reschedule? I'm stuck at work.

After a moment, he texted back. *All good. Everything ok?*

I stared at the phone for a moment. *No crisis.* It would feel weird telling him I forgot our date because I was waiting around for a student. *I'm sorry!*

I watched for a reply. Nothing. Was he mad? But Stephen never really got mad.

And then: *No worries.*

I breathed a sigh of relief and started typing again. *Susan is on my case about my annual report.* That was true. *I feel like I accomplished nothing last year, maybe I should just turn in a blank page.*

Ha don't stress. You'll get it done. Miss your face.

Thanks. I hit SEND. Then—*Miss yours too.*

I put my phone away. Through the crack of my office door, the hallway dimmed as my colleagues clocked out for the night. I clicked open the overdue assessment form and filled in the first line: Name. I growled and picked up my phone. Maybe Safie was around. I could just walk down the hall and check, but I didn't want to chance running into Susan.

I texted: *Are you still here? Come over and distract me.*

A moment later, Safie texted back. *Mark Lausson working late?*

I smiled. *More like "working."*

Sorry buddy I'm at that new bar by your place with some history folks. It's cute here, we should check it out. The bar was at this recently opened hotel. It was just a few blocks from me but I hadn't been. Safie was always better about putting in the effort and exploring. *But I'll see you in the morning.*

The morning? *You will?*

Department meeting.

Nooooo. Sent. Then, *At least we'll be together.*

I put the phone down, picked it up, checked the time again, put it back down. How much practice did the soccer team need? I said I'd be working late before I thought it through—I just kind of blurted it out. I felt bad—Tyler seemed so worried about falling behind. In any case, now I was stuck waiting.

I pulled up the college website and searched the calendar of activities for info. Nothing. I found the page for the soccer team— also nothing helpful. There was a tab of player profiles. My finger hovered over the keyboard and then I clicked, scrolling until I found him. Tyler Cunningham, starting defensive midfielder. A photo popped up: face disappearing into a cartoonish grin and a deep squint, one eye peeking open. It was not a flattering shot; it was odd that he wouldn't mind it being up there. I read through the accompanying paragraph. He was a sophomore, from Charlotte, North Carolina. He had played in high school, on a good team it seemed—they'd gone all the way to state.

I shut the browser, anxious to be found snooping around about a student on the college internet. Could they track these things? I reopened the site and clicked through all the other players, scattering a trail of cyber breadcrumbs. When I was done with that, I went through the women's team as well, just to be safe.

Finally, at eight, I gave up, hungry and annoyed. Clearly, Tyler was not coming. I'd wasted a night for nothing. I closed up my office and stepped into the dim light of the hallway. Outside Walton Hall, the campus felt deserted. The sky had gone charcoal. A slap of thunder cracked the silence and a torrent of rain unleashed—great. I dashed under an overhang. I could sit out the storm, but I'd squandered enough of my night. I lifted my backpack over my head to shield myself from the lashing rain and ran into the dark and silence of campus.

The second greatest mystery of the universe is other people. My sister Cassie said this to me one night. I must have been ten years old, she fifteen. Our parents were away for the weekend. A quick business trip for my father, my mother along for some sightseeing and a break from us kids. I don't remember where they'd gone, but they left money for a pizza and put Cassie in charge. We were in the backyard, plunged into darkness, stretched side by side on two beach chairs Cassie had dragged across the lawn. The warm fuzz of music floated around us from the small battery-powered radio our father kept as part of his hurricane supplies. The radio was, as he constantly reminded us, "for emergency use only." Cassie found it in the garage when she went looking for the chairs and together we pawed through the cluttered kitchen junk drawer, searching for a fresh pack of batteries. "Seems like they should be a little more accessible," Cassie said, and dipped her voice to a stagey baritone, "*in case of emergency.*"

The night sky whirled above us. Cassie was taking astronomy. The class was known to be for aspiring dropouts who wanted an easy "A." Cassie had joined that crowd the previous year, much to our parents' dismay. While my mother was terrified Cassie would get pregnant, my father worried—with Cassie's loose hair falling like rope around the shoulders of the drab green jacket she refused to take off, even in the height of summer—that no one would want to date her.

If Cassie had taken the class to be with friends, it turned into something else. As we sat together late into the night, she pointed out constellations and told me what they'd been learning about quantum mechanics, the idea that something could be in two places at once. We could see the pulse of one of Saturn's moons, and when a shooting star made its blistering arc across the heavens, Cassie explained that it had died out thousands of years ago. What we saw was merely its last spark echoing across the chambers of the Milky Way. I strained my eyes to track the fizzing star until it faded from view. We sat in silence for a long while.

Finally, I asked the question on my mind—"Do you think we'll ever find out if there's really life on other planets?" I felt it was kind of silly of me to wonder, but I knew Cassie wouldn't think so.

"I'm not sure," Cassie said. "As much as scientists have figured out, I would still say almost everything about life is unknown. Starting right here on Earth—forget about other planets."

"What do you mean?"

"Just like, the state of existence—of being alive—is ultimately mysterious."

"Really?"

"Totally." She laughed and then, after a moment, said, "I think the second greatest mystery of the universe is other people."

"What?" I had no idea what she meant.

She laughed again. "Just like, you can never really know another person, like what they're thinking or feeling. I mean, you have your ideas of something, like being sad, but you can't know exactly what sad feels like to someone else. Or happiness, or love. Not truly." She reached over and ruffled my hair. I had already entered the stage of dodging our parents' attempts to touch me, but I smiled beneath her hand.

"Okay," I said. "Then what's the first greatest mystery?"

"Ourselves," she said. "Obviously."

CHAPTER 2

That night I had a dream I was walking to campus. I saw a house I didn't recognize and then I realized: It was my childhood home, where I lived until the abrupt move my freshman year of high school. How had the house transported itself from Florida to Ohio? The door was cracked open and I walked in. Everything looked exactly the same, nothing out of place. Suddenly, a great storm erupted and a flood rushed through. I raced, frantic, through the halls and rooms, looking for my parents. The tides rose to my ankles, then calves, then thighs, until the swirling floodwaters produced a kind of vacuum effect and I found I couldn't pull myself free. The heavy scent of the water, earthy and acrid, filled my nose and throat. I woke in a tangle of bedsheets, damp with sweat. I pulled myself free and checked my alarm clock. Shit—already running late.

I didn't teach on Wednesdays, but had to go in for the English Department's monthly meeting. (The life of the mind is mostly just meetings.) The week before we met, Susan would send out an agenda with a request for further items. An avalanche of proposals followed, most of which had nothing to do with our department: sexist rants about the clothing choices of female students, with suspect references to "rap music"; indignant demands that something be done about the noise from the Computer Sciences construction project; and convoluted plans for overhauling the campus recycling program *especially urgent in this, the dawn of the*

Anthropocene. Last year, after a spirited but unsuccessful campaign to have our meeting extended by an hour, one of our more senior colleagues, Mary Ackels, sent a desperate plea that we intervene in the "devastating tragedy of the Congo." For emphasis, the email's several thousand words were written in a wide range of colorful fonts in various sizes. While Safie was impressed with Mary's formatting skills, I remained unsure of what use the Congolese might find a bunch of semioticians and Mark Twain scholars in Ohio. Each month, Susan relegated these addendums to a section of the agenda titled "Further Business." We never got to this section before Susan adjourned us for the following month, when all those unaddressed items went missing and a new crop of hopefuls took their place.

We met in a conference room on the top floor of Walton Hall. A bank of tall, mahogany-framed windows looked out across a densely wooded grove at the south end of campus. The beautiful view depressed me. After a year staring out those windows watching the seasons change, I knew that the leaves of the great black ash trees, today crisp and resplendent, would soon enough fade, desiccate, and die. I felt I was watching my own life pass me by, and I didn't like the looks of it.

The assembled were talking in twos and threes or poking at their phones. Susan sat at the front, arms folded across her middle, leaning back from the conversations around her. I scanned the room. There was a seat next to Colin—*ugh*—and then I saw Safie waving me over and lifting that gigantic bag she brought everywhere from the seat beside her.

"You're a good friend," I said. "Why haven't we started? Susan is such a stickler about time."

"Hal hasn't shown up yet."

"Hal? I thought we were rid of him."

"He's giving a report on the trustees meeting. About the new health sciences school."

Hal Smith, a colleague from the department, had just started a new appointment as dean of Humanities. Hal imagined himself an iconoclast, a British Marxist still talking about May 1968 like he started it all. When the promotion came through, he jokingly called himself a sellout for joining the managerial class, but he adjusted quickly to his new status, swapping his leather jacket and jeans for a suit and tie. (His silver hair remained gelled into one sharp spike in front, a conspiratorial wink that said, *I'm doing it all for the proletariat.*) I'd run into Hal the week before. Since the promotion, he had started speaking from the point of view of "the College"—as in "the College expects this" or "of course the College supports tenure track faculty, but . . ." etc., etc. I joked about it to Safie and she diagnosed him with *institutionalitis.* "That's when you lose the last of your soul and stop seeing yourself as separate from Sawyer," she said. "It's fatal."

"What's going on guys? Make some room."

I looked up as Colin dragged his chair over to the other side of Safie. He wedged in and then managed, somehow, to expand—all shoulders and elbows and youthfully worked-out muscles just going soft. How do straight guys do that—rearrange space around themselves wherever they go? I didn't dislike Colin, exactly. But if junior faculty got grades, he'd be a grade-grubber, volunteering for every task force and initiating service-learning trips. His team-player attitude made the rest of us look bad.

"We're just waiting on Hal," I said.

Colin glanced to the front of the room. "Susan looks pissed." It was no secret Susan had been gunning for the dean position. She had spent two decades doing grunt work in the department, keeping things running, but, of course, in the end the promotion went to a man. "I heard she filed a formal complaint about the search passing her over."

"Maybe that's why Hal is taking his sweet time getting here," said Safie.

"Or maybe," said Colin, "it's because of his impending divorce."

"What's that now?" Safie raised an interested brow. Colin's grubbing ambitions meant he was well connected and thus a consistent source of gossip. I still found him annoying, but Safie shifted the blame to me. "Knowledge is power," she said when I complained about him, "and you're a dead end—you don't talk to anybody." I couldn't argue with that.

"I heard Elizabeth has moved out," Colin said, leaning in.

Safie made a sound like *hmmph*. "Good for her. I wonder if Hal is up to his old tricks—" but before she could continue, Hal blustered into the room, a flurry of apologies about running late. "You know how it is," he announced to no one in particular, like we were all in on something. "But the College"—I smirked and beside me, Safie snickered—"is very eager to catch you up on our plans for the year."

Susan, arms still crossed, stood and announced, "Well, I guess we can finally start."

The meeting droned on around me. I never paid attention at these things. I figured if anything important came up, the news would find me. My thoughts drifted to the previous night. I was ticked off that Tyler had stood me up. After all that anxiety about falling behind, he didn't even show? And when I checked my email there was nothing—no apology, no explanation. I still hadn't gotten any notification from the registrar's office. Maybe I'd make him sweat it out a little, say it was too late to sign up, as punishment for wasting my night. But that was petty—he's just a kid, and I was the one who offered to stay late. I wondered what it was like to be at Sawyer on financial aid, surrounded by so much wealth. It wasn't all the students, of course, but I'd learned you couldn't trust their accounts; the baseline was so high, kids whose families didn't own multiple homes thought themselves poor. *I* had found it overwhelming. My first semester, when I griped about a student in my Comp course to Safie, she replied, "Oh, the Saudi prince?" I laughed. He was obviously wealthy, gaudily sporting an enormous wristwatch you could trade in for a car—a nice one, not like mine. But Safie wasn't kidding; he was an actual prince. The student had done a miserable job with his final presentation. He argued that the ban on women driving in Saudi Arabia was good for the economy, as everyone just hired a private chauffeur. "Everyone?" I asked. "Yes, of course. Every family has a driver." He had no idea. When I later explained his low grade, he tried to bribe me to reconsider. He said I should let him know the next time I was in the Middle East—his family owned a chain of hotels and would set me up. It was weird enough having royalty in your classroom—I don't know if I could have handled living with them in the dorms.

When I was applying to college, I'd heard of Sawyer, of course, but why anyone would go to college in Ohio was beyond me. From the limited vantage point of a state school in Florida, I couldn't see how the world worked, the unmarked networks that run between places like this (Sawyer, Wesleyan, Brown, Smith) and funnel directly into New York, San Francisco, Los Angeles. While in grad school at NYU, I became acquainted with the beneficiaries of these circuits for the first time, people in their mid-twenties already

advancing in careers in arts administration and magazines and
PR, worlds of work I had no clue how to enter. (That's the thing
about being naïve—you don't know you are.)

I had gotten completely lost in these thoughts and was snapped
out of it by an eruption of conversation and people standing to
leave. The meeting had ended.

"Back with us?" Safie asked.

"What did I miss?"

"Honestly, not much."

"I kind of like knowing what's going on at my workplace,"
Colin said.

"And that is just one of our many differences," I said. "I want
the minutiae of this job to occupy as little space in my brain as
possible—I don't have much to spare."

On our way out of the room, I tried to dodge Hal, but he saw
me and turned from his conversation, waving a hand for me to stop.

"Mark, you'll get that email to me?"

"Yes, yes," I said. "Sorry to be slow," and then hurried us
through the door before he could say more.

In the hallway, Safie faced me. "Are you secretly conspiring
with Hal?"

"Yeah, what was that about?" Colin asked, trying and failing to
sound casual.

"Nothing, really," I said. "He invited me to do one of those
talks. Sawyer Scholars or whatever."

"Really?" Colin asked. "I didn't realize they were working out
the schedule already." I could tell he felt slighted; I would gladly
trade places.

"That's great," said Safie. "I don't know why you wouldn't tell
us. But you're doing it, right?"

"I mean, it's not really an invitation you can refuse, is it?" It was part of Fall Fest, when alums and parents came for a weekend of showboating and fund-raising. Sawyer mainly treated junior faculty as undeserving of our jobs, so the talk was considered something of an honor. But I was left puzzling at the sequence of choices that led to a life in which I was meant to feel lucky to spend a Friday evening reading from a bunch of printed pages to a sparsely populated room of semi-interested people.

Colin offered some laudatory words and Safie repeated hers. And then Colin asked if we were going back to our offices.

"I think I might just head home." Although I had planned to spend the day on campus, I could tell that my efforts would be futile. I was too tired and distracted.

"I have another thing," Safie said. "Pre-tenure orientation."

"They should have you running the meeting," I said. Safie was turning in her dossier at the end of the academic year, going up for tenure next fall. "You're a shoo-in."

"I don't know about that."

But she was, anyone could see it. The students all loved her, she had published a million articles, and her book would be out with Duke in the spring. Safie was doing everything right.

"Well, you guys should come watch the match with me tonight," Colin said. "It's important to show your face at things. And soccer is Sawyer's only decent sport."

"Soccer?" I asked.

"Yeah, why?"

"Nothing," I said, suddenly shy about showing interest. "I just didn't know they were playing tonight."

Safie laughed. "I mean, extracurriculars aren't exactly your deal."

"I'm not that bad. I go to things sometimes."

"When I drag you."

"Fine, drag me tonight."

"For real?" Safie looked genuinely surprised. "Okay, pick me up on your way."

"Great," said Colin. "It's a plan."

Safie had started at Sawyer a few years ahead of me. Our first real conversation followed my initiation into department meetings. I remember she was wearing this bright green vintage dress, something that on anyone else would look weird, but on her was exactly right. And she had that leather bag plopped on the table in front of her, like a barricade. The bag was so big, I spent half the meeting wondering what was in it. When the meeting closed, as we filed out, Safie stopped me and asked how I was adjusting to Sawyer. I said something noncommittal and polite, and when she gave me a look, I asked, "Are the meetings always like this?"

"That was one of the good ones." She made a sad, sighing sound. "Let's go, you're coming with me."

She took me to her office, where neat stacks of file folders and books and PDF printouts covered every surface. On one wall, she had hung a gigantic calendar, each square packed with small, precise print, outlining her tasks for the day. I leaned close, squinting: deadlines for grants, page numbers to revise, books to finish reading.

"I usually don't know what I'm doing in ten minutes, much less ten days."

Safie shrugged. "I'm a planner. I want to know everything is under control. Anyway—" She scanned a shelf lined with small tins of tea, satchels, neat brown paper bags with handwritten

labels. "Do you want green, black, or red? Or something herbal—
I've got a nice mint somewhere."

"That is a lot of tea."

She laughed. "I have this thing whenever I travel. I find a shop
selling something I can't get anywhere else." She stepped back and
looked at the shelf. "It is maybe a little obsessive. I don't know, I
find something about the hunt relaxing. I was in Portland for a
conference once and took three buses to get to this shop that spe-
cializes in rooibos. I had to leave the hotel at five in the morning so
I would be back in time for my panel. That tea is the only good
thing about Portland."

She heated water in an electric yellow kettle and I noticed her
nails—they were painted with an intricate design, black to purple
to pink at the tips. I complimented them—there wasn't a lot of
style on display among faculty. Safie fanned her fingers. "I get them
done in Cleveland, when I go up to do my hair. They can't handle
Black hair in Sawyer."

That morning I discovered one of my favorite things about
Safie. Despite her meticulous and ambitious daily plans, she
wanted to talk about anything but work. We discussed television,
where to eat in Cleveland, where not to eat in Dayton; she told me
about her previous summer (in Lisbon) and where she was thinking
of going next (maybe Mexico, or back to Lisbon if she could justify
it as research and get some funds together). I only got the story of
her career by grilling her about past girlfriends. There were a lot. ("I
might be a bit picky," she said. "But I don't have time to date anyway.
First tenure, then maybe a girlfriend.") She had dropped out after a
semester of community college in Virginia and then moved to San
Francisco "to become a lesbian and a line cook, but maybe that's
the same thing." She spent the next years working her way through

the food world, eventually starting a small catering company. A woman she'd been dating—"an insufferable poet"—took her to a lecture by a famous feminist philosopher. Something in that room, the philosopher's live brilliance, the play of ideas—Safie realized what her life had been missing. She sold her company. She enrolled at Merritt, transferred to Berkeley, and kept going until she had a PhD. She made it sound easy—like each door just opened to the next. I suspected there was more to it than that, and also that I shouldn't pry; already I understood that Safie was in charge of our conversations, and maybe everything else. But I expressed surprise she seemed happy in Ohio.

"I am happy," she said. "I like it here."

"But you must miss San Francisco?" I had moved to Sawyer just weeks before, and already felt restless.

"After twenty years, California is totally grating. I think I prefer the blatant racism of the rust belt to the backhanded jabs of the precious Bay Area."

Most of my life, friendship eluded me. I felt more at ease on my own, though I knew something was not quite right about it. My mother brought it up once, my loner ways. It was my last year of high school; all my classmates were celebrating graduation, but I had nothing planned. My mother asked if I wanted to have a dinner before I left for college, with them and some friends. "Isn't there anyone you'll miss?" she asked. I'd said no. After a moment, she said, "Well, we will miss you," and I could feel her hurt and knew that someone else, someone better with people, would have the words to ease it.

College was less solitary, but, still, everything felt so temporary I didn't invest much in those friendships; I knew we'd finish and move on. When I got to New York for grad school, I mostly hung out with people from my program, at program events. I dated a bit, guys I met at bars downtown, but that was it, and nothing really lasted; a few weeks, sometimes a few months. Once I left the city for Sawyer, I stayed in touch with only a few people from my grad cohort, mostly through group emails I would halfheartedly skim and then delete.

And so Safie's welcoming me into the warm ambit of friendship was an unfamiliar and at times unnerving experience. Some part of me understood that her options were limited in a place like this; in a bigger school, a real city, what I—a random white gay guy from Florida—had to offer might be less compelling. Nevertheless, here we were. One night woozy with drink at her apartment, I said I couldn't believe my good fortune at finding her. Safie said she felt the same way. When I responded with something dismissive, joking that she had no discernment about men, she had simply said, with no judgment, "I know what you're doing, trying to keep that little distance between us, but it's not going to work." And that was it.

I drove home after the meeting. I lived in what constituted Sawyer's downtown, a few miles south of campus. A small distance made greater by the college's fickle relationship to the town. The trustees had contributed some funds to a revitalization program launched by a young and hopeful mayor, now in his second term. A few blocks from me there was the new hotel, together with some restaurants and bars, mostly struggling; two had already opened and closed. Most faculty lived in a ring of reclaimed Victorians encircling campus or in the suburban sprawl on the north side of town, really bedroom communities for professional classes working in Cleveland or Akron. Colleagues often expressed surprise at my choice of neighborhood, saying "Good for you" like I was doing charity work, living among the locals. But I liked knowing I wouldn't run into colleagues every time I stepped outside; I didn't want the job to define me, and I found the separation a comfort. It helped me imagine that my life meant more than work.

My apartment was in an old brick building, converted from a former bakery abandoned for decades. It was just three floors, an empty storefront on street level, and one unit above that; a guy in his late twenties lived there. He worked in Columbus and mostly stayed down there with his girlfriend. I had the impression he kept the apartment as an insurance policy, a tether to his previous life. On the top floor, above his, sat mine. The apartment was fine, nothing special. It could be nicer but I hadn't done much with it. I ate my meals at a small table tucked into the kitchen. My bedroom was just a bed and a chair and dresser; my living room—a couch, a coffee table and end table, a bookcase with my records, which I hadn't listened to in forever. The under-furnished aspect gave it a temporary feeling. I guess there was something disappointing about it. After the grad student hustle in New York, I thought moving anywhere else, I'd live like a king—but these felt like forgotten rooms set aside for a minor duke, at best.

The rest of the morning and afternoon crumbled away. I passed the time, or it passed me, but nothing much happened. I tried to catch up on reading for class, but couldn't focus. Finally, I started getting ready. It wouldn't kill me to make some effort—put on a good showing, like Colin said. I got dressed, undressed, tried again—jeans in different shades of black, a white Oxford, then a blue. Nothing looked terrible, but nothing looked great, either. I stared at myself in the mirror. I had a slouchy air about me—I was not at my best. My running years, my body held that vibrancy of purpose, but my marathon days were behind me. I hadn't even set foot on a jogging trail in . . . how long? I'd lost the routine to the demands of grad school and kept thinking any day I'd pick it back up. Still, I wasn't bad-looking, I knew that. But even at my most fit, I was never someone who inhabited my body with a lot of confidence, more like a sense of acceptance—this is what I have to work with. I leaned close to the mirror, pushing at the half-moon shadows under my eyes—I couldn't get away with a bad night's sleep as I had in my twenties. My dark irises and heavy eyebrows created the impression of a band across my face, like a nighttime intruder. I changed my shirt again, back to what I first had on, and pushed the unruly dark waves of my hair into place. Good enough. I checked my watch—it was still early, but I headed out.

I texted as I pulled up to Safie's. She rented an apartment over a garage behind an old clapboard house with a kind of charming, cobbled-together appearance. She brought the same care to her home as she did to everything in her life. She'd painted the walls a soft pink. Yellow curtains pooled on the floorboards, the thrift-store sofa reupholstered in a green checkered print, paintings done by an ex hanging behind it. Safie's landlords lived in front. Loren ran the Black Studies department and her husband, Eugene, was a sculptor. He welded giant abstract pieces that stood sentinel on the lawn, patinated rust mirroring the rough-barked trees. It was a humid night, one of those autumn days that gets warmer as it goes, summer reasserting itself one last time. I had the windows up and the AC on so I didn't notice Safie until she was tapping at the window. I let her in.

"Sorry to make you wait," she said. "You're early."

I pointed to the dashboard clock. "I'm on time."

"On time for you is early. No Stephen tonight?"

"No Stephen. Why?"

"Everything okay there?"

"Of course." I hadn't thought to invite him, but that didn't mean things weren't okay. "We're allowed to do separate activities."

"Relax." Safie smiled. "No one's trying to curtail your freedoms."

Safie had invited Priya, who was waiting when we arrived. Priya had just been hired into the department, teaching South Asian diasporic lit, and she bubbled with effort, as if she were still on the interview. She thanked Safie for the invitation, repeating it three or four times. Safie waved it off; she was the kind of person who includes the new kid and is gracious about it. Truthfully, I felt a little jealous—I had been the new kid last year. Sometimes Safie's friendliness made me feel, maybe not replaceable, but not entirely special, either. Or it reminded me that I needed her in a way she didn't need me. As we waited for Colin, Priya asked about my research. "You're working on a book about serial killers?"

"Kind of," I said. "Like—cultural discourses of gay sex and murder. Or that's the idea."

"That sounds fun."

"I guess—if you're into sex and murder."

Priya laughed, but talking about my book stressed me out; with the tenure clock running down, I felt the pressure mounting. Sometimes I wanted to gay murder myself to get out of doing it.

Finally, Colin arrived, apologizing for getting caught up at work.

"We're glad to see you," Safie said, "but no one wants to hear about everything you accomplished today."

Colin smirked. "Har-har."

The stadium sat low-slung and sleek. A swooping walk funneled us toward the entrance. It was part of the new west side of campus; I never had reason to come this way.

"This is really nice," I said. "I expected to be standing around in a field."

"They use it for other things," Colin said, "but they built it for soccer."

"That seems random," said Safie.

"Some loaded alum from the nineties decided Sawyer should have a real soccer team. He dumped a ton of money into it, so the College basically bought its way into Division II." We went in, Colin leading us up the stands.

"Do this many people always come to watch?" Priya asked.

Colin explained that local families made up much of the crowd. "Northside," he said—meaning families with money. He steered us up some steps toward the back of a middle section. "I like an aerial view," he said. "Better for the big picture." On either end of the field, each team had assembled in tight groupings, waiting to begin; Sawyer was down to our right. Colin talked about the previous season and the head coach, in his second year, poached from San Diego, apparently a coup.

The music playing over the sound system cut out and the start of play was announced. The teams hustled into formation and my eyes landed on Tyler, jersey number seventeen—I recalled it from the website. He took his position, jumping in place, warming up. A sharp whistle sliced the silence. A moment later, the opening kick—the ball shot out and the field erupted. I instantly lost track of Tyler in the frenzied play; I couldn't follow him and also the game, despite the announcers' broadcast and Colin narrating beside me. All at once, everyone cheered; Colin jumped to his feet. Sawyer had scored.

The first half stretched on with no more points. Colin was getting worked up about the new health sciences school. The idea was to begin offering a few master's programs, Sawyer's firsts.

"The debate feels so precious," Safie said.

"How do you mean?" Priya asked. I noticed that she had been asking questions all night but rarely offering opinions of her own. Earlier, Colin had explained the entire scoring system (as if it were confusing; you kick a ball into a net). Only after he finished did Priya mention, almost apologetically, that she had played in college.

"Yeah, what's precious about it?" Colin asked.

"This narrow idea of what a liberal arts college should be," said Safie. "Like it can never evolve."

"To be honest, I find the whole thing kind of crass, it's just a moneymaker, these professional degree programs," said Colin. "This is a liberal arts college, not a trade school. What even *is* a master's in health administration?"

"Lots of these kids"—Safie gestured across the stands and field—"they don't have to worry about what's next. Most people don't have that luxury. Like it or not, there are jobs in health care."

"Fine, okay," Colin said. "But there are plenty of places to get that degree. Cleveland State, or Kent. Sawyer can't be all things to all people."

I stood. "I'm going to find a bathroom." Around me, the crowd let out a collective sigh. A missed shot or something. Colin, too— somehow he could issue a defense of elitism and also pay attention to the game. Before anyone could try to join, I slid from our row, only turning when I started down the steps. "Be right back."

I walked down the stands and passed a group of students who called out hello—they were from last year, but which class? I waved and kept going, circling to the restrooms. I didn't actually have to go. I stood around and rinsed my hands. I pulled out my phone—had the crack on the casing gotten bigger? I hadn't gotten a new phone in . . . I couldn't recall. Five years? It was a message from Stephen. I started to check it then put it away—I'll text him later. I passed a concession stand and stopped for a soda. I sipped at it, sharp and sweet, then tossed most of it in a trash bin.

And then I realized—I was stalling. I wanted to be on my own. Rather than turning left and heading up the stands, I went right, walking the lower ring, above and along the perimeter of the field. I stationed myself at a low wall, before the curve to the other side began.

From here, I had a clear view. The other team had the ball and our players moved in from either side. It was a kind of ballet, beautiful and almost brutal: bodies in total command of themselves and yet completely, wordlessly in sync. Team sports had never been my thing. Or any sport, until I found track in junior high. Even then, I didn't participate in the relays. I preferred the solitary experience of cross-country; I wanted to feel fleeting, unattached. Suddenly, I spotted Tyler within a cluster of players, closing together then parting. He was easy to follow, the lines of him distinct in the tangle of bodies. He jumped, round calves flashing. He was drenched—the humidity had only increased—his hair swinging in threads as he ran.

I lost him for a moment and then a whistle blew and he broke away, sprinting in my direction. For an absurd moment I thought he was running to me. But he stopped short at the edge of my sightline, below to the right. Someone passed him a water. He drank from it, deep, fast gulps. He handed it back and then, in one quick motion, pulled his dripping jersey up over his head and let it fall to the ground. He was heaving, out of breath, bent at his knees, small swells of his chest rising and falling. He stood and stretched—the bright lines of his ribs. He lifted his thin arms into the air and sniffed at himself, nose dipped close. He grabbed back the water and splashed it across his face, letting it run down the front of him.

Just then, he turned and raised his head. I jerked and looked away, mortified—had I been caught? I waited a moment and glanced back up. Tyler wasn't watching me—he faced the nearby stands. He'd seen some friends, someone he recognized, and shouted something, laughing. I tried to see who it was and then a buzzer sounded and the commentator announced halftime. The crowd rose, blocking my view, and jostled me out of the way.

The second half dragged on forever. I gave up trying to keep track of anything. A whistle sounded; the crowd cheered. Sawyer had won, two to nothing.

"The next matches are away, but they play here in a few weeks," Colin said. "We should all go again." Priya said she was game, and Safie, too.

I shrugged. "I had fun, but I think this was enough for me."

"I guess we should have expected that," Safie said. "But we're glad you gave it a shot."

Priya had walked from another part of campus and needed to get back to her car. When Safie offered that she and I could drop

Priya on our way, Colin cut in, saying Safie lived in his direction, he'd take care of both of them. I felt relieved, and then guilty, but didn't protest. I was ready for this day to be over.

At home, the night drew itself around me in slow, tedious loops. I tossed in bed, flipping onto my back and over again. I ripped back the stifling sheets, itchy on my skin. I couldn't shake the image of Tyler from my mind. The labor of the game visible across him: his breath in quick gasps, skin slicked with sweat. I retraced the lines of his body, the tendons and angles, the stretch of him. I felt a surprising kind of grief—I can think of no other word for it—that the stolen glimpses of his body, taut with its wires, were all I would ever get. In my recollection, everyone else disappeared. There was only Tyler, solitary in the field, burning pale and hot. Why had this hold come over me? There was something in the unself-consciousness of the gesture as he stripped, the lack of either pretense or shame. And smelling himself, that animal impulse.

I lifted my own arm and inhaled. A faint musk. I wondered if we smelled anything alike and, at the thought, I got hard. I hesitated, then pushed my nose into my armpit, deeper this time, searching out the scent beneath my deodorant, imagining it was Tyler's, his skin damp across my face. I reached down and took hold of myself. My cock was thrumming, already wet. I pulled at it, rubbing my thumb along the head and down. I moved slowly at first, tentative, and then quickly, with an urgency I couldn't pull back. My body tensed and I came, spilling across my stomach. I lay awake in the dark, heart pounding, breath in shallow gulps, the sour taste of myself lingering on my tongue.

CHAPTER 3

The whole next morning, a vague shame stuck to me. I reasoned with myself it was nothing—just sex. Not even sex—the thought of sex. Still, I couldn't shake the sense that I'd done something wrong, crossed a line I shouldn't have.

And I surprised myself. I never thought of students like that. Before coming to Sawyer, when I was teaching adjunct classes across the city, I got questions about it all the time—from dates, or guys in bars trying to flirt. Had I slept with students? Did I want to? Did they try to sleep with me? At first, I was caught off guard by the curiosity—I found nothing sexy or titillating about my job. But the questions came so regularly I realized they really had nothing to do with me. I was the occasion for a fantasy of—something. Power, youth, transgression? Whatever it was, I'd thought I was immune.

I felt disjointed and irritable all through my Composition class—the students seemed extra needy. As my next class drew nearer, and, with it, the fact of seeing Tyler, I felt increasingly anxious, like he would be able to tell just by looking at me. (*Just by looking at me*—an old fear from childhood, harder to shed than I wanted to admit.) And with that anxiety, my irritation at him not showing up to my office grew. If anything, that was the infraction. Tyler had actually done something wrong—blowing off our appointment like it was nothing—whereas I had only *thought* something. Some part of me understood that I was stoking my anger at him as a cover for myself—what a therapist I briefly saw in New York called compensatory something or other. Whatever it was, my anxiety and upset fed off each other, so by the time I was headed to Taft for our class, I was a jittery mess.

When I arrived at the classroom, students were streaming in and I saw, at the tail end of a group, Kennedy and Tyler. I stopped, waiting for them to go in, and then Tyler saw me and waved. "Hi, Professor Lausson."

The rest of the group went in as Tyler waited. I couldn't just stand there, pretending I hadn't seen him. I smiled hello and approached. He started talking immediately—he'd gotten up really early to finish the book—he couldn't put it down. He'd discovered Highsmith had written a whole series and wanted to read the rest. I was nodding along, half listening, waiting for the part where he apologized for the other night, and then realized—the apology wasn't coming.

"I'm glad you liked the reading," I said, "but you know—I was surprised you didn't show up for our meeting on Tuesday."

"Our meeting?"

"Office hours. You said you were coming by after practice?" Did he really not remember?

"Oh, right." Something passed over his face, an indiscernible wave, and then it was gone. "I'm really sorry. Coach kept us so late, and then I got caught in the rain and had to go back to the dorms to change. I figured you wouldn't still be there."

"Oh—I see."

"You didn't wait for me, did you?"

"What? No, I—"

"Oh, good." He let out a nervous laugh. "I'm really sorry."

Maybe he was right. I was making a big deal out of nothing. And the storm had been intense—I'd been soaked by the time I'd gotten to my car.

"Don't worry about it."

"Okay," he said, and smiled. "Oh, I wanted to ask—did you have fun at the match?"

I felt my whole body jump, a quick kick from within.

"What?"

"Last night. I think I saw you in the stands. Did you enjoy watching?"

My face went flush, cheeks burning.

And just then Constantine arrived—"Hello, professor." I'd never been so happy to see him.

"We should get in there," I said, and then hurried in and down to the front of the room.

I stumbled through class, watching the clock the entire time, willing it to be over. I ended early, announcing I had a meeting to get to, and then hurried from the room. I couldn't bear another moment of my humiliation.

Stephen and I had rescheduled our date for that evening. There was something easy about spending time with him. Undemanding. He always seemed happy just to be with me—I didn't quite get it, but I was trying not to question it. And a movie was feeling very appealing—I wanted to shut off my brain and disappear into the dark for a few hours.

I was getting ready when my phone rang. I thought it would be Stephen, saying he was downstairs, "but no rush." (He, unlike me, was never late.) But it was my mother. I panicked a little whenever she called—my parents were getting old enough that I worried bad news might be coming.

"Mom? What's going on?" I could hear some background noise. She was speaking to someone in the distance. And then I heard my father's voice and relaxed. "Mom? Are you there?"

She laughed. "Sorry, Marky. I'm here. Your father got this new thing for the television and he's convinced he shouldn't have to spend a hundred dollars to have the guy set it up. But now there's nothing. No channels, just some blue screen."

"Is that why you called?"

"No, it's just—he's driving me crazy. I needed a distraction." She laughed again. "I don't know why I called." She asked about the semester, my new classes, the students. I told her everything was going fine, busy. I got dressed while we chatted, going through the same rotation of shirts from the night before—I needed some new clothes. She asked how Safie was doing. She always asked about Safie—I think she loved that I'd found a friend. And then she wanted to know if I'd been thinking more about Thanksgiving. I'd made an offhand remark that I might come down, and now she brought it up every time we talked. "Don't wait too long. The tickets aren't going to get any cheaper."

"Don't worry, I'll figure it out." My phone vibrated with another call—I glanced at the screen. "Listen, Stephen's here. I'll call again soon." She also liked when I talked about him—any sign that I wasn't "all alone out there," as she put it.

"Maybe he wants to come down with you. Get out of that cold for a few days."

"He probably has plans. But I'll ask him, okay? I have to go."

*　*　*

When I got outside, Stephen stood beside his car and waved, gregarious sweeps across the air, looking like a commercial for something healthy. We had met in the spring. The president of the college was hosting a reception—a new grant, a step up in rankings, I don't remember what. Safie took me. "I really don't want to," I whined when she stopped by my office to walk over. I made some excuse about grading and Safie shook her head and said I could do better.

We walked to the president's house, a wide rambling structure of slate and shingle on the other side of campus. The house sat deep behind an iron gate, hugged on all sides by a carpet of flush May grass, just mowed. It was warm inside and the oily funk of cheese platters and nervous sweat soaked the air. Safie left me next to a fern and wandered in search of drinks. I couldn't tell if the fern was real or fake; I wanted to touch it but also didn't want to know. Around me, attendees stood in awkward groupings, plastic cups of thick purple wine clutched in damp palms. The gathering brought to mind a very brief stint in my local synagogue's youth group during ninth grade. "We're not really that kind of Jew," my mother said when I expressed interest in going. When I asked what she meant, she said something like "the kind who joins in." And I understood; we were the kind who feels left out, apart from things. But those years I grabbed at any way to pull myself from beneath the heavy shroud of silence blanketing our family home. There was so much we were pretending wasn't happening, it felt like we had agreed to mostly avoid each other—rushed, quiet dinners, weekends spent hidden away in separate corners of the house. If I had arrived at the synagogue seeking out some room to breathe, I quickly discovered the suffocating feeling of spending time with people who had no business being together, except they had nowhere else to go.

Safie came back balancing two quite full cups in one hand. With the other, she pulled along some man by the sleeve of his dark sports coat.

"Drink this," she said, nudging a cup at me. She released her charge and introduced him. "This is Stephen, from Math." Someone waved at Safie from across the room. "I'll be right back," she said, though of course she wouldn't be—Safie was always in demand at social events.

"Come here often?" Stephen smiled at his own bad joke. His face was wide, plain but not unhandsome. His jacket fit well, rare among male academics, who usually looked like they were wearing a larger brother's hand-me-downs. I glanced at my own jeans and wondered if I was underdressed, or Stephen over.

"How did you end up here?" I asked.

"I met Safie last week. At the meeting for the new safety commission," he said. "She told me to come."

"Ah. Safie loves to give instructions. And she does it in this way that makes you feel like, of course—it was obvious all along—this is what I should do."

Stephen laughed. "She does have a persuasive personality. But she didn't mention this?" I shook my head. "Sorry, but I think you've been set up."

"Oh." I hadn't put it together. That Safie would think someone could be interested in me—it wouldn't occur to me. "You're probably the one who deserves an apology. I'm not much fun at these things."

My warning disregarded, Stephen stood with me next to that real or unreal fern for the better part of an hour. We talked about the year, my first, his second, and plans for the summer. As he spoke, Stephen rotated his plastic cup between the fingers of one hand, as if setting up a magic trick. There was something calming in the repeated motion and maybe that's why I let myself talk with him for so long; the spell was working.

I didn't usually date other academics (I try not to shit where I eat), but when Stephen emailed the next day and suggested we get dinner, signing off with a smiley face, I accepted the invitation. We met again the following weekend, and then again the next. After the first time we had sex—it was gentle and quiet and sweet, like him—Stephen asked about past boyfriends. At thirty-four years old, I was embarrassed to admit that nothing had ever lasted long enough for someone to call me that. To think of me as theirs. I was worried I didn't know how to be in a relationship, but Stephen was patient, and, truthfully, did a lot of the work—a weekend afternoon antiquing in the small towns between here and Akron, getting tickets for a concert in Cleveland. I did my part by trying to stay out of the way. Sometimes I wondered if it was love, and I remembered someone in grad school saying that if you had to ask, you knew the answer. But I wasn't so sure I would be able recognize love. Whatever we had, I knew it was a good thing, and I could try to let it be good.

We drove across town to a strip mall of local chains and big box stores. We got to the theater ridiculously early, even for Stephen. We bought tickets at the box office and then Stephen pointed at the cell phone store next door.

"We have enough time. Wanna look around?"

"Maybe after," I said, knowing it would probably be closed by then. "We should head in."

He and Safie had both been nagging me to replace my phone for months. The battery died constantly, and the back was held together with tape. I don't know why I was so resistant to a new phone. It felt unnecessary—I hardly used it.

"Mark, come on. Just to look."

"Okay, sure. Just to look."

The guy in the shop had a round shiny face with dark eyes like little pins. I passed him my phone and asked if he could just replace the battery. "I mean . . . I guess," he said, turning it over in this hand. "But fixing it would probably cost more than this thing is worth. I can't believe you still have a flip phone. My niece has one of these."

He led us across the store and gestured at a display case. "We finally got the Five." I had no idea what he meant. He had one himself and pulled it out. It was one of those new kinds, compact little computers that did a million different things. He loved it—that's what he kept saying, "I love this phone, I love it." And now he couldn't live without it. He spoke in a rush, never pausing for a breath, heavy eyebrows bouncing over his pinprick eyes. "We still have the Four. It's cheaper, obviously. But honestly, the Five—this thing is incredible." He rattled off numbers: megabytes, data, pixels. Beside me, Stephen made little sounds of approval—"Yes, yes"—and nodded along. The guy showed us some game about unhappy birds and his high score. "And check this out," he said. "Facebook finally came out with a decent app." That's what he called the applications, "apps." He pressed it open, moving his thumb around. A photo filled the screen: a young kid holding a popsicle, cherry-red smear on her fat cheeks. "This is Louisa!" And when I didn't react, he said, "My niece!" And indeed, her other hand clutched a phone exactly like mine. I didn't feel like I needed all the bells and whistles, but the guy was so insistent, with Stephen egging him on, I finally agreed. He wanted to set it up right then, move my number over. It seemed like a whole process.

"I don't want to be late for the movie," I said, though we still had plenty of time. "Can't you just give me a new one?"

"You want a new phone number?" Stephen asked.

I shrugged. "Who do I have to tell? You, Safie, my parents."

"I suppose," Stephen said. He had a look on his face, I couldn't tell what it meant, but he didn't argue, and so the guy rang me up and handed over the box, grinning.

"You're gonna love it," he said.

The theater was mostly empty, just an elderly couple down in front, some teenagers to the side, giggling and pawing at each other. As low-budget ads for used car lots flashed by, we caught up on our week. Stephen had been working on a grant application, a big one. If it came through, he'd be set for the next few years, and probably for tenure. I asked how it was going.

"It's almost there," he said. "I think."

"Did you get any feedback from Amit?" Stephen had sent a draft to his chair. He nodded. "And what did Amit say?" I asked, though I had a good idea at the answer.

"He had a few small tweaks."

"And?"

"And he said otherwise it was good to go."

"Those were his words?"

Stephen sighed, but smiled. "He said it was a stellar application."

I laughed. "So send it in."

"I will, I will. I just want to go through it one more time." He tossed a handful of popcorn from the jumbo-sized container into his mouth—Stephen was serious about his movie snacks. "How were your classes today?"

"I don't know—fine." I didn't want to think about my classes.

"Fine works. How about the new one? Are the students liking the sex and death?"

"I mean, who doesn't like sex and death?"

"It's what keeps us going, isn't it? Running toward one, and running from the other."

I laughed. "It's true."

Stephen shook out some candy and then passed me the box. "I bumped into Colin today."

"Lucky you," I said.

"He said you all went to see the soccer game last night?"

"Right." I hadn't meant to hide it, it just hadn't seemed important enough to mention. "Didn't I tell you?"

"I think I'd remember, I was kind of surprised. Not that you didn't say anything. That you went at all."

"You know—Safie made me."

"Well, did you have fun?"

"Sure, I guess." To my relief, the lights went down; I lowered my voice. "Movie's starting."

Stephen had picked the film. A sci-fi thing about time travel. As soon as the first images came onto the screen, my mind returned to the conversation with Tyler. When he asked if I enjoyed watching, did he mean the game, or him? I was horrified to think he'd seen me, and I was kicking myself for going in the first place—a stupid idea. The theater felt overly warm and I couldn't settle—the unforgiving chair, its plastic angles and scratchy armrests. Stephen leaned close, his breath buttery on my face. "You okay?" His hand drifted to my leg and cupped a knee. I willed myself to stay still but the resisting thought only made me more antsy.

Finally, the movie ended. At the first flash of credits, I jumped up and pulled Stephen toward the exit. The parking lot was a sea of SUVs and Camrys. Stephen had done a master's in physics and was explaining the field theory behind the storyline. I half-listened, eyes wandering the lot.

"There's just something really interesting about translating these ideas to film," he said. He waited, and then—"At least I think it's interesting."

I realized he was waiting for a response. "I'm sorry. Do you remember where we parked?"

"We're right there." Stephen pointed across from us, where his car sat, surrounded by empty spots.

"Jesus."

At the car, Stephen stopped me. "Everything okay?"

"What do you mean?"

"You seem distracted. You're sure there's nothing?"

"I'm just stressed." I leaned against the car and stared at the stretch of open asphalt. The parking lights hummed orange overhead.

"What about?" he asked.

"Nothing, really. Sometimes I just find work mentally exhausting."

"Well, it does involve a lot of mental activity. It's kind of in the job description." He smiled.

"I don't know. . . . Do you ever suddenly look up in class, at all these students staring at you, and just think—who the fuck are these people? Where did they even come from?"

Stephen laughed. "Did something happen in class?"

"No, nothing. I don't know what I'm talking about. I'm just tired."

"So we'll have an early night and get some sleep."

He started to pull me in for a hug when all at once I was aware that a car had stopped in front of us and there was a shout and a crash of something and the screech of tires and the engine revving as the car pulled away. And I saw that the crash was one of those gigantic sodas from the theater. They had thrown it from their car and it had exploded, spilling ice and its contents across the asphalt at our feet. A spray of it had caught my leg, splotches of dark against the denim. And it was not so much that I realized what they had yelled from the car, but I heard it, on delay. They had shouted *faggots*.

I couldn't look Stephen in the eye. That was the worst part, that he had witnessed my humiliation. And that's what it felt like: mine. Something in me had brought this on.

When I did look up, Stephen's face was leaned close, still and open. "Are you okay?"

And then another humiliation: my weakness in caring.

"Can we just get out of here?"

As Stephen pulled toward the exit, I asked if he could take us to my place instead of his. He paused a moment, considering. "Sure, I can stop back at home in the morning. I don't have an early day."

"Oh." He'd misunderstood, or I'd been unclear in my asking. "Could you just drop me off? I think I need a night alone."

His head ticked, just slightly. "Are you sure?"

I nodded.

We drove in silence. At the front of my building, Stephen kissed me, hand against my face. The seat belt sliced my collarbone. It would be easy enough to take him upstairs, get into bed, fold against one another. But instead I said, "Let's make another plan soon," and bolted from the car.

I lay on the couch, staring across the room, and noticed the box from the cell phone store. I sat up and opened it. The phone felt strange in my palm, surprisingly weighty, my thumb slipping across the slick surface. It hummed to life and I moved around its layers. I opened the camera and found the way to flip it around, so my face filled the screen. I scowled at my image and clicked it shut. And then I saw the little square for Facebook. I had an account I never used—someone in my grad cohort had insisted we all sign up. I guessed at my password, the same one I used for everything. People I hadn't spoken to since coming to Sawyer populated the little screen. Someone had landed a new job, the announcement followed by a chorus of praise. There were photos of babies and somebody's dog that had just died. That seemed an odd thing to broadcast to the world.

There was a message at the top asking me to update my information. My location was still set to New York. It felt sad to put in Sawyer; like accepting defeat. But then it occurred to me—would Tyler be on here? It took three attempts to type his name into the tiny search bar—how did people get used to a phone without keys?—and then his page appeared. A whole world revealed itself to me, but in a code opaque and undecipherable. I couldn't make heads or tails of what Tyler and his friends were talking about, although Sawyer and what it meant to be a Sawyer student was a running dialogue. What they took for jokes felt harsh or inexplicable. Tyler posted photos that had nothing to do with him, spelled things wrong on purpose, made bold proclamations and then contradicted himself on the next line—about television shows, bands, food, anything. There was something annoying about it, or cloying. Something typical of his generation. A performance for its own sake.

Moving backward in time, I got to Tyler in high school, in Charlotte. Some photos from soccer, overblown snapshots with friends at house parties. A mound of bodies squeezed into a car. A gathering in a clearing in the woods. In almost every photo, six-packs and enormous plastic handles of cheap liquor. Lit joints lifted in grand, hubristic gestures. Did none of these kids have parents? It wasn't my idea of fun, but there was a togetherness, and I felt a kind of envy. This had been Cassie's life, perhaps, but not mine. Not then, not now.

I clicked another photo: Tyler prone across the roof of a car, arms spread wide, reaching through the black surrounding space. Looming above him, a shirtless guy in baggy khaki shorts gripped a bottle of something at his crotch, fat tongue spilling out. Liquor streamed from the bottle into Tyler's mouth, like piss. It seemed embarrassing for Tyler, playing at masculinity to fit in. In the comments someone had called him a "homo," but he replied with a joke, a funny admission. And I understood: Tyler wasn't trying to fit in, he just did. There was no secret here, nothing to hide. And then I felt embarrassed for myself.

I opened another album. Childhood photos. I clicked one. A picture of Tyler with a woman. Even in the small, grainy scene, the resemblance was immediate. His mother. It looked like a camping trip: a hardscrabble of trees, gray river just visible in the background. Other Sawyer students had spent their childhood summers on Martha's Vineyard, at art camp in Italy. His mother's mouth was set in a thin line, hand at her hip. I could imagine Tyler's father coaxing one more shot, the mother impatient. Beside her, Tyler crouched on the ground. Twelve, maybe thirteen years old. His child's face had not yet grown around his changing features, which looked misplaced or uneven, stretched out like putty. That distorted look of early puberty, his next self straining to emerge. Tyler held a snorkel in hands too large for their skinny arms, clutched in front of a bare, concave chest, his skin flush with sunburn; a pink ring marked where his shirt had been. I stared at the photo, my chest buzzing—and then a tidal wave of surprise crashed over me. I tossed the phone, hurling it away. What the hell was I doing?

I looked up at the clock on the opposite wall. Over an hour had passed. It was like I had blacked out and just come to. I reached for the phone and picked it back up. I pushed on the Facebook app, like the guy at the store had shown me, and deleted it. It melted into the ether, making a small, satisfying sound, like completion.

CHAPTER 4

We moved into October. The air shed its summer stickiness as the temperatures dropped. I gave in to the rhythm of the semester and let it organize my weeks, pulling me along. I taught my classes; I hung out with Safie, I hung out with Stephen. He and I had recovered from the situation at the movie theater (and that is how I thought of it—the situation). Or I had, and he had accepted my tacit plea that we not speak of it. We did a weekend away in central Pennsylvania, at a cabin in the mountains Stephen booked for us, taking turns picking CDs for the drive out. Stephen grilled and I mixed us drinks and we made a fire, reading until we were drowsy and going early to bed. I worked in fits and starts on my book. My talk at Fall Fest loomed, a specter of regret. Feeling ambitious, I had proposed presenting a new chapter, yet unwritten. I thought the deadline would offer some momentum, but I felt stalled out, my attention watery and thin.

Tyler showed up each class with Kennedy. They would arrive with coffees in hand just before the start and take their same seats toward the back. Kennedy chimed in more as the weeks went on. She was smart (majoring in Classics, I learned) with a funny, unexpected edge—I could see why Tyler liked her. And she knew how to handle the boys and their egos. She'd even gotten Constantine to back down. One discussion, she cut him off, saying, "I really don't think everything we read needs to be compared to *Infinite Jest*." I would see her and Tyler around campus sometimes, always with Addison, the roommate. They were a striking trio—they had a way of carrying themselves apart from their surroundings. I'd never had that kind of thing in college, my friendships all felt somehow interchangeable. Meanwhile, in class, Tyler always got caught up in his own thing, scribbling notes and scanning pages of the books for who knows what. Despite his thoughtful showing that first day, he never again participated. Many of his classmates stayed quiet, but this felt different somehow. College students were so much more like children than they realized, just playing at adults. And, like children, they were chemically attuned to their peers—for acknowledgment, approval, acceptance. You could sometimes feel the anxiety of those needs fueling class discussions. But with Tyler's way of being alone in the room, it felt like he didn't care about anyone else. He was figuring it all out on his own. He never lingered after class, or showed up at my office with questions or concerns. I got an email from him one afternoon, but it was only a forward, a message from the athletics department with a schedule of away games: *Students' first priorities are their educations, they should be held accountable for any missed sessions, we appreciate you working with them*, and on and on.

When the class submitted their first assignments, Tyler's stood out. He was doing some real thinking. There was nothing superficial—he made keen, attentive observations. And his writing had a light touch, unusual for his age. Most of his peers struggled to string together a meaningful sequence of words. The more competent ones, trying to sound smart, constructed complex, labyrinthine sentences, clauses opening upon one another like a series of corridors their author got lost within, so the meaning at the end bore no obvious relationship to where they'd begun. Tyler's essay carried no trace of effort, the easy flow of an intellect that felt no urge to prove itself.

The quality should have pleased me; it demonstrated a serious engagement with the course. But I was strangely annoyed. I felt excluded from an experience he was having all on his own—it felt like it had nothing to do with me. At the bottom of the final page I scrawled, *Nice work, well written and conceived. You might push the analysis a bit further next time.* The latter, I knew, was unkind: vague and impossible to apply. I gave it an "A" and then in a rush added a minus and shuffled it to the bottom of the pile.

I was working at home one Thursday evening—well, working is an overstatement. I sat in front of my laptop, staring at the screen, when I received a message from the library. Another book I'd requested had come in. I jumped up, grabbed my jacket and keys, and headed out. I had gotten what I wanted: a reason to give up for the night.

Campus had a muted gray quality of desertion, the stone-faced buildings tucked quietly back from the empty paths. It was almost nine, I was rarely here so late. I entered the library—hushed and practically empty, the lights tawny and warm. A familiar, comforting musk washed over me: the sweet, pitched scent of softened leather and mildew. All my life, libraries had offered sanctuary. While other kids rejoiced at the end of school years, facing the interminable summers of my childhood filled me with dread. My father found virtue in the mere fact of being outdoors and would cast me from the house, chastising my deficiencies of sun and air, my body a wan and wasting thing to him. I would wander our suburban streets for hours. I dragged a stick along, the knobby end catching against the rough asphalt, talking to myself. I rejoiced when a summer storm would overtake the skies, driving us indoors. My mother

would load Cassie and me into the minivan—"I can't be cooped up
in the house with these kids all day," she'd announce. She'd drive us
to the local branch of the library a few miles away. We'd dash across
the lot through torrents of rain and into the bracing cold of the air-
conditioned rooms. During these years when they still got along,
Cassie and our mother would settle into the upholstered club chairs
by the periodicals, wordlessly passing magazines between them. I
spent the hours on my own, huddled on the floor in a low-trafficked
stretch deep in the furthest stacks, books piled in my lap.

A student was alone behind the circulation desk, highlighter
skimming photocopied pages. I gave my name and she returned a
moment later with the book. I thumbed through it. It was an autobiography published in the 1940s. Its author, a Chicago industrialist, lived a life less compelling than he imagined: I could find only
a single copy in print, sent over from a university in Montana. I
was not interested in the author himself but the fact that a second
cousin's son was Nathan Leopold, the subject of the chapter I was
currently struggling through. In 1924, Leopold and his rumored
lover Richard Loeb, just teenagers themselves, neither yet twenty,
had kidnapped and killed a fourteen-year-old boy. For decades the
industrialist kept a daily journal. After his death, his estate ended
up with a sister, a philanthropist whose marriage took her to
Columbus. I had just learned that her papers had landed at Ohio
State, his diaries among them. I was planning to make a trip to the
archives in the next few weeks to see if the diaries held some
account of the trial, which had been closely followed in the media,
but of which few firsthand accounts existed. I hoped the autobiography might give a sense of where to begin.

I turned to place the book in my bag and saw the three of them,
huddled around a long table heaped with backpacks, books, and

papers: Addison, Kennedy, and Tyler. Addison and Tyler sat side by side, Kennedy across from them. They each leaned forward, heads close, deep in conversation; a rapt energy rippled off them. Kennedy was talking, head bobbing in emphasis, hands like fins slicing through the small space between her and the boys, nodding along. She finished whatever she was saying and shook back her hair without touching it, shiny waves across her shoulders. Addison said something then, tipping back in his chair and spreading himself like wings, and made the group of them laugh.

A moment later, Tyler shot up, lifting his jacket from the back of his chair. He pulled it on and stepped from the table, leaving behind the papers arrayed before him.

I turned and hurried from the library, hoping I hadn't been seen. Outside, the black and quiet of night were a startling calm. I stopped, halfway down the steps, unsure why I was rushing. And then I found myself unable to move, my feet weighted in place. I heard the whoosh of the door opening and then Tyler's voice.

"Professor Lausson, is that you?"

I turned and squinted into the lights of the library entrance— framed by grand white columns on either side, the golden outline of him stuttered and fuzzed.

"Tyler. Hello."

"It's funny seeing faculty on campus so late. What are you doing?"

"I was just grabbing a book and—it's such a nice night, I suppose I wanted a moment to enjoy it."

"It's gonna get cold soon. I hate it. We have winter in Charlotte, but not like here."

"And you? Are you leaving?"

"Just taking a break." Tyler glanced down at his hands, a pack of cigarettes in one, a small black lighter in the other. "I know we're

not supposed to smoke here. And I shouldn't be smoking anyway.
I just—"

"It's okay," I said. "I'm not going to call the police on you."

He let out a breath and smiled. "Want to sit?" Before I could
reply, he hopped down a few steps. I followed, sitting above him,
conscious of keeping a measured distance between us. The dull
cold of the slate steps pushed up from below. Tyler tapped the pack
against the flat of his palm, gliding a cigarette right to his fingers
then lips. The lighter flared, his waxy face lit up in the flash: a
ridge of zits across his forehead, faint mustache of sparse brown
wisps, the lines of his jaw soft like a pastel drawing. I hadn't gotten
such a close look at him since our first conversation. Kennedy and
Addison were more obviously attractive, good looks cultivated
over generations of wealthy breeding. Tyler had a kind of raw
beauty that reveals itself in a shift of angle or light. Not perfect, or
immediately apparent; something mercurial—unfinished. He drew
in, exhaled slowly, and then, as if suddenly remembering where
he was, slapped the smoky air back and forth to dispel it.

"You're fine," I said. A few students walked by on the path
ahead but paid us no attention. I stared across the otherwise empty
quad—this is where I had first seen Tyler, fighting with Addison.

Tyler pulled the cigarette from his mouth and looked at it,
pinched between his finger and thumb. "I know it's gross. I quit
for a while this summer but something about being back in classes.
It's just a way to take a break I guess? Coach would kill me if he
saw this."

"You'll figure it out."

"It's strange running into you actually," he said. "I was just
thinking about class."

"What about it?"

"I don't know." He laughed at himself. "I shouldn't have said anything. I mean I'm thinking about it a lot."

"I'm glad." I hesitated, and then—"I wasn't so sure. You've been quiet."

"I know, I'm sorry."

"You don't have to apologize, I don't mean to put you on the spot. But you have good insights. Your classmates might want to hear them."

"I don't know about that, but thanks." He laughed again. His cigarette was burning down and I wondered if he wanted to be smoking it rather than talking to me. "I don't know," he said, "sometimes I just feel like, I'm either way ahead or way behind. Like the conversation gets interesting or gets to something I think is important and then we change topics and I'm still hung up on where we were. Like I'm still figuring it out. I don't know if that makes sense."

"It does."

"Or I'm somewhere else entirely. I don't mean smarter." He looked down at his own hands, thinking. "But just like, my mind is a thousand miles in some totally different direction. And I don't want to be annoying."

"You don't have to worry about the rest of the class. That's my job."

"Okay." He smiled. "I'll try." He didn't say anything more but didn't seem inclined to go. I let a moment pass and then asked about his other classes. He said he was regretting Anthropology and just trying to get through it. But enjoying his history course, on the Roman Empire; that's why he was in the library, working on an assignment. "But I'm kind of stuck. I don't know if it's the library or if I'm doing something wrong, but they never have the books I need. Or maybe I just don't know how to find them."

"Sawyer's collection is pretty small."

"I found this one that looked perfect. They have a copy down at Ohio State but it's too late for me to put in a loan request. It won't arrive in time."

Behind us, the door to the library banged open.

"Kennedy's wondering where you are, dipshit." Addison emerged beside us. I saw his eyes fall on me and the flicker of recognition. "Oh, I'm really sorry, Dr. Lausson. I didn't realize that was you." Even standing still, he exuded a jocky swagger, the hard lines of his face and muscles, his easy smile.

"It's no problem." The sense I should explain myself pressed at me. "We just ran into each other."

"This guy and his nasty habits," Addison said, eyes on the burned-down stub of Tyler's cigarette.

"Please no lecture tonight."

Addison shook his head, but smiled. "I'm just looking out for your well-being." He was giving Tyler a hard time, but genuine concern lay beneath. And then I felt bad: I shouldn't have been so approving.

"Are you headed out?" Tyler asked.

"Yeah, I'm going back to P Building." Addison turned to me. "I'll have to check out what you're teaching next semester. Tyler can't stop talking about your class."

Tyler let out a dramatic sigh, more a growl. "I thought you said you're leaving."

"Relax. See you in the room." And to me—"Enjoy your evening, Dr. Lausson."

Addison bounded down the steps, long gliding strides bisecting the void as he cut through. He wore a nylon athletic jacket. Two crisp white stripes ran across each broad shoulder down the sleeves, marking him against the surrounding night. Tyler and I watched until he disappeared from view and then, in unspoken agreement, we both stood.

"I should get back in there. Kennedy hates being left alone."

"You know"—I paused, thinking over what I was about to say— "I'm actually going down to OSU tomorrow to do some research. If you give me the title of that book, I could grab it for you."

"Really?"

"It's no big deal. Sawyer faculty have borrowing privileges." I hadn't planned to visit the archives until I'd had some time with the autobiography, but maybe this was impetus to stop procrastinating. "I could leave it here for you to pick up."

Tyler looked down, then past me. I wondered if my offer was too much, a gaudy and misplaced eagerness to please. But I felt suddenly important—and I didn't want the feeling to end.

"I don't know if this is okay to ask," Tyler said, "but could I come with you?"

"To Columbus?"

"A change of scenery sounds really nice." In the moment as I took in his request, a shadow of distress passed over his face. "I shouldn't have asked. That's totally weird."

"No, it's not weird. It's fine." I thought it over. And inside that thought, another pushed through: Don't think too much. "Sure. Why not?"

"You wouldn't mind me tagging along?"

"I wouldn't mind at all."

At Tyler's suggestion, we arranged to meet the next morning off-campus—just a few blocks away, but it felt like miles; this was townie territory. An enormous, mostly vacant parking lot surrounded a small plaza of shops. Side by side sat a liquor store, a doughnut place, a laundromat, and an empty storefront; the punched-out awning above announced its former tenant, a Chinese restaurant. No sign of Tyler. Maybe he wouldn't show. I checked the time. Just a few minutes late.

And then he stepped out of the doughnut shop, a coffee in each hand. I pushed opened the door—embarrassed a bit by the state of my car, which felt on the brink of another breakdown. Tyler climbed in, laughing. "Thanks." He raised one of the cups. "I didn't know if you would want any?"

"That's nice, thank you."

Tyler passed it to me and I could smell the scalded heat of it. He reached into his pocket and pulled something out. An orange plastic vial; prescription pills. With just one hand gripping the bottle, he popped the cap, shook out a pill, and tossed it back. He swallowed it dry and looked over at me. My eyes shot away; I felt I'd been watching something I shouldn't.

But if Tyler cared, he didn't let on. "Adderall," he said. "I keep getting off them then going back on." I wanted to say he didn't have to explain anything, but before I could speak, he pointed ahead. "Have you ever been inside?"

"The doughnut place? No."

"It's kind of crazy in there. It's covered in posters from Poland, I think. Like tourism posters? But the photos are really awkward and ugly. It doesn't really make you want to visit."

"Honestly, I didn't even know about this place."

"That's kind of why I like it. There's never anyone from Sawyer over here."

After getting home from the library the night before, I almost emailed Tyler to cancel. But then I worried about creating evidence a plan had even existed. In a panic, I tore through my hall closet for my copy of the faculty handbook—shoved on a high shelf, never opened. Trips with students out of town for academic purposes were fine, and only overnights, for athletic events or conferences or group outings, required prior approval. So we were doing nothing forbidden. But I wondered if the anonymity of our meeting spot was why Tyler had chosen it. Did he mean to keep our day a secret?

I pulled from the lot and drove through town, eyeing the speedometer, driving at exactly the limit. Columbus was almost ninety minutes away and I'd been nervous about the ride; it felt like a lot of time to fill. But Tyler was absolutely at ease. He asked if he could put on the radio and clicked through the buttons, landing for a moment and then punching to another station and settling there. "I love this song."

We turned onto the freeway and sailed along. Traffic was light; it was always light. The outskirts of Sawyer gave way to smaller towns and Mennonite communities. We passed a stretch of farms, some active, others fallow, and some bought out by agricultural giants only to be shut down.

"You're going to do some research today?" he asked, and I nodded. "What about?"

I explained my book was about popular narratives of murder cases involving gay suspects. My research kind of jumped around in time and place, which made it feel a bit unwieldy. But I was trying to track something about shifts in how we think about queerness. He asked for an example of what I meant. "Like Andrew Cunanan—do you know who that is?" He shook his head no. "He killed this fashion designer, Gianni Versace. Shot him dead in front of his mansion in Miami Beach." I explained this was 1997, when there was still all this early panic about AIDS, mixed up with racist anti-immigrant discourse. "All that kind of shaped how Cunanan's story was told. There was this totally fabricated theory that he found out he had HIV and so went on this killing spree. And the media was obsessed with his so-called 'inscrutable ethnicity,' like that was a crime, too."

"What do you mean?"

"People couldn't immediately tell what his background was. And he made up different versions, for different places. For a while he was telling everyone he was Jewish. He kind of messed with people's assumptions."

Tyler laughed. "He sounds like a Tom Ripley."

I smiled. "He was a bit." In fact, I was writing about parallels between the Highsmith novel and Cunanan's story. I was pleased Tyler picked up on the connection.

"That's cool," he said. "I mean, not the murdering." He laughed. "But the project. I hope it's okay that I asked."

"I don't mind." It was true—talking about it helped me remember why I was bothering in the first place. "It's nice. Students don't usually show a lot of interest in what we do outside of class."

"I'm definitely interested." He laughed again. "When I was a kid, I saw this thing on TV about Jeffrey Dahmer. I was terrified but couldn't stop watching. My parents had gone to dinner or something and left me with my cousin, Emmy. And she was in the backyard on the phone all night. My parents got home while I was watching and, oh my god, they were so pissed and Emmy was freaking out. Mom threatened to have her arrested for child neglect."

"Really?"

"She can be pretty dramatic. I don't know, I guess that's where I get it from." He turned and looked out the window. He was quiet for a bit, and then spoke again. "Ohio is so weird and flat."

I laughed. "It is both those things."

The rest of the drive, Tyler talked nonstop, carrying on with his observations about the scenery, changing stations and rattling off facts about the songs. He told stories about other students, from classes and soccer and the dorms. I didn't know any of them but didn't mind listening. He mentioned Addison and I asked how they'd met. They were placed in the same dorm first year, both with roommates they couldn't stand, and had engineered a switch. Addison was from Los Angeles. His father worked on the business side of the film industry, his mother was some kind of important lawyer. "His parents are loaded," Tyler said, "even for Sawyer." Tyler had spent a week that summer at home with Addison. "More a compound than a house," he said, an enormous pool in back and a tennis court behind that. Tyler was shocked to discover that Addison's parents had a live-in maid, but more so that Addison never mentioned it. When pushed, Addison said something about how she'd always been there. Addison was majoring in economics, which Tyler found predictable and boring. "What's the point of studying money when you've always had it and always will?"

As Tyler talked, the mile markers clicked by and when a sign announced Ohio State in two exits, I was surprised. The time had passed quickly.

The campus was a small city unto itself, roads looping past immense green lawns, sprawling plazas of brick and stone. Sawyer would fit within it several times over. I drove slowly, trying to make sense of the map I'd printed out—I still felt confounded by my new phone and hadn't figured out how to use the GPS. I scanned the signs directing traffic to various buildings bearing the names of donors; I recognized a few we shared.

"This place is massive," Tyler said. The temperature had ticked back up. A golf cart coasted by and mobs of students rushed through a crosswalk beneath a cloudless sky. A giddy energy rolled through the crowds, bouncing off the sun-streaked buildings. "I thought about transferring here last year."

"Really?" It was disarming, the idea that our students could just leave; and, of course, eventually, they all did. I couldn't imagine spending my entire career at Sawyer, as many of my senior colleagues had, and junior would. But I also couldn't see a way out.

"Don't get me wrong, I like Sawyer. Sometimes it just feels so small. But their soccer team is really good, better than here, even though OSU is Division I. Plus Sawyer gave me a scholarship to play."

"That's great," I said. "I don't know how anyone affords it."

"Seriously," he said, turning to look out the window. "Maybe it's stupid to care so much about soccer, it's only a game."

"I don't think it's stupid." On the drive down, Tyler had mentioned that Addison played water polo in high school, and while Sawyer had a team, he gave it up because his father believed athletics were for leisure and not a serious pursuit. I had wondered if Tyler felt implicated in this assessment, but he didn't offer and I didn't ask. I stopped at an intersection, peering at a sign. "I'm pretty sure it's this way."

Eventually, I found visitor parking, grateful I hadn't gotten lost. We headed to the library. I felt antsy walking with Tyler beside me, rattling away. I reminded myself that we were doing nothing wrong. No one even knew who we were; we were indistinguishable in this anonymous mass. But I would feel better once we got inside.

The library was built at a scale to match the rest of the campus. A soaring atrium of glass shot through the center. Students filled the tables circling the perimeter at each level, looking down and over the open space in which we stood. Tyler craned his neck.

"No wonder all the books I need are here."

We took a wide set of stairs to the special collections. I checked in at the front desk and the librarian stepped aside, flipping through a binder. I had called that morning as soon as they opened, worried that I wouldn't get in on such short notice. I was absurdly relieved when it worked out—I didn't want to have to fabricate tasks to justify the trip; anxiety about maintaining that charade for an entire day had kept me up half the night.

The librarian returned. "You want the fourth floor. You can take the elevator behind you. Just show these passes." She slid two small pink cards across the counter; I'd said I was bringing a research assistant. "And we have this for you as well." She set Tyler's book on the counter; I had requested it for him.

"Wow, amazing," Tyler said, and turned to me. "Thank you, this is so great."

"It's nothing." But I was pleased he was happy about it.

We headed toward the bank of elevators and then Tyler stopped.

"What time do you think you'll be done?"

"The archives close at seven. Is that too late?"

"No, that's great. I think I'll just meet you back here."

"You're not going to work on your project?" We hadn't discussed it, but I'd assumed that's what he'd be doing.

"It's so nice out, I don't want to be stuck inside." He laughed. "No offense."

"What will you do?"

"I don't know, I'll figure it out." He looked at the pink card in his hand. "I guess I don't need this."

He passed it to me, turned, and was gone.

I wandered a hall in one direction, then the other. I checked the suite number, forgot it, checked again. I headed down another hallway, the numbers going down when I wanted them to go up. Finally I found it, a set of double glass doors, directly across from the elevator where I'd begun.

"Dr. Lausson, yes? You're here!" It was the archivist I had spoken to that morning. Lucy. She looked like a bird, sheathed in a bright blue dress that shimmered in the overhead lights, a plume of dyed orange hair. I liked her immediately. I thanked her again for arranging my visit. She grinned—she was happy someone was interested in the collection. "We went through so much trouble acquiring these papers. I'm glad they'll see some use." Lucy looked past my shoulder, behind me. "I thought you were bringing an RA. Just you today?"

My cheeks flushed. "Yes. Just me."

She led me to a private room, the table laid with the materials she'd pulled. She apologized for the smallness of the accommodations; they were short on space today. It did feel a bit like a cell, strangely high walls with no windows. "No, this is perfect."

"I'm jealous you get to spend the day with these. My day is just email, email, email." She laughed and left me alone, the door clicking shut behind her.

The whole trip suddenly seemed ridiculous. I didn't know what to think of Tyler's hasty departure. Did he have some reason of his own for coming down? He hadn't mentioned any friends. I tried to push my worry aside. He was right, it was a gorgeous day. And I would get better work done on my own; he would probably just talk my ear off with all his stories about people who meant nothing to me. I pulled the first box toward me. Legal documents and lease holdings. Nothing of immediate interest. Strange what survives the passage of time. What's remembered, what's resigned to the dustbin. There is something so arbitrary in it. Why—I lifted a sheet from a stack, a report from an accountant in 1939—these papers and not something else? But maybe this is what always remains of a life: columns of addition and subtraction, a balancing act.

Lucy had pulled a guide as well. I scanned it and opened another box. A stack of the journals. The author was long dead, and he meant nothing to me—he was just a way to get at the story of Leopold and Loeb. Still, I felt a voyeuristic thrill as I lifted out the first of the notebooks. The industrialist accounted for his days with an almost comic sense of self-importance, recording mundane details with hallowed specificity. As I read, the piling up of insignificant facts—times and locations of meetings, a list of phone numbers for hotels in New York—became oddly compelling.

I was about to move on to another journal when I paused on a longer entry—many were just half a page, but this one ran for several. Throughout, he referred to individuals by their initials, and my eyes landed on F. L.—Florence Leopold, Nathan's mother. I checked the date. March 6, 1924. A few months before the murder.

F. L. joined for lunch today. She was impressed and said so several times; the new cook is doing an excellent job. I told

F. what a chore the hiring had been. You cannot depend on others for that, I explained. You must take responsibility for your staff. The meal was served on the new China which the manager at Marshall Field's had set aside especially and which F. also admired.

She was accompanied by N. He has always been a strange child to me. Well, he is a young man now but he has the air of a child about him still. He holds himself with a petulant disdain. He reminds me of a ferret, darting eyes and flared nostrils. N. has a friend R. who stopped at the house just before two o'clock; I was surprised and not pleased by his unannounced arrival. They were to attend a lecture at the university. R. is a handsome fellow but there is something undignified or presumptuous in how he intrudes upon a space. Just a look from him and he seems to be leering at you. I do not know what it is but there was something I found . . . repellant is too strong a word. Off-putting is fair. Truthfully, I was happy when they left.

Later that evening, went with M. to the Athenium for a show. It was not very good.

Historians have debated whether Nathan Leopold and Robert Loeb were actually gay and, if so, actually lovers; only later accounts referenced this explicitly. But in the uncle's depiction—an overgrown, petulant child and an undignified, leering intruder—the wheels of homosexual panic churned already. I felt a quick and satisfied kick. This was a great discovery. I took photos of the pages and made some notes.

There wasn't time for a deep dive; I would just familiarize myself with the papers for my next visit. I was eager to get to the arrest and trial and moved ahead. The cousin's account was lurid but sporadic; at times the murder and its aftermath dropped out completely; for him it was a sideshow, a minor affair. But what was there was great—no one had written about this. When I'd started the project as my dissertation, I had gotten so fixated on the technical details of murder cases I took an internship in a forensics lab. I wanted to find out how they talked about things so I could better interpret the texts I was examining. My peers thought I was crazy; lit scholars don't usually sully themselves in the trenches. But I had a feeling of an unknown world waiting to be unlocked. And I got that feeling again, poring over the journals.

I was cross-checking some dates when there was a knock at the door and it opened—I jumped.

"Sorry!" It was Lucy. She sounded surprised at her arrival as well. "Sorry, sorry!"

I laughed. "It's okay. I was deep in it." How many hours had passed?

She leaned over me to look—I could smell her perfume, robust and powdery. "Find anything interesting?"

"Definitely. I'm excited." And I was.

"Wonderful—I hate to stop you. But we're starting to close. We can arrange for you to come back soon, of course."

"I got so caught up, I didn't realize it was seven already."

"Oh no, did I not mention we were closing early at six? I've been so scattered. There's an event. They're taking the entire floor and just told us last week. Like we don't have things to do. It's a bunch of local elected officials and some board members—something for funders." She rolled her eyes at the last word as if to say—*you know how they are.*

The sun had started to drop, the air cooling in its descent. I had an hour to kill. I was hungry, I'd skipped lunch. When I told Safie I was coming down (omitting Tyler), she told me about a Middle Eastern place. "You have to go," she said. "And get the lamb." I had mapped it, not far from campus. Maybe Tyler would be hungry, too. I could wait; it seemed okay to share a meal down here.

I set off in no direction—it felt good to stretch my legs. Sawyer stifled: smaller buildings, narrow paths, fewer people, the same faces day after day. I felt a buzz at being somewhere new and unfamiliar, surrounded by strangers. I wondered what Tyler had been up to. Had he been alone all day? He seemed like someone who could slip seamlessly into whatever place he landed. Not me. As I walked, I found myself looking for his face among the packs of students.

I kept checking the time; I was nervous not to be late. As I wandered, the sun set, and in the cobalt blue of dusk, the buildings and paths became indistinct. I moved in hurried strides, headed in what I hoped was the right direction. I had wandered farther than I meant to, down some steps to a walk along a heavy stone wall circling a small lake, its black waters depthless and still. I spun around, searching out the stairs I'd come down, and caught a scent of something. I lifted my shirt and sniffed: nervous sweat and library funk.

A young couple, walking close and bent over a phone, passed by.

"Can you point me toward the library? I've gotten lost."

"Which one?" the girl of the pair asked.

"The main one, I think?" Though I'd spent the day there, the name escaped me. "Lots of glass?"

"Thompson. That way." She motioned behind me; I'd just come from there. "It's like a ten-minute walk or something."

"Shit"—it was already seven; I would be late—"pardon me." But they were walking away, back at the phone. I hurried off, wishing I had taken Tyler's number. What if he was looking for me and got lost? The faculty handbook must have rules against misplacing students.

But I hadn't gone far when I saw him, standing alone at the edge of a road. Something was off: shoulders braced, limbs tensed. He had his phone at his ear and then shoved it away. In his other hand, he held a cigarette. He drew it to his mouth, took a quick puff, and then flicked it, still smoldering, to the ground.

I called his name and he turned, languid eyes unfocused like he didn't see me. I jogged the last steps toward him. "Sorry"—I stopped and caught my breath—"they kicked me out early. I went for a walk and got turned around."

"It's fine," he said, voice flat and empty. I waited for more but nothing came.

"Well, I'm glad I found you." The library was ahead, easy to spot now that I knew where to look. But still the equivalent of several city blocks away. What was he doing over here? "Were you looking for me?"

"No, not yet." He sounded completely disinterested, unbothered. "Is it seven?"

"It is." I was running in frantic circles, stressing out about being late, and he hadn't even checked the time. "Is something the matter?"

"No. Why?"

"I don't know. Just—I don't know, I'm asking." We stood in silence, his reticence a solid thing between us. My stomach growled and I felt light-headed with hunger and adrenaline. I needed to eat. "Listen, I should get some dinner before we head back. Are you hungry at all?"

He shrugged. "Sure."

It wasn't really a yes, but I didn't know what else to do and it seemed he wasn't going to make it any easier. I couldn't tell what was happening. He was upset about something, but what? We could be quick about it. We walked without talking, Tyler standing apart, hands in his pockets, eyes down. I kept checking the map, straining to make sense of it in the dark, worried that I'd get lost again. Finally, we made it to a broad street at the edge of campus. "It's this way," I said. "We should be there soon."

We crossed the street and, as we got to the other side, Tyler stopped in the middle of the sidewalk.

"I'm sorry," he said.

"What do you mean?"

"I'm being a total brat." He looked away from me and down.

"Look, we can just go back to Sawyer if you want."

"It's not that."

"What then?"

He picked at something on his lip, tugging. "Just some stupid thing with Addison."

Ah, of course. I thought back to the fight I'd witnessed between them in September. "Want to tell me about it?"

"He's just so frustrating. He acts like he's the center of the universe. Mostly I can handle it but sometimes he just pushes me over the edge. He can be so clueless."

It didn't seem like much—teenage concerns. But I nodded and said, "That sounds annoying."

"It's not *annoying*." Tyler spat the word, startling me, his face splotchy and red with a rush of heat and anger. "It's fucking infuriating. He's had every little thing handed to him in life and he has absolutely no idea. I just—" His eyes narrowed and flashed, his hand ripped through the air, as if grabbing for the words; a delivery guy dodged out of the way. "Forget it. Whatever." He pressed a cigarette to his lips—I hadn't noticed him pull out the pack. His face twisted in the lighter's flare.

We stood there, Tyler smoking, neither of us speaking, pedestrians streaming around us. And then, as abruptly as the moment had erupted, it passed, as if a curtain had lowered and then lifted, Tyler's whole body shifting in an instant. The tightness gone, a looseness returning. "I'm sorry." He shook his head, whisking something away, smiled and laughed. "Don't pay any attention to me, it's nothing, just silly college shit. I don't want to bore you." He laughed again.

I wasn't sure how to make sense of the sudden shift in mood. "I'm not bored. You're sure you're okay?"

"Really, I'm fine," he said, and genuinely seemed it. "Forget about it." He swiveled and scanned the block. "Look at all this." It was the kind of street that radiated from college campuses across the country: Irish pubs, Thai restaurants serving gooey, sugary heaps of noodles, suburban fast-food imports. Throngs of students clogged the sidewalks, coming and going with the urgency of youth. "I forgot what it's like to be in an actual city."

"I think our spot is at the end of the block. Are you up for it?"

"Definitely, I'm starved."

But we took just a few steps and then Tyler stopped again. We stood in front of a bar. A thick-necked bouncer manned the entrance, flirting with two girls.

Tyler pointed at the door. "Actually, let's check this out first?"

"I don't know." Tyler was underage, I knew that, but I didn't want to say anything—I didn't want to set him off again. "This restaurant is supposed to get pretty busy. We might have to wait." The door opened as a group exited. The crowd's cacophony and the sour smell of old beer rolled out with them.

"Just a quick drink." Tyler chucked his cigarette and grabbed the edge of the door before it shut. The bouncer turned from the girls but before he could speak, Tyler said, "We just stepped out for a smoke," and leapt inside. I followed.

Riotous music blasted at us. Bodies packed together into the narrow space, peeling walls slapped in murky black. "This way." Tyler edged into an opening. Before I could say anything, he shouted an order for two beers. "That okay?" he said, without waiting for a reply. When they arrived he asked for some cash, laughing—"Sorry, I'm all out." Great, I thought—now I'm buying an underage student drinks. I dug out a twenty and passed it to him. We shoved back through the crowds, the over-full pint spilling down my hand. We found a corner, a high table loaded with empties. Tyler gulped from his glass, draining the half of it. "That's perfect," he said. "I'll be right back." He set down the beer and spun, weaving through the crowd toward the bathroom, leaving me on my own.

Somehow I'd gone from a bad idea—bringing Tyler down to Columbus—to something much worse. I should have just taken us to the car when I'd found him. I resolved: When he returns from the bathroom, I'll get us out of here, and we'll head back to Sawyer. As I waited, I looked around. Students filled out the entire space. Guys crowded below television screens, watching whatever game was on, shouting and clapping each other on the back, as if they had achieved something. Girls perched at high-topped tables, wrapped in tight dresses too nice for the setting and not warm enough for the season. I had been to bars like this a few times in college, but not since. There was nothing appealing about it. I felt conspicuous, and old.

I kept an eye toward the bathrooms for Tyler but apparently missed him, because he returned to our corner from the opposite direction. His eyes shone glassy and bright, darting around in the dark of the bar, lights blinking off his pupils. "Sorry, there was a long line." He lifted his beer and tapped it absentmindedly against mine, head shifting left and right, searching for something. He finished the rest of his drink. I lifted my glass to do the same; I didn't really want it, but I wanted to get out of there.

Then Tyler called out to someone, waving. A guy in a baseball cap, auburn curls bursting out. He gripped a pint in one hand, balancing three shots in the other.

"Perfect," Tyler said, passing a shot glass to me and grabbing one for himself. "This is Jason."

"You know each other?" Panic seized me; was he from Sawyer?

"How would we know each other?" Tyler laughed, liked I'd asked something absurd. "We met in the bathroom."

"What's up?" Jason shouted over the din, louder than necessary. At the edge of his nostril, a trace of something white. Tyler, maybe seeing me notice, motioned at Jason, brushing his own nose. Jason wiped it away. Were they doing drugs in the bathroom? They tossed back the shots and, unsure what else I could do, I followed. Tequila. It singed my throat, hitting my empty stomach with a slap. Jason and Tyler got to talking. I couldn't make out what they were saying and then I stopped trying. Jason looked like any frat boy in any college town, and I couldn't imagine what Tyler would want with him. I thought of Tyler's high school photos on

Facebook. I had assumed he hung out with that crowd because he was trapped in North Carolina with no better options. But is this who he would choose?

Jason finally left—he said something I couldn't hear. I turned to Tyler. "We should probably get going."

"Yeah," Tyler said, looking around. "This place is so funny."

"What do you mean?"

"Everyone looks exactly the same."

It was true, they did. Or most of them did. There was a guy, older than the rest, in a button-down and tie, sleeves rolled up, talking with the bartender and looking our way. Beside him stood the bouncer.

"Tyler"—his name felt funny in my mouth, or maybe it was the tequila and beer—"are you ready?"

Before we could move, the guy in the button-down approached.

"Good evening, gentlemen. How's it going?"

"Fine." Tyler said. "How's it going with you?"

"Seems like maybe there was some confusion at the door earlier." He wore a nametag—MATT, MANAGER. His eyes roamed between us. "Just wondering if I could see some ID?" It was addressed to Tyler, and not really a question.

Tyler looked about to speak, then took his time. "Why?" He chewed on the word, gummy in his mouth.

Matt's face flinched, in surprise or annoyance. "It's not a problem, is it?"

"No, it's not a problem." Tyler pulled out his wallet and passed him a card. "I'm just asking."

"Thanks," Matt said. "I'll be right back."

He started to walk off when Tyler spoke again. "Wait." Matt turned and Tyler pointed at me. "You didn't ask for his ID."

"Tyler."

He ignored me. "Well, you didn't."

Matt gave a sharp smile. "I am sorry, sir. Do you have some ID I could see?"

I handed over my license, humiliated. Matt the Manager walked back to the bar.

"Tyler, what are you doing?"

He ignored my question and a few moments later Matt returned. He looked at Tyler. "We have a policy of confiscating fake IDs." Matt stepped aside, making space in front of him. I was conscious of the eyes around us, tuning into the fact that something was happening. "I'll need you both to leave."

Tyler pushed off from the wall, spring-loaded, storming to the exit.

"Mark, right?" Matt glanced at my ID then back at me. "I'm going to do you a favor and assume you didn't know you were accompanying a minor to a bar. But, honestly, this doesn't look good."

Across the street, Tyler stormed in a tight, furious circle. I dashed through the traffic. A car honked, the driver shouting.

"So stupid," Tyler said, waving a cigarette. "I've been going to bars since I was fifteen. Now I have to pay a hundred bucks for another ID."

"Tyler—this isn't a joke."

"What's the big deal?"

"Are you kidding me? We could have gotten in serious trouble." Rage and panic coursed through me. "Do you understand?" He said nothing. "Tyler, are you listening to me? This isn't a fucking joke."

"Mark." His voice had changed, gone soft and low. His eyes widened. "You're hurting me."

And then I saw. I had grabbed him, gripping his shoulder. I didn't even remember reaching for him. I let go, my fingers humming with the afterburn of strain. I looked at my hand then down. Tyler had dropped the cigarette, or I had shaken it from him; it smoked at his feet.

"Let's just get back to Sawyer," I said, and turned from him, already walking away. "This is a goddamn mess."

We drove home, the drone of silence cut only by the low whoosh of an occasional car passing by. My hands were shaking and I squeezed the wheel to steady myself.

I had been a complete fool—and for what? What did I think was going to happen today? Tyler's disappearance from the library, his lost hours, that idiot from the bar, cocaine or something on his face—how had any of this become part of my day? I didn't know what was going on between Tyler and Addison, and I didn't want to. He said it himself, it was silly college shit. What did that say about me? I couldn't shake the image of the bar manager taunting me, holding my license like it was my fate. I could have been seriously fucked. And I had gotten so angry, I'd grabbed Tyler without even knowing it. What if I had done worse?

We reached our exit. I retraced our route back to the parking lot. The doughnut shop was closed, and the laundromat, too. Only the liquor store was open, its neon sign casting a lurid green across the lot. I parked and shut the engine. For the first time since we'd gotten in the car, I turned to Tyler. He looked at me, calm and expectant, the curve of his cheek pulsing in the lights.

"Listen," I said. "I'm sorry about what happened. I didn't mean to grab you—"

"It's fine."

"No, it isn't." And when he tried again to interrupt, I cut him off. "It's not. I'm sorry. I lost my head."

"Don't be upset. Really, it's okay, I get it. I know I can be a lot."

"I didn't think this day through. I shouldn't have brought you along."

"Don't say that. It was my idea."

"Okay. But I'm the adult here."

He snorted. "I'm nineteen."

I let out a long breath and closed my eyes. And then I felt a hand on my arm—my eyes sprung open: Tyler's fingers, light on my sleeve. I looked from his hand to his face.

"Let's just pretend it didn't happen, okay?" His voice wavered and cracked, eyes holding mine. "Everything turned out fine, right?"

"I don't know." I wanted what he was offering: forgiveness, reprieve. "Maybe it did."

He sighed and pulled his hand away, his smile a shot through the dark. "Okay, good. We're good." I could feel the soft press of his fingers on me still. "I'm telling you, last time I got busted with a fake ID, it did not go that well."

I laughed, I couldn't help it. "I do not want to know."

"You really don't." And Tyler laughed as well. "I never asked how your research went. Did you find what you were looking for?"

The archives seemed a lifetime ago.

"I did, actually. It was a good start."

"That's great, that's what matters." He smiled. "Don't worry about tonight."

After Tyler left, I stayed in the parking lot. Hunger clenched my stomach but when I thought about returning to my apartment, standing alone in the dim kitchen light, I didn't want to go. So I sat in the car for a long time, doing nothing.

CHAPTER 5

"H ere." Safie passed me a wooden spoon and pointed toward the stove. "Stir that."

The tomatoes bubbled in their juices, pinking from the butter. A burst of oregano hit my nose. Beside me, Safie bent over the counter, coaxing paper-thin slices from a purple onion. The kitchen window above her framed the last ruddy light of the fading autumn afternoon.

"This was a good idea," I said. It was a Friday. At Safie's insistence, we'd ditched work and come to her place to cook an early dinner. "Thank you."

"No, thank you," Safie said. "I hate eating alone. Did you make up your mind about the Friedmans?"

"No," I grumbled. "I don't know."

Elaine and Robert Friedman were campus figureheads. They'd been teaching in Sawyer's Anthro department since the 1980s, arriving fresh from Fulbrights. They'd become famous—well, academic famous—for their joint research on an isolated community in the Brazilian Amazon. Despite attempts by larger and richer schools to lure them away, the Friedmans had stayed loyal to their Ohio enclave all these years. Every fall toward the end of October, they hosted a party at their gigantic house. They served beer Robert brewed in the basement and complicated dishes seasoned with spices Elaine smuggled back from their travels. It was by invitation only, a rotating guest list of senior stalwarts and junior faculty deemed worthy. Safie, of course, scored an invite every year. (She thought out of white guilt; I thought, sure, but with some real affection thrown in: Everyone loved Safie.) This year, Stephen got invited and wanted me to come along. We'd argued about it— there was something about showing up as a plus-one, without an invitation of my own, that felt a little degrading. I knew I was being unnecessarily difficult, but I guess that's what being difficult is.

"It's just a party," Safie said. "I don't see what's the big deal."

"It's not a big deal. So why does it matter if I go?"

Safie laughed.

"What?"

"Nothing. I just sometimes forget you're the kind of person who would say no to a party on principle."

"I'm not a kind of person. I'm just not thrilled about giving up a weekend to kiss ass and chitchat with a bunch of work people."

Safie turned from her chopping and looked at me. "I'm sure it's not intentional, but when you say things like that, you sound like you think you're better than the rest of us."

"I didn't mean—" It was a shitty thing to say. What had gotten into me? I'd been cranky and out of sorts for weeks, picking little fights with Stephen, avoiding my parents' calls. And now this, with Safie. "I'm sorry."

She waved the knife in her hand, dismissing it. "It's fine. But it would probably make Stephen happy if you went."

"Did he say something?"

"No, it's just a guess." She held a pepper grinder toward me. "Now this."

I twisted and watched the tiny flecks disappear into the sauce. Maybe Safie was right. It didn't really matter if I wanted to go or not; I could do this for Stephen. We hadn't had a proper date in a while. I kept claiming work, which was true enough—I was scrambling to get ready for the Fall Fest lecture—but then why did I feel like I was lying?

The day of the party, I waited at the curb, the collar of my coat pulled against a bite in the air. I needed to sort my Thanksgiving plans—a few warm, swampy days in Florida could be a nice break. Stephen pulled up and I jumped in, almost landing on a bouquet of flowers. I picked them up and lowered my face, the hothouse sweetness bursting at me.

"These are nice." Maybe he felt bad for pressuring me to come along. "What's the occasion?"

"Oh." Stephen glanced between me and the flowers. "They're for Elaine and Robert."

Elaine Friedman greeted us at the door, wrapped in a bright and flowy caftan totally out of place for autumn in Ohio. Looping strands of ceramic beads and painted wood circled her neck. She looked like someone from SoHo who'd spent a year throwing pottery in Taos.

"Stephen, Stephen!" Elaine took his cheeks in both palms, the jewels of her heavily ringed fingers sparkling against him. She turned his face side to side, as if inspecting her firstborn home from war. "I am so delighted you're here. Robert can't wait to see you." It turned out Stephen had grown up going on family fishing trips to the same lakeside town in eastern Michigan where the Friedmans spent their summers.

"Elaine, this is Mark Lausson. And these are for you." Stephen motioned toward the bouquet he'd insisted I carry in. I'd forgotten it, pressed to my side.

"Aren't freesia just perfect?" she said, lifting the flowers (apparently freesia) from me. She barely touched the bouquet; it seemed to float between the fretwork of her fingers. "And Mark, what do you do?"

"He's at Sawyer," Stephen said, and I thought I heard a catch in his voice—like he was embarrassed that nobody at Sawyer knew who I was. "In English."

"Really? We've never met, though. Is this your first year?"

"Second, actually. Somehow, they let me come back."

Elaine laughed, a light trill in her throat. "I am sure we are lucky to have you."

"Mark is doing a Sawyer Scholars lecture for Fall Fest," Stephen said.

"Wonderful, wonderful," Elaine said, but I felt annoyed, as if Stephen were trying to prove I wasn't a liability. "You know I gave the very first one."

Stephen offered to help put the flowers in water and Elaine steered him toward the kitchen. He turned, mouthing *Be right back*, and was gone.

The Friedmans were of an era when academics still had, relative to their surroundings, money to spend and social standing to match. The house, with its rooms opening onto more rooms through French doors of wavy-glassed panels, felt almost ostentatious. Artifacts from research trips crowded bookshelves and low side tables and hung from the walls: rugs and bowls and masks of broad, plaintive faces pining for escape. I stationed myself in a corner, a long, carved stick topped with a straw tassel like a flaccid broom at my back. Clusters of Sawyer's best and brightest filled the room. I recognized some faces and occupied myself guessing at the home departments of those I didn't. Nearest me, a group of men debated the last election. While their generic dress was hard to place (dark jeans, wrinkled Oxfords), the ubiquitous beards gave them away immediately as sociologists. Another male-only crew inspected an enormous, framed map hanging above a rolltop desk: political scientists (dressed like the sociologists, but clean shaven). To their right, a professor of film studies (hair dyed with purple streaks, thigh-high black boots) clinked glasses with an economist (clean, classic, old money). Given the Friedmans' own department, a healthy number of guests sported chunky but tasteful jewelry (the women of anthropology) or T-shirts (the men). As I gloated in the corner judging everyone, I knew that I, too, could be easily pegged as an English professor: white, gay.

I headed toward the kitchen. Caterers buzzed over serving plates lining the long stretch of countertop. Stephen and Elaine were gone. The young staff were dressed in white shirts and pressed black pants. I recognized the name of the catering company printed on a satchel slumped on the floor, and it explained the presence of Latinos in Sawyer; they were down from Cleveland. I apologized for intruding and moved from a side door into what must have been an addition to the original house: a wide glass-walled room, two steps down, abutting the backyard. While the yard lay browning and dry, awaiting the first snow of the season, the sunroom brimmed with life, gargantuan yellow-green plants and rows of engorged, spiked succulents. The warmth of the room had a disorienting effect, out of sync with the season. I found a cooler of Robert's home brews and grabbed one. It was labeled with a piece of tape sharpied in the neat blocky print of an older generation. *August IPA.*

For me, work functions were like poker night: Show up, shuffle things around like you know what you're doing, and accept your losses. I scanned, trying to figure out where to place myself. Safie was talking with Loren and Eugene, her landlords. I was about to join them when Colin pulled me into an adjacent group: It was him, Priya, and two of the bearded sociologists—a skinny one with bad posture and a short one. The skinny one was going on about the failings of qualitative research. The short one nodded along in vigorous assent, a pained expression on his face, like he needed everyone to know he agreed. "Qualitative research has its merits, of course," the skinny one said, "but in practice, begs for rigor." Academics never fail to disappoint with a lack of range. A conversation among more than two inevitably turns to our own sorry lots in life, circling the drain of our profession, the suck of it irresistible: complaints about the administration, complaints about students, and lamentations about the declining state of the field. Whichever field the participants belong to is presented as the most in decline; today it was sociology.

"But isn't methodological diversity good for a field?" Priya asked.

The skinny sociologist was ramping up, his beard damp with beer and dismay, continuing as if Priya hadn't even spoken. "How are we supposed to interest our students in statistical methods when our own colleagues can't perform a basic linear regression?"

"I can see where you're coming from," Colin said. "In the humanities there's a skepticism about science that really doesn't serve us well. Sometimes I feel like our fixation with the literary will make us obsolete."

Priya pushed back in. "Are you saying English should abandon the study of literature?"

"Of course not," Colin said.

"Literature has its place," the skinny one said. "But you're not going to solve, say, the immigrant problem with literature."

At this, Safie turned from Loren and Eugene. "Who said anything about an immigrant problem?"

The skinny sociologist stammered, and the short one looked away, trying to distance himself. "It's just an example."

"An example of what?"

He cleared his throat, eyes lighting on Priya. "Of the need for replicable measures of social problems." His voice had risen an octave.

"A funny example to go to," Safie said, and then turned from him. "Who needs a refill?" She took Priya by the arm, guiding her toward the kitchen. Colin excused us and we followed.

"Wow," I said. "Social scientists really know how to have a good time."

Priya let out a whoosh of relief. "Thank you for that."

"Immigrant problem? Seriously? Write your irrelevant articles and leave us out of it." Safie lifted a bottle of wine to inspect. "Something to dull the memory?"

Just then someone popped a head in. It was Elizabeth Chen. She'd cut her hair shorter since I'd seen her last, blunt at her chin, framing cheeks rosy with the warmth of the house. "Oh. Wrong room. Hello everyone." She wiggled her fingers and disappeared.

After a long enough moment had passed, Colin said, "Divorce is looking good on her."

"No more Hal?" Safie said.

"No more Hal," Colin said. "It's officially over."

"What happened?" Safie asked. "Did he take up with another student?"

"Elizabeth was Hal's student?" asked Priya.

"I don't think so," I said. "I don't remember hearing that."

Safie grunted. "She was a grad student at Rice while Hal was there. And the only reason she wasn't his student is because the school found out about the relationship and took Hal off her committee."

"Is that how they ended up here?" I asked.

"I guess Elizabeth got her partner-hire and doesn't need him anymore," Colin said.

"That's kind of sexist, don't you think?" Priya said.

Colin's face flushed. "My apologies," he said, trying to make a joke of it. "Anyway, I don't know why Elizabeth left. But I haven't heard any rumors about Hal and a student." Colin turned to me. "Have you?"

"Me? I don't know anything." I picked at the label on my beer, my thumbnail getting gummed up from the tape. "I'm just here for the drinks."

"It's so obvious—sex with students. What a cliché," said Safie. "Are you so unimaginative that you can't see a world beyond this?"

Colin smirked. "I don't remember you talking about clichés last year with the Annabelle debacle."

"That was different."

"How so? Because she's a woman?"

"Yes," Safie said. "Of course."

The year before, Annabelle Cleremont, assistant professor of French, had been unceremoniously let go when it came to light that she was sleeping with not one but two students, both from her Intro course. (As Safie said, "*Comme c'est audacieux.*") When the first student found out about the second via a thinly veiled Facebook post in the middle of lecture, he went nuclear and brought the entire thing crashing down on all three of their heads. (This struck me as somehow appropriate to the language, and something that would never happen in German.) Naturally, Annabelle was the only one to suffer consequences. In fact, she was the first case of a Sawyer professor getting fired over sex with a student;

administration cited "creating a hostile learning environment" as cause for termination.

"I don't know why that matters," Colin said. "There's the same power differential."

"Not exactly," Priya said. "I'm with Safie. Not that it's some radical feminist act for a woman to sleep with a student. But there's power at play in terms of gender as well."

"If there's sex, there's power," Safie said. "Otherwise, what's the point?"

I finished my beer and set down the bottle; I'd ribboned the label to shreds.

"I should look for Stephen. I haven't seen him since we arrived."

"Maybe he met someone else," Safie said, smiling.

"Here?"

I found Stephen coming down the stairs and climbed to meet him at a landing where the wide planks turned, the golden finish rubbed down. A stained-glass window cast an aqueous blue light across him. Robert had taken Stephen to the upstairs study to show him an album of photos from the lake house in Michigan. While that seemed like torture—photos of somebody else's vacations— Stephen didn't mind. "That place is special to me," he said. He picked something from my sleeve, a bit of leaf from the orangery. (On my way to look for Stephen, I'd passed Elaine and that's what she'd called it. "I'm so pleased you've enjoyed the *orangery*. It's absolutely vital in winter.")

"I'm glad you had a good time with Robert." I meant it—it was nice seeing him happy.

Stephen seemed to consider his next words. "We should go out to the lake some time. Maybe at the end of spring term, when the weather warms up."

The end of spring seemed impossibly far away. "I don't know, I'm not much of a fisherman. Fisherperson."

"There's a lot more to do than fish."

"Like what?"

Stephen's eyes narrowed, and I could hear how I sounded. "If you don't want to go, you can just say so."

From below, Elaine appeared. "Come, come," she called, fingers spread, hands waving across the yawning space at the foot of the stairs. "Robert is going to make his toast."

She whisked away and I touched a hand to Stephen's arm. "I'm just stressed about this stupid lecture. A trip to the lake sounds great. We should do it."

"Really?"

"Of course." I kissed him, a light brush on his lips. "Let's go downstairs."

The guests, numbering forty-odd, had crowded together, forming a dense, lopsided horseshoe in the sitting room. (Again, Elaine's designation—"Everyone into the sitting room," she'd cooed, ushering us like baby chicks back into the pen.) I knew from Safie this signaled the beginning of what would be a long and meandering speech by Robert, reflecting on the year and imparting some nonconsensual pearls of wisdom. Elaine squeezed Robert's arm and shook back her hair. She wore it long and loose, white streaks against carbon. I caught Safie's eye and she braced herself: a slight dip of her lip, a sly commiseration just for me.

Around us, the catering staff swooped, clearing away half-full glasses and greasy paper napkins folded around final, discarded bites. Something in their silent labor brought back a memory from when I was twelve, the summer before seventh grade. My parents' twentieth wedding anniversary. My father had recently switched jobs, hired into a promotion. Cassie and I understood it was a big step up, although we were never clear on exactly what he did. Something about accounting and global shipping—the mysteries of fathers and their lifetimes spent at the office. My mother once joked she wouldn't mind living in a nunnery, if they would take a Jew, because then you wouldn't have to decide what to wear every day. With my father's new position, she became a woman concerned with her appearance: taking a standing appointment to color her hair at the chrome and white salon in the fancy new mall; fretting about repeating a dress for one of the weekend functions that increasingly took them away from us. We had no nearby relatives and though a few old friends attended, the invited guests were mostly new acquaintances from the company, my father's coworkers and their wives. When I asked why they would celebrate something that seemed so personal with a bunch of strangers, my mother replied, "We have to put on a good show," and I couldn't imagine what she meant. They hired a company to manage the party, stressing about the cost but feeling they had no choice. The staff arrived in two white vans early in the morning and swarmed through the house, getting it ready. A crew set up a large tent in the backyard. The summer sweltered and I felt bad for the workers, in their heavy pants and long sleeves.

Adolescence came on slowly for me, and late. That July, I was still a child, soft skin and shiny hair, so my mother allowed me into a private orbit from which puberty would soon exclude me. I stood beside her as she got ready at her bedroom vanity in a slip and bra, brushing powders across the bow of her cheeks. I was wearing the outfit she'd bought new for the occasion: a cardinal blue tie cinched uncomfortably around my neck, a short-sleeved button-down, my sticks of arms swinging from it with no sense of where to go. She sprayed a cloud of perfume above her head and it settled around her. I dashed out a hand to catch some of the wet dust on my fingertips. I carried the faint and purloined scent around with me the rest of the day.

My parents had decided the event would be adults-only and Cassie felt this meant she and I should be pardoned from attending. "Don't be absurd," my mother said. *Absurd* was a new favorite word, lobbed at Cassie in regard to everything from her clothing choices to her proposal to put off college for a year and join her new friend Meg, who planned to backpack across Australia working on farms. While I wouldn't admit this to Cassie, I felt relieved that no other kids would be at the party. Whenever children gathered, a ranking quickly emerged. Navigating these hierarchies, with their unspoken yet cruelly enforced rules, was an exhausting enterprise: the constant calculations of how to hold my body, of what topics I should feign ignorance about (the daytime soaps I watched on sick days; what girls various teen heartthrobs were rumored to be dating) and in which ones I needed to mimic interest (mostly just sports and cars)—though not so much interest as to elicit questions, only enough to keep the conversation moving past me. My efforts to remain undetected often failed, and some boy sniffed me out, targeting me for ridicule, if not worse. If the girls took any notice of me—it was a saccharine attention, the same cloying affections they directed at kittens and babies—this only inflamed the boys' annoyance, escalating their attacks.

In the company of grown-ups, however, I felt at ease. There, I found the invisibility I desired. I spent the afternoon of the party floating among the guests, weaving between their suits and dresses, the just-laundered fabrics holding the cool of the air-conditioned house when they stepped outside. I ate mouthfuls of unrecognizable foods as they zigged by on trays and eavesdropped on the conversations around me, searching out some window into the opaque lives of my parents. I was looking for a clue, an indication that in the universe of adults, awaiting across an interminable chasm of time, I might find escape from the lonely terror of childhood.

I wandered from the backyard tent to the side of the house. Cassie was there, out of view of the party, talking with one of the caterers. They stood close together, backs to the wall, leaning at a shared angle. I'd seen him earlier. He had muddy brown hair pulled into a ponytail at the nape of his neck and a small, dark patch cut into a neat rectangle below his lower lip. He'd been setting up wineglasses with another caterer, and she'd said something about it, asking why he shaved his face like that. He grabbed at her backside, saying, "You don't like my flavor saver?" I didn't know what that meant, but I could hear in the lilt of his voice it was something teasing and private. She called him gross and swatted him away. I stood still in the clipped grass, watching Cassie with him now. He said something and she laughed in this weird loud way that didn't sound like her. The guy waved his hand in front of her face and I saw the spark of a lit cigarette.

Cassie noticed me then and called over. "What's up, Marky?" I shrugged. "Come here. This is Dave."

Dave was tall and as I looked up at him, I could see dints in a line around his ear, where he'd taken out earrings. He cleared his throat and spit, a fat yellow hock into a shrub. "Enjoying the party, Marky?"

"My name's Mark."

"Okay, Mark," he repeated, my name a taunt in his mouth.

"Where's Mom and Dad at?" Cassie asked. I shrugged again. "Well, what have you been up to?"

"Nothing, really. I accidentally ate caviar. And I think raw tuna."

"You liked it?" Dave asked.

"Yeah. I guess."

"Tastes just like pussy, right?"

Cassie shoved at him, not hard. "He's twelve. Don't be nasty." But she laughed again, a sharp snort. Dave grinned and the hair under his lip spread itself out like a dirty stain and I understood the crudeness of his joke before.

"Relax, he thinks it's funny." Dave smashed his cigarette out against the wall, leaving a charcoal smear behind. He dropped it and it landed on a broad leaf, waxy and yellow. "I should get back inside."

"Find me later?" Cassie said it like a question, a hesitation in her voice I didn't recognize.

Dave didn't respond but put a hand on my shoulder and dug his thumb in, sharp. "Don't rat me out, Mark."

Cassie sat and I joined her. I pulled on a long blade of grass missed by the mower and the ground released it, thick and fibrous between my finger and thumb. Cassie and our mother had battled about her outfit. When she'd found a dress laid across her bed, Cassie burst into shouts. Things escalated like that those days, from spark to conflagration in an instant. I was in the hallway outside her room and a girl from the catering team who'd been using the bathroom came out. She turned her head toward the sound of my sister's yelling, then looked at me, guilty, and scurried away. Cassie was outraged that our mother had gone through her things. When our mother said that, God forbid, Cassie try to look nice for once, Cassie snarled back, "You mean like a painted clown, like you?" My father said, *Watch yourself,* the words even and slow, the warning so soft I could almost not hear it. Cassie won the right to choose her outfit but compromised on a dress. It was black and fit tight in the middle, its stretch pulling across her. She reached into the front and pulled out a pack of cigarettes. She smiled. "He forgot these. Want one?"

I had smoked a cigarette with this weird kid Wayne on the last day of school. Wayne was crazy, everyone said so, and there was a rumor his dad was in prison. Wayne didn't care, though. He didn't have friends but he wasn't picked on, either. He lived in some other world, outside the pecking order of junior high. I guess that's why I said yes even though I was worried about getting caught. I detested our school, but, unlike Wayne, still longed to fit in. I wanted to learn his secret. As his cigarette burned down to the stub, Wayne bent and extinguished it against himself, pushing the cherry into the skin of his scrawny ankle. The sour smell of singed hair surged at me. I retched and Wayne giggled. The inside of his leg, the entire length of it, was dotted in small circles, smooth, shiny rounds of pink and white.

Cassie pointed the pack at me and I pulled out a cigarette, placing it at the very edge of my lips like Wayne had done. Cassie lit one for herself. Smoke ribboned around her face. She leaned forward, pushing the lit end to my own.

"Suck in."

I did and a rash of smoke swelled into me. I coughed so hard the cigarette flew from my mouth. Cassie laughed, her true laugh, gauzy and bright. My coughs turned to laughs as well and I picked up the cigarette.

"You'll figure it out." The skirt of Cassie's dress fanned across her folded legs. As her hand looped through the space between us, flakes of gray ash dotted the skirt and disappeared. "What time it is?"

"I don't know. Almost four, I think?"

Cassie growled. "This day is never going to end."

"It's not so bad." I twirled the cigarette in my fingers, hoping it would burn down so I didn't have to smoke it.

"Dave said there's some party tonight. A bunch of his friends are going."

I had never been to a party without grown-ups but, based on what I gleaned from the young adult novels I was secretly checking out from the library, I didn't want Cassie at one. Especially not with Dave. I didn't understand why she would want to hang out with him.

"Are you going?"

"I don't know," Cassie said, and flicked a stray flake from the tip of her tongue. "It could be fun."

"Do you think Mom will let you?" I wanted to plant a seed of doubt in her mind so she would let the idea go.

Cassie let out a sigh, more a moan. "God, she's been acting like such a cunt."

"What?" I'd never heard Cassie say that word before—not in any of her complaining to me, not in all the screaming fights. I had never heard anyone say it. It made her face turn at the edges, ugly.

"I'll just tell them I'm staying at Meg's. If Mom had her way, I'd spend my life stuck inside this house with the rest of you."

I said nothing. The long ash of my cigarette drooped and fell under its weight. I pulled the last of it to my lips and inhaled, holding the smoke in the cave of my mouth. I squeezed my eyes shut, willing myself not to cough. Bursts of neon light flashed in the dark behind my eyelids. The noise of the party rolled over me in waves, ebbing then rising again. The high pitch of a woman exclaiming cut through the din. "You did not! I don't believe it!" she yelled, her voice a squeal. I opened my eyes and exhaled. The smoke billowed out. My cigarette was done. I tucked the soft end into my pocket and stood.

"I'm gonna go inside."

I went to the kitchen where I hoped to find some orange juice to wash the dirty taste from my mouth. Caterers crowded the space but, to my relief, Dave was not among them. My mother stood with one, discussing which trays should go out next. As I slipped toward the refrigerator, she saw me.

"Where have you been?"

"Just outside." I opened the fridge, pushing my face into the cold blast.

My mother made a sound with her throat. "Crap." I turned to look. Her necklace had gotten caught in the collar of her dress, the gold chain twisted upon itself like a worm. "Marky, help me with this? My hands are sticky, I don't want to get anything on me."

She bent toward me and I reached for the chain. My mother's nose wrinkled and she grabbed my fingers, pulling them to her face.

"Were you smoking?"

Around us, the noise of the kitchen tamped down. I had never been the target of our mother's anger—it was reserved for Cassie—but something in the vibrating pitch of her voice scared me. I yanked my hand away. "No." My mind scrambled for something else to say, but I came up with nothing. "No."

And then, from the other side of the kitchen—"Jesus, Mom. Calm down."

We both turned to the sound of Cassie's voice, unaware until then she was there.

"You gave your brother a cigarette?"

She sprang toward Cassie so quickly, I heard the crack of her hand before I realized what was happening. Cassie's cheek glowed with a hot, pink streak. Her hair had fallen into her face but I could see the shine of water welling in her eyes as she fought to hold back tears. I braced myself for the insult she would hurl at our mother. I was frightened she would anger her further with some cruelty I didn't think she deserved, even if she had just hit Cassie. But Cassie was silent. The caterers kept their heads low, sweeping from the room so just the three of us remained.

Finally, it was our mother who spoke.

"You disgust me," she said, her voice drained of heat, and walked from the room.

Cassie said nothing and made no move. I couldn't look at her. The shame of my betrayal consumed me. I trained my eyes at the floor and traced a thin, spidery crack running through a tile until it disappeared under the edge of a cabinet. I stayed there, frozen in place, listening to the sound of Cassie's breathing—short, quick swallows of air, one after the other.

Robert's speech was long, as Safie warned. The room simmered with restless energy. I whispered to Stephen, "I'll be right back."

"Everything okay?"

"Just a bathroom break."

I stepped from the crowd, looping through the house. I stopped at the kitchen—empty—and went in. I pulled out my phone. The muted rumble of Robert pontificating echoed from the other room. I opened up Facebook. (After a few weeks cycling through deleting, downloading, deleting, I had given in.) I glanced side to side then clicked on Tyler's page. There was a new post, something from Kennedy. Addison had commented and then Tyler replied with a photo of a cat in giant sunglasses; for some reason I couldn't glean, most of their posts seemed to be about cats. As usual, I could

make no sense of any of it. Tyler and I had kept our distance since
Columbus. Despite our talk on the library steps, he remained mute
in class. If we passed each other in a hallway or quad, he nodded
hello, nothing more. It felt we were becoming strangers to each
other—which should have filled me with relief, but somehow was
making me desperate to know more about him. I wasn't totally
sure why. Boredom? Maybe, but not only that. His life in college
seemed so different from mine—he was connected to the community, comfortable in his skin. Nothing like my own solitary, awkward years. And this despite the fact that Sawyer must be a totally
different world from North Carolina. But he seemed completely at
home, and some part of me wanted to understand how. I'd check
on his page throughout the day, when I first woke in the morning,
during a lull in office hours, at night before bed. I was gathering
moments of his life, like bits of sea glass on a beach; the act of accu-
mulation made them precious.

I pushed the small square of Addison's profile photo. His page
showed restraint compared with Tyler's, more composed. Lots of
family photos, each scene dripping with wealth: heavy, rich drapes
framed towering windows in the backdrop of group portraits; ski
trips to Vail, scrubbed and glowing faces squinting in white light
bouncing off virgin snow. Addison was someone whose entire life
would go exactly as planned; whatever he wanted, he could have. A
golden existence.

Tyler had left two posts on Addison's page since that morning;
a still from a movie I couldn't place, and a single line of text—two
exclamation points, nothing else. Despite living together, Tyler
and Addison were in constant communication via their pages. The
friendship had a boyish quality, or it was puppy-like; in photos

together, they were always proximate, touching. I wondered if there was something more than friendship between them. I'd found photos of Addison's high school girlfriend; she disappeared after his first semester at Sawyer. I'd seen many students cling to hometown romances but they rarely survived the transition to college. It was a normal progression, but maybe there was some other reason here, something to do with Tyler. Kennedy appeared regularly as well. The three had taken a road trip the year before, during spring break. From what I could gather, Addison's car had broken down in the middle of Texas. They stayed in whatever town for two days and then paid to have the car towed all the way back to Sawyer before flying home. What was that like for Tyler, having friends who could drop money like that? Had Addison paid for Tyler's ticket as well?

A round of applause and polite cheers sounded from the other room.

"Hiding out?"

I jerked my phone to my chest and looked up. "Sorry." Elaine stood before me.

"Not at all." She smiled. "Robert can go on a bit."

I lifted the phone. "My mother," I lied.

"Mothers come first," Elaine said. "Although not for me."

"Motherhood's not for you?"

"That, too. Where's yours?"

I explained that my parents lived in Florida, where I'd grown up. Elaine remarked that she worried she and Robert would end up down there. She said it seemed an inevitable destiny that all Jews finish their days in South Florida, with nothing to do but get skin cancer and complain.

"Some of us begin there," I said. "Complaining from birth."

"You're Jewish?" she asked, and I nodded. She tilted her head, sizing me up, and clucked her tongue. "Yes. I see it now."

"You and Robert seem happy at Sawyer."

"Happiness, I've discovered, is something made not found. Same as misery. It doesn't happen to you."

"Are you sure you're a Jew?"

She laughed and it made me glad. I liked Elaine, her costumey clothes and ridiculous house.

"Stephen's great," she said.

"He is."

Two of the caterers came in, a young guy and a girl, both early twenties, both with jet-black hair and huge luminescent eyes. I could see it immediately—they were siblings. It was time to serve a dessert round, slices of dark, wet cake on ceramic plates. The girl of the pair sneezed, so light it made no sound, and reached for a dish.

"Throw that out," Elaine said.

"What?" The girl froze, fingers skimming the edge of the plate.

"You sneezed on yourself and touched the food. Throw it out and wash your hands."

The girl looked stricken and rushed for the sink, mumbling an apology. The boy lined his arm and moved from the room. The girl followed a few paces behind.

Elaine sighed. "It's better, you know, to tell them when they make a mistake. Mexicans don't have the same standards of hygiene. It's not their fault, it's cultural, but you're not doing them any favors, letting it slide."

A scattered crowed remained in the sitting room. Stephen was talking with Safie. She was laughing at something he'd said, her smile broad and easy. Stephen waved his hands, reenacting some scene, and I thought about the care he put into his stories. It was an invitation. He wanted you to share the experience—the meal he'd eaten, the book he'd stayed up all night finishing, an unexpected view on a drive that took his breath away. Elaine might be racist, but she was right about one thing: Stephen *was* great. There with Safie, he looked handsome in the late afternoon light. I felt bad about earlier on the stairs. Why did I act this way?

"He returns," Safie said.

I smiled and squeezed Stephen's arm. "Do you want to get out of here?"

"Had enough?"

"I've had a nice time, actually. You were right."

"See?" he said. "Sometimes I know a thing or two."

We stepped into Stephen's house, shutting the door on a cold gust behind us. Before he'd even taught his first classes at Sawyer, Stephen had closed on the house, a compact new build. "I just wanted to feel like this is home," he'd said. He bought all the furniture at once, matching sets for the living and dining rooms, one for the main bedroom and another for the spare. A guest room seemed like something for another life.

I pulled two of Robert's beers from my coat. "I grabbed these for us." I dropped next to Stephen on the couch and passed him a bottle, taking a pull from mine. "We should order something. I'm starving."

"There was so much food at the party."

"I'm so gross when I eat. I didn't want to force that sight on everyone."

"You're not gross." Stephen lifted my legs across his lap.

"Come on. You've seen me eat."

"Alright, you are a little gross. Sometimes it seems like you don't know where your own mouth is."

"Right here." I gulped at the beer and bent forward, kissing him roughly, biting at his lip.

"Someone's feeling frisky." He kissed me back, his breath yeasty and warm. I smiled against his mouth. *Frisky* was a funny word, I thought—for old ladies trying to flirt with the bag boy at the grocery store.

I sat up and pulled Stephen to his bedroom. I shoved him onto the bed, clambering on top. He was bigger than me, pleasantly solid, thick around the torso. He smelled good, a mulchy mix of sweat and cologne. His scent was the thing that had really turned me on our first night together, and there in the bedroom I felt it had been a long time since I'd taken in the smell of him. I pulled at the buttons of his shirt. He raised his hand and I pushed him away, his wrist thick in my palm. "Let me." I ran my fingers from his chest to his shoulder. The hair grew in patches across both shoulders and he shaved it off, but the stubble had come in and I wondered why he didn't just leave it. He shifted beneath me, lifting his hips and mumbling softly.

"What did you say?"

"I said—" he exhaled, voice rough and thick—"I said I want you inside me."

I pictured a miniature version of myself, like a Russian nesting doll, tucked into him. I tried to hold back a laugh, but it spilled out.

"What is it?"

"Nothing." I laughed again. "Sex is just so weird if you think about it."

I pulled off the rest of his clothes and then my own and hoisted his legs, probing. I rubbed the head of my dick against the edge of his asshole, coiled with hair.

"Hold on."

Stephen reached into the bedside table. His hand swum around and found it—a bottle of lube. He squeezed some out and rubbed it against himself. He grabbed a condom and passed me the bottle. I oozed some into my palm.

I closed my eyes and Tyler filled the dark of my head, unbidden, pulsing and bright. I saw him in the soccer field, the twist of his body, his face lowering to himself. The white, white of his skin, the spun golden-blonde of his hair. I grew hard. I ripped open the condom and mashed it on. I leaned and licked at Stephen's mouth, maneuvering my dick toward him. I stared past him to the window-sill. A lone houseplant perched there, one droopy leaf leeched of color. For all his competencies, Stephen could not keep a plant alive. I pumped in quick thrusts, trying to hold thoughts of Tyler at bay.

"Let's try this." I rearranged us, moving the angle of Stephen's legs. I bore down, shifted again, and then my penis popped out. It was going soft and the condom sagged around it. "Hold on." I pushed with my thumb against his hole. The hair, gummy with lube, splattered around it. My thumb slipped; the condom slid off. It stuck, plastered to his thigh.

"Shit." I rolled onto my back. A faint stain bloomed in a corner of the ceiling. Had that always been there?

"What's the matter?"

"I'm sorry. I think I drank too much on an empty stomach."

Stephen nuzzled against me, hand moving in loops across my stomach. We stayed like that for a while. I got up and went to the bathroom. I stood around, doing nothing, waiting for enough time to pass. In the mirror, a face stared back, slack with disappointment. I flushed the unused toilet and ran the tap. When I returned, Stephen was sitting on the corner of the bed in a T-shirt and boxers. He'd brought in his stash of take-out menus. They were fanned out, dog-eared and grease-stained, across the empty space of the mattress where I had been.

CHAPTER 6

I bolted awake and checked my phone; not yet 6:00 a.m. My Fall
Fest lecture was at 5:00—I had eleven hours. Why had I said yes?

Fall Fest was Sawyer's version of homecoming, but without the
football games and ridiculous pageants. Admin wanted a more
dignified affair. "Homecoming for nerds," Colin said; he'd done
undergrad at Penn and thought Sawyer was denying us all a good
time. Student clubs hosted events: Smart Tech for Social Problems
and A Conversation about Sex Trafficking—Karaoke After. Art
majors curated an exhibit of student work in the campus gallery.
The theater department hosted a showcase of experimental mono-
logues, about which Safie said, "Those parents must really love
their kids." And one suspected they really did; the weekend was
Sawyer's biggest fund-raising event of the year.

It had become lucrative for the town as well (although the town
would need more than a few flush days). As the weekend approached,
Sawyer's streets and shops filled with visiting parents and siblings
and nostalgic alums. It was disorienting; one got used to the near-
deserted feel of living here. Restaurants and the few hotels and inns
offered specials. A street fair took over the downtown blocks
around my building. The nearest Mennonite community, ten or so
miles away, transformed an unused stretch of field into a "tradi-
tional village experience." Horse-drawn buggies took visitors from
the parking lot to a circle of tables laden with items for sale, dense
cakes and wooden bowls with the MADE IN CHINA stamp scratched

off. The women behind the tables, saddled in heavy, drab smocks, lived in suburban tract homes and had discreetly parked their leased sedans behind an abandoned barn. They named the site Amish Land because most people didn't know the difference.

I had been working at the lecture steadily; in fact, I wasn't doing much of anything else. I'd seen neither Safie nor Stephen outside campus the past few weeks. But I felt like I was going in circles. I'd gone back to Ohio State a few times and was building a real relationship with Lucy—youngest child of six, third-generation librarian. I had uncovered a number of surprising details about the court proceedings in the archives. The industrialist seemed to think Leopold was the innocent victim of Loeb, seduced into a lurid life of sex and crime—no one had written on this. Despite these discoveries, each day, as I sat down to work, a growing dread greeted me. I started dreaming up ways to get out of the lecture: I'll just quit; I don't like this job anyway. Or I could say my grandmother died—it worked for students, an alarming number of whose senior family members seem to conveniently croak around midterms and finals.

I checked the time again. Almost 6:30. Ten and a half hours. Anxiety pressed me to the bed. I used to be excited about research—I had chosen this life, hadn't I? In grad school I discovered that many of my peers were the children of academics. For them, the path was set: four years at a private college like Sawyer, if not Sawyer itself; one year being humanitarian work in Latin America or Africa, just long enough to generate material for an application essay; and then a PhD. These students carried a heavy burden: Realizing their parents' unachieved ambitions earned both praise and resentment; the petty jealousies of the academy spare no one, not even your offspring. Worse off were my classmates from tense and unhappy families of actual doctors. These peers attacked their work with exhausting drive, desperate to prove that a deconstructive analysis of *Swann's Way* was a meaningful contribution to society, even if it might not save any lives. (*Might not!*)

Of my life and what should be made of it, my parents had no real expectations. I got through high school with them hardly aware it was happening. By senior year, I could produce an uncanny facsimile of my mother's signature, and I wrote my own checks for my college application fees. I applied only to in-state schools; the logistics of loans and winter clothes felt overwhelming, too much to figure out on my own. I got in everywhere and enrolled at Florida State in Tallahassee, kissing distance from Georgia, across the entire length of the peninsula, because it was the farthest away.

I arrived at college with no idea what I wanted to study or what my interests might be. I signed up for a gender studies seminar because this girl from my dorm who had purple hair and didn't shave her legs told me to. The professor, Marianne Wahls, was new to the school. Our first class meeting she announced, "I will not pander to you. We are not going to keep journals or look at our cervixes, although I encourage you to do both. We are going to work hard." A few weeks in, she assigned Michel Foucault, *The History of Sexuality*. I read the first ten pages over and over again until the library closed and they kicked me out. I couldn't understand what I was reading but I knew there was something there, a promise reaching toward me. By the week's close I had made it to the end, having scribbled the near equivalent of a second book in the back pages and margins. In class we debated the central premise of the book, the question of whether sexuality was a true thing inside you, waiting to be discovered, or whether society had erected an entire apparatus that made you *feel* there was something inside you called "sexuality"—a thing you must find, understand, and name. The conversation was electrifying, dizzying, and I felt I was getting both closer and farther away from understanding who I was—and that was the point. And being in those conversations, with kids my age who wanted to question everything they'd been told—it felt like, here's the truth of who I am. I was testing a new way of seeing myself and the world, and feeling for the first time that I might have a place within it.

I took every course that Professor Wahls offered and when we ran out of classes senior year, we set up an independent study. We met in her office on Fridays, late in the afternoon. The sun would often set before we finished. One night, she asked about my plans after graduation. I didn't know what to say. I hadn't thought of it and until then, no one had asked. "I think you should consider a PhD," she said. I tried to recall the last time someone talked to me about my future but came up with nothing. I remember sitting in her office and thinking—if she cares enough to ask, she must be right. And so I did.

Seven in the morning. I made a pot of coffee and sat at the kitchen table. It got the best light during the day; I hoped it might illuminate my path forward. I set to work but whenever I found a thread it slipped away, leaving me grasping at nothing. Tyler had missed class again yesterday—he'd been absent a lot, another away match. Without him, the time dragged on. I had gotten used to an expectant, uneasy feeling in his presence which, strangely, I found myself missing. Again and again, I checked the clock and its slow progress. Afterward I found an email from him. I rushed to open it. It was just his make-up assignment and a single sentence: "Thank you for accepting this work and for your support of athletics at Sawyer." A boilerplate message, copied and pasted. He didn't even bother to sign his name.

I got up to brew a second pot of coffee. My stomach rumbled. I opened a cabinet, looking for a snack—and then suddenly I remembered: Tyler's Adderall. A few days after our trip to Columbus I found the bottle rattling around beneath the passenger seat. I had meant to return it. As more time passed and the silence between us grew, it had started feeling like the trip never happened, which somehow made me morose with regret. The pills were proof it had. I reached to the top shelf where I'd hidden them—it was weird stashing them like this, I knew, creepy even—like a serial killer's trophies. I found the bottle of pills and pulled it down, the cheap plastic light in my hand.

I was old enough to have missed the Adderall craze—kids at my elementary school didn't have ADHD, they were just hyperactive or, if they weren't white, they got labeled "troublemakers" and that was it. Scores of Sawyer students were on it, part of the chemical mix propelling them through their days: Adderall or Ritalin to amp them up, Xanax to calm them down, a steady rotation of weed and alcohol to smooth out the transitions. I felt bad I'd kept them from Tyler. What if he couldn't get a refill? I wondered what it felt like to take, if it could help with my focus. In grad school, of course, tons of people used it, prescribed or otherwise—someone I know even slipped in a thanks to "Dr. Adderall" on his dissertation acknowledgment page. And then, before I quite realized what I was doing, the bottle was open and I was swallowing a pill, bitter and chalky on the way down.

I sat down at my desk, waiting to see what would happen. In a short while, it started working, spreading a fuzzy electric charge across me. And then it hit like a bolt of espresso, or like that time I did coke at a party in New York—this girl I'd met in the bathroom line so pushy about it I finally said yes. But this was without any jangly harshness. I felt the space inside my head expand. I could see the thoughts as they came to me, I only had to write them down. Whatever worry and doubts had clouded my thinking broke apart, dissipating in a hot and scopious light. And as I wrote, rolling beneath the ideas falling into place, another chain of thoughts: Is this how Tyler's body feels? This soft rush and warm charge? I felt I was learning him from the inside and the feeling of that kept me company as I worked.

The day passed like that and suddenly it was 4:00 p.m. I had just enough time to shower and get dressed. The pill had worn off but a residue remained, a low combustion across my skin. I was stepping out from the apartment when I remembered—I'd left the bottle on the counter. We would go for drinks after the lecture and then Stephen was staying over. I went to stash the pills again. As I picked them up and reached for the cabinet, something I'd seen but hadn't registered clicked into consciousness. I turned the bottle over in my palm. There, along the edge of the pharmacy label, in small block letters: Addison Stewart Mitchell.

It was not yet five o'clock and already the afternoon's tepid light had leeched from skies putty-gray like wet ash. The talk was in a small auditorium, a satellite of the campus outside its original walls. In recent years, the college had been gobbling up real estate: collapsing houses local families barely held on to for decades snatched for a song and demolished. The new building glimmered, steel and dark glass. Cantilevered wings stretched at oblique angles across a small plaza, the reflecting pool drained for winter.

As I approached, I was surprised to see Addison and then did a double take, the surprise (and then embarrassment) that I also recognized from his Facebook page the two people beside him: his parents. I tried to get by unnoticed but Addison called my name, his arm cutting a wide arc, waving me over.

"Great to see you, Dr. Lausson," he said, reaching to shake my hand. "These are my parents." The father introduced himself— "Charles Mitchell"—his grip almost painful. "Lauren," his mother said, both of her hands soft around mine. "Lovely to meet you." She sounded luminous, like she meant it. Charles was even more striking in person, as tall as Addison, same wavy curls, silvering edges. Lauren's flaxen hair fell blunt to her shoulders; a sharp profile, cheekbones like open plains. She could almost pass for a student but was set off by a poise that came from experience. Even under the wool heft of her sleek trench, she held herself like an exclamation point. Together the family was almost unbearable to look at it, as if the beauty of each amplified the others. I pulled at my shirt; I felt like my clothes didn't fit right, my shoulders too narrow. Standing between them, Addison radiated, a hand at the back of each, as if posing for a photo.

"Where are you in town from?" I asked, as if I hadn't been tracking Addison's life online.

"Los Angeles," Lauren said, with a slight roll of her eyes that conveyed—*ridiculous, I know.*

"Sorry about our weather."

"Honestly, it's a nice change from the relentless sun," Lauren said. "We couldn't make it last year—work was crazy for me." She mentioned they were staying at the new hotel downtown. I said I lived nearby but hadn't been; I'd heard the restaurant was good. "It's lovely," she said. "So refreshing to stay somewhere with personality and charm. Not like all these new places that feel like an airport, or a mausoleum. Same thing everywhere you go in the world."

"And what are your plans for the evening?" I asked.

Addison looked puzzled by my question and then a smile cracked across his face. "We're here for your talk."

"Oh." I laughed, suddenly nervous. "By no means feel obligated."

"Not at all. We're looking forward to it," Charles said.

"Absolutely," Lauren said. "Part of me always regretted I didn't do a PhD instead of law school. I'm a little envious."

Addison checked his phone. "Tyler's inside. Holding us seats."

My skin tightened, the hair on my arms pricking alert, my body tensing at the news. I should have put it together—of course Tyler would be here; he and Addison were inseparable. A wave of adrenaline rushed though me—the pill's afterburn or the anticipation of Tyler or both. We went in, Lauren commenting on the building, a hand tucked in Addison's arm, Charles asking how I was finding Sawyer.

In the hallway, Safie stood with Susan, speaking in low tones. Safie's eyes caught mine, sharp with some strain that said I shouldn't interrupt. "This is it," I said, steering us to the auditorium. "Last chance to change your minds."

Tyler sat halfway up in the middle of the room. He called the Mitchells over, and then waved to me. I nodded hello and even that felt like too much: my excitement at seeing him uncontainable. In the front row, Colin sat with Priya. "Man of the hour," he announced.

I stood at the lectern, scanning my notes. When Safie and Susan came in, I thanked Susan for helping organize the night. She made a small huffing sound and left Safie with me.

"You're looking sharp," Safie said.

"Thanks, I did the best I could. Dazzle camouflage to hide my dread." I lowered my voice. "What was going on in the hall?"

"Nothing," said Safie, eyes on Susan wrestling with the coffee station at the side of the room. "Tenure stuff."

"What kind of stuff?"

"Concerns about me going up."

"What? You're kidding me."

"I guess P and T met last week"—the promotion and tenure committee—"and raised some questions about my work and its 'intellectual merits.'"

"They cannot be serious."

"Susan seems to think they are. She said they might recommend I take an extra year."

"That's absurd," I said. And it was. "They've told us all along—a book and a couple articles. That's it. You've gone way beyond that."

"I thought so, too."

"They say you hit those benchmarks and you're fine."

"That's what they say, until they say something else. Anyway—" Safie shuffled the air with her hand—"I don't want to talk about it anymore."

"You'll be fine—I'm sure of it."

Safie looked toward Colin and Priya, bent close in their row. "Is something going on there?"

"I was going to ask you the same thing," I said. "Seems like an odd choice, for Priya at least."

And then—"Here you are."

I looked up. Stephen. He pulled me in for a hug, mashing my arms to my sides. I felt on display, there in the front of the room.

"It's just a lecture," I said.

"Well I'm excited about it. But I thought we were coming over together?"

"Oh fuck. Sorry." I had completely forgotten. "I was writing all day. I lost track of everything."

"It's fine, I figured," he said, but I couldn't tell if he meant it.

"Well, we're all here now. Let's grab some seats," Safie said. "While we still can."

Stephen squeezed my arm, mouth a straight line. "Have fun with it."

Some minutes later, Hal scrambled in, apologizing for running behind. I stepped aside and gave him the podium. He welcomed the assembled group. You would think he was recounting the history of NATO, the gravity with which he spoke of the humbling experience of being in charge. The display of false modesty made me think of Cassie. Fake, for Cassie, was the greatest insult that could be attached to a person, a band, an outfit, an idea. Listening to Hal drone on, I felt grateful Cassie had inoculated me against the great fakes of the world.

Hal had asked Susan to introduce me after his opening remarks. I knew this because she grumbled about it for weeks, as if it were something I had done to her. But Hal must have forgotten, because he launched right in, reading from a printout of my faculty page and butchering the titles of two of my publications. Susan grimaced in her seat. She lifted a sheet of paper from her lap, folding it in half, and then half again.

Hal finished his remarks and I stepped forward. It was a full house, a bigger crowd than I expected. Some colleagues I recognized, and students from various classes. I stole a glance in Tyler's direction. He leaned forward, eyes intent. Waiting for me to begin. I held back a smile and looked down at the pages in front of me: They glowed a brilliant white.

"If you have come to hear a heartwarming story about queer resilience," I started, "you have come to the wrong place. There are no heroes here." Some laughter. "But if you are looking for the stories of some very bad gays, you might leave satisfied." Laughter again, the room warming up.

"This project started, like many, as an argument, this one with a colleague from grad school. We often got into a debate about how to tell gay stories. In fiction and films, this colleague felt, gay life only appeared as tragedy. Why, he would ask, must gay stories always end in misery and death?

"A movie came out a few years ago—I won't go into it, you know the one—and this colleague could not have been happier. The story tracked two well-adjusted white gay guys living problem-free, well-adjusted lives. When I heard about it, I thought, well who wants to see that?" More laughs. "Most of America, it turned out.

"I was annoyed. I hated this desire to make gay good, to take everything messy and troubling about queer sexuality and recuperate it into some sanitized version. And so I decided to commit myself to finding the worst gays possible—unrepentant murderers, preferably repeat offenders—and spend all my time with them.

"So tonight I'll share a bit of what I have found so far. This is not an account, though, of why these figures killed. I will leave that question to the dubious science of forensic psychologists. Instead, I want to think about why we find these stories fascinating. What they tell us about how we imagine depravity—sexual and criminal. And, ultimately, what we can see in these stories about ourselves—or as French philosopher Michel Foucault might put it, the 'mirage in which we think we see ourselves reflected—the dark shimmer of sex.'

"I am going to focus on a case from 1924, the kidnapping and murder of a young boy by the infamous maybe-lovers, Leopold and Loeb. Let's see what we can learn from these extremely bad gays."

The room broke into bright applause. From the front row, Stephen grinned—wide and warm—and Safie winked. I smiled back and lifted my eyes toward the middle of the auditorium: Tyler—upright, smiling, clapping along.

Safie and Stephen hung back, chatting with Priya and Colin as the crowd filtered out. Hal said some genuinely kind things while congratulating himself for thinking of me. "Looking forward to the book," Susan said, which felt like praise but also a threat, but I took the compliment. Marissa from class had brought her mother, who looked like she couldn't shake a foul stink from her nose and said it was a "very interesting topic." Marissa's face contorted in apology, and I smiled and thanked them for coming.

"We really enjoyed it," Charles said, as he and the others made their way down. "When this one—" he squeezed Tyler's shoulder "—insisted we spend Friday night at a lecture, I wasn't so sure."

"Really, just fascinating," Lauren said. "I would never be able to do that. Thinking out loud like that, with an audience."

"You do it all the time in court," Addison said, laughing.

"For a bunch of legal bureaucrats and corporate hacks. Nothing like this."

Tyler, who had been standing beside them, finally spoke.

"That was really great," he said. "I have like a million questions, but I'll save them for later. My mind is totally spinning." He laughed at himself, almost giddy.

"Alright," I said. I was smiling as well, I couldn't help it, or I didn't care. Tyler's pleasure felt like a gift, and I wanted to accept it. "I look forward to that."

"I hate to tear us away," Lauren said, "but we should get back to the hotel. Dinner reservation—it's been so busy in there."

"You should join us after, when you're back downtown," Charles said. "Let us buy you a drink."

I politely declined—"I wouldn't want to intrude"—and we said our goodbyes. The rest of the room had emptied out, so there was just the group of us left: Stephen, Safie, Colin, and Priya.

"You were amazing." Stephen grabbed me, planting a wet kiss on my cheek. If he'd been annoyed with me before, it had passed. "It's nice some students came."

"I guess there isn't anything to do in Sawyer on a Friday night."

"Come on," Stephen said. "They obviously love you."

"I don't know about that."

"You were really on tonight," Safie said. "And very funny. You had the crowd in the palm of your hand."

"You think so? Some of the parents seemed a little surprised."

"They should be," Priya said. "It's good for them."

"You nailed it," Colin said, "you really did," and he sounded sincere. "And now, where to?"

This led to a debate about the Stacks, the closest bar to campus, but Safie thought it would be overrun. Stephen suggested a place on the northside, but Colin didn't think it was worth going that far. Priya thought that would be fine, but she said she was fine with anything, really. Safie knew some people from History who were going to O'Reilly's. Colin liked O'Reilly's; they had a decent burger. I stood silently as the merits of the burger were

considered, thinking about Tyler and how happy he looked. I
smiled to myself at the image.

"Okay, it's decided," Stephen said. "I'll take Mark and Safie."

Outside, the skies had thickened; it looked as if it might snow
in the night. As we walked across the plaza, I paused, saying something before I realized I would.

"I think I might just head home."

Stephen stopped and turned to me. "But it's your night."

"I don't think I'll be any fun," I said. "I'm completely wiped out."

Stephen's face blanched, holding something back. "Okay," he
said. "Sure. You can leave your car here and I'll take us back
to yours."

"I can get myself home," I said. "You go. Enjoy it."

Safie shot me a look.

"Really, I'm fine."

"Well, I need a drink," Safie said. She laced her arm through
Stephen's. There was something protective in the gesture that
irked me; she was my friend.

"Are you sure?" Stephen asked.

"Yes," I said. "Go."

Servers swooped in quick loops from the side rooms to the center
bar and back. It was packed, the feeling augmented by the compact
design of the space: low ceiling and dark walls, dimly lit. The noise
of crowds deep in conversation and drink reverberated from all
directions at once. It was odd to feel such life in Sawyer, and I was
overwhelmed in an instant. This was a mistake.

I was about to turn to leave when I saw Lauren stepping from
the restrooms.

"You made it!" She gripped a small leather purse. Between two freshly painted lips—oxblood red—her perfect teeth gleamed.

"My plans ended early and I thought—I don't mean to crash."

"Nonsense. The boys will be thrilled you're here." There was a swell of noise around us and she raised her voice. "We're in back. It's quieter there." She caught the attention of a server and pointed at me, motioning that I would need a drink. She rested a hand on my arm and I bent to hear. "The food is really quite good, but the service—well, I guess they're still figuring it out. In L.A. every waiter thinks you might be their big break. They bring a bottle of Evian and it's an entire production."

She pulled me into a paneled room, moody in the low, warm lights. She was right, it was much quieter, the noise dampened. "Look who I found. Charles, make some room."

Tyler's face lit up, eyes and smile wide. "Here." He moved Addison and then himself down the booth, so his space was open for me. The leather upholstery still held Tyler's heat and as I sat I was conscious of his closeness; just a shimmering slice of air between us.

Charles sat across from us, next to a man I didn't recognize. "Really glad you made it," he said. He pointed at me. "This is the star of the night." The guy—I didn't catch his name—in a dark suit, perfect fit, was a friend of theirs. He lived in Chicago but was in Cleveland on business. "Sawyer's a great school," he said. "Terrific. I never could have gotten in with my grades. Much less a job here."

Somehow Lauren had already maneuvered to get another place setting and was piling it with food. "You have to try this, really," she said. "Addison complains there's nothing to do in Sawyer, but I think this is wonderful. It's all from local farms."

You wanted to hate the Mitchells; no one should be that beautiful and that rich, one should have to choose. But there was something comforting just being in their presence. They emanated a gracious energy, nothing cliquish about it; they invited you in. Charles was raising money for a new film, a staggering amount, hundreds of millions. He relished it, all of us in the grip of the story as he played it up, saying he couldn't reveal a thing. "These days, they've got NDAs for every possible scenario." ("Non-disclosure agreements," said Lauren, leaning across the table.) But Charles dropped enough hints that we all knew which actress had signed onto the lead. "Don't say a word!" he said. "Dad, come on," Addison grumbled. "Give it a rest." But he was grinning.

And they clearly loved Tyler, whose own family wouldn't be able to afford this trip, probably not even this meal. Charles and Lauren asked about a class project and egged on his ridiculous stories. The visiting friend asked after the soccer season. They had just narrowly triumphed over Carnegie Mellon. The day of the match, the assistant coach, a new hire, a young guy who had just graduated from Michigan, showed up reeking of booze and brutally hungover. An hour outside Pittsburgh, he threw up on the bus. "The driver went ballistic," Tyler said. It was a charter bus and the driver didn't feel he owed the college anything. He pulled over and insisted the assistant coach get off, right there on the side of the highway. He wouldn't listen to any pleading on the coach's behalf. "And he did! He walked right off. Or staggered off, actually," Tyler said, swooping his body in imitation, and everyone laughed. Somehow or other, the coach had found his way to Pittsburgh, arriving right at the start of the second half. Tyler lowered his hands and his arm brushed mine. I tilted my face toward him, the slightest shift, and caught the sweet punch of his breath.

"But Mark." Lauren turned to me, chin resting on clasped hands, ice blue eyes intent. "I can't stop thinking about your lecture. Did you really work in a forensics lab?"

"Well, I interned. Just a few months."

"That must have been fascinating. But forgive me, a little gruesome."

"Go easy, honey," Charles said. "He's not on trial."

"It's okay." I laughed. "I guess I've always had a bit of a morbid streak."

"I suppose we all do," Lauren smiled, "buried somewhere inside. But what was it like? Tell me everything."

Our private little room grew in warmth as the night went on, not stuffy heat but a cashmere prickle, the amber lights glinting off the flocked wallpaper and bathing us in a tactile glow. The rumbling bass of the classical music piped overhead and the softening murmur of the dissipating crowds beyond our walls melded into a soundtrack just for us. We stayed for hours, Charles ordering bottles of wine in twos, making a big fuss about letting Addison and Tyler drink. He grinned at me, wolfish—"Don't report me." He lifted my glass and a maudlin wave of sadness crashed over me. Did everyone have a family like this?

On my walk home, the street fair was still going strong, raucous even, surging with an end-of-the-week energy. Strings of vivid white lights laced across the blocks between lampposts and street signs. Against the murky, blank sky they emitted a phosphorescent bubble, producing the sense of a world severed from itself. Packs of locals drank from funnels of beer. I shivered at the thought; it had gotten quite cold. I passed a row of game booths, a young woman whooping as her toss hit its mark.

When I reached my block I found they'd closed it off for parking. A guy was stationed there, working security—he had an enormous walkie-talkie clipped to his pants, dragging them down; they looked like they were about to fall off. "Street's closed."

"This is my block."

He said nothing, just pointed in the direction from which I'd come.

I circled back and looped down a side street, coming at my building from the other way. My phone dinged. A text from Stephen.

You were great tonight. Sorry if I was weird, I just wanted to celebrate you. Hope we can do that soon.

Then another ding. A second text. *I love you.*

I stared at the screen, unsure what I should say. Or what I wanted to say. I felt bad, sneaking out after I'd ditched on our plans. But I'd enjoyed myself, I really had. And Stephen said it was my night. Shouldn't I spend it as I liked?

I put the phone away and pulled out my keys; I'd reached my building. And then I heard my name.

"Hi, Mark."

Tyler stood on the sidewalk, thin jacket loose against the cold.

"Tyler. Hello. What's going on?"

He looked at the keys in my hand and then rocked, heal to toe, eyes scrolling my building's façade. "Do you live here?"

"I do. Where are the others?"

"Addison is staying with his parents tonight, they got a second room. I was supposed to meet up with Kennedy but my phone is dead. Actually—" he clutched his phone and waggled it in the air "—do you have a charger I could use?"

I turned and looked at my building, its obdurate red bricks. Above our heads, the light from my kitchen window blared yellow; I'd forgotten to shut it off.

"You could use my phone. If that's easier."

Tyler's face wrinkled. "I don't know her number—I know, I'm an idiot. I can't remember anything. It's like this phone is my brain."

And then a shout from behind us—"Hey! Coming through!"

We both jumped back. Two guys, stumbling. One had his arms wrapped around the other's torso, straining to keep him upright. They swerved in a wide arc, then back, hurling themselves down the street.

"Wow, people are wasted out here." Tyler laughed, his own pale cheeks flush with drink, or maybe the cold. "But don't worry about it, I can just go back to the hotel."

"No—of course it's fine. Come on up."

He followed me inside, down the narrow entrance hall. We walked in silence up the creaking flights. At the landing I fiddled with the doorknob, struggling before I realized I was holding my office key. I found the right one and let us in. I flipped on the lights: my apartment looked small and dingy, in need of a fresh coat of paint.

"There's an outlet over there." I pointed next to the door. "Just let me find the charger."

I went to my bedroom. I picked up the charger from the chair beside my bed. I stood in the dark, holding it in my hands, not moving. If I stayed in here long enough, maybe Tyler would just leave.

When I returned to the living room, Tyler was looking at his phone, face glowing in the flare of its screen. "You're back." He glanced down at his phone and laughed—that soft laugh. "I guess it wasn't dead after all."

"I guess not." I looked at him, standing in my living room, small shoulders stooped, a half-smile on his face.

"Can I ask you a question?" he said.

I nodded. "Sure."

"I was wondering—did you have plans tonight, for after the event?"

I nodded again. "I did."

"And you bailed on them? To come meet us?"

I opened my mouth, as if I might say something else, then simply admitted it. "Yes."

"I thought so. Or maybe." The half-smile bloomed, spreading across his face. "I'm glad you did."

I don't remember crossing the room, if I went to him or Tyler came to me, but then I was kissing him, his open mouth under mine, tongue against my teeth, breath gamey with wine and nicotine. He slipped from his jacket and lifted his T-shirt over his head. I watched my hands skimming up and down the length of this body I had conjured so many times, the ridges of his ribs rippling under my fingers. He dug into me. I pulled him closer, lifting his face to my own. From low in his chest, an animal moan rose up.

He pulled away and we faced each another. A quick panic seized me—was that it? And then something else came over me and I felt in that moment, with absolute clarity—this is my chance to become somebody else. I tore off my jacket—I still had it on, I was baking inside it—and undid my shirt, the small buttons slippery under the rush of my fingers. I threw the shirt to the floor and Tyler reached for my torso, fingers grazing me—I started at the live wire bolt of his touch on my skin. I grabbed him and spun him against the couch, pushing into him from behind, holding him there—his back against my chest, breathing in sync. I reached around and unsnapped his jeans, slid the zipper down. "This okay?" He nodded and whispered, "Yes." The edge of his underwear peaked out, black briefs. I hooked my thumb into the waistband and peeled them down with his jeans, just enough. I stepped back and looked down—his exposed ass, the taut swell of its muscles.

I took him by the wrists, my hands easily encircling him, and knelt. I leaned forward and inhaled, my body seizing in disbelief. I let go of his wrists and his arms hung slack with surrender. I thought—how is this happening? And then I yanked down his underwear and jeans—he gasped, a sharp cry of surprise. The clothes bunched at his ankles, the backs of his legs rosy from the rough rubbing of elastic and denim. I pried his thighs apart, opening him up, and he growled, pitched and low, holding the back of the couch and bending forward. I licked at the inside of one leg and then the other, my tongue leaving a trail of spit behind. A dank heat poured off him, I could smell it. The hair of his legs was coarse and brown, darker than the hair on his head. It became soft and almost invisible as it reached his ass cheeks, a coat of pale down. I rubbed my face against it and gripped his hip bones, pulling him to me, pushing in my eager mouth. My tongue searched him out, lapping up the pungent, alloy taste of his asshole. He made tiny, whimpering sounds like it hurt, a hand clutching the back of my head.

I stood, pressing into him and undid my pants. I pulled out my cock—the relief of pressure a kind of aching. I tapped it against him. "Oh fuck," he said, and giggled. I pulled back, making space for him. He kicked himself free of the bundled clothes and turned around, naked. His damp hair was matted across his forehead. The skin of his face splotchy and almost swollen from the blood-rush of leaning over the couch. Violet pinpricks of pimples dotted his cheek and chin. I looked down. He had a small dick. It curved toward the flat of his stomach in a tight, hard loop, like a finger calling you forward. It was a shiny scarlet against the dark of his pubic hair, which he'd clipped short. He wasn't circumcised and the foreskin had pulled back, revealing a bright, round head glistening with precum; I could see a string of it hanging like spittle. I pulled him to me, kissing him roughly, and then lowered him, guiding him to the floor. He looked up, eyes yellow-green slits, mouth open. I spit on my fingers, rubbing my saliva across the dark pink of his lips. I slid my fingers into his mouth. He sucked at them, his tongue whirling over my knuckles, down the groove where they split.

I hooked my fingers to his teeth and pulled, forcing him open. I rubbed my cock against his face and bounced it along the curve of his cheekbone—it made a popping sound against the hollow of his open mouth. "Wider." He did as I said and I forced myself in, over my fingers and into his mouth, to the back of his throat. He grunted and with my other hand I grabbed his hair, greasy in my palm. He sucked at me wildly, too hard, teeth scraping. I pushed in deeper and then pulled out and hoisted him up. We looked at each other, heaving, the wildness I felt inside myself reflected across his face. I turned him around, against the couch again, my palm cupped beneath his chin. "Spit."

I felt around for the nub of his hole and rubbed his spit against it, coaxing it open. I eased in the tip of a finger, waiting for him to loosen around it, and then another. The inside of him was warm and pulsing, warmer as I pushed deeper, twisting inside him. I moved my fingers in and out, getting him ready. My other hand skated the front of him: the small, hard edges of his abs, the dip of his breastbone, over the razor edge of his collarbone and up to his neck, pressing along his jaw. I licked at the salt of the back of his neck and then around to his throat, my tongue trailing across my own hand.

"Should I get a condom?"

He took shallow, quick breaths and for a moment I thought he couldn't speak. But then he said, "I don't care."

I curled my fingers inside him. "Are you sure?"

Above my hold, his head nodded, the smallest movement, up and down.

I slid my fingers from him. They were gummy with saliva and a thicker mucus, a taint of rusty-orange from shit or blood or maybe both. I wiped them against my leg. I spit on myself, rubbing it around. Slick lines of sweat ran from Tyler's armpits down his sides, tracing the length of him. I gripped his neck again, tilting his chin. His throat hummed. I guided my dick to his hole and nudged the head to the opening, flicking against his wetness. His breath caught.

"Okay?"

"Yes."

I pushed in. He shuddered and pushed back, straining against me. I bore up, moving inside him, slowly at first and then faster, his shoulder blades pressed to my chest, his elbow digging into me as he twisted himself in his hand. I paused, catching my breath and he bucked into me, urging me on with a soft howl. I barreled in, pushing myself deeper, seeking out the furthest part of him, the most inside, some unknown place I could tell myself no one else had ever been.

CHAPTER 7

The ecstasy of sex is also its betrayal: In the tangled and delirious heaving, the self obliterates. But only for a shattering moment before you return to your body and life, the same ones you'd left behind, but now, uncertain and depleted. These small deaths we are consigned to repeat again and again.

Tyler and I lay splayed on the floor, our damp bodies at a cross hatch, his legs over mine, his head out of view past the edge of the sofa. My hand, brown against the white of him, clutched the swell of his calf, its rough hairs shedding heat beneath my palm. The silence of the apartment was cut by the gasps of our desperate breathing, as if we had fucked the air from one another. It seemed the room was spinning but it was only me. What have I done?

Tyler snapped in his legs and jumped up. He stood over me, slick and shiny with the aftermath of our sex. "Where's your bathroom?"

I gestured. "That way. Through the bedroom."

"Let's take a shower."

I always felt uneasy sharing a shower with someone—following sex, I want to hide, not expose myself further. But Tyler jumped right in. "This is great. The showers in the dorms suck." The water's steam enveloped us. Tyler rambled on about a plumbing problem the previous year that left them without working toilets for two weeks. He turned into the spray and passed me the soap. "Can you get my back?"

I drew the bar in slow circles down the small curves of him, skimming a line of pimples along his spine. I knelt and continued down his ass, reaching gently to clean his hole, the lip of it softly swollen. Then his legs, carefully lifting and balancing each foot in turn. When I finished, I stood and swiveled him to face me. "Okay, rinse."

He stepped back and shut his eyes. The water sliced past him in sheets. I watched, taking in the uncommon stillness of his face. He pushed his hair back and opened his eyes.

"What?"

I startled, caught. "What do you mean?"

"I don't know. You're so quiet. You look like something's on your mind."

I almost laughed—the absurdity of his observation. "No, nothing. I'm just glad you're here."

"Me, too. I needed that." He pulled back the curtain—"Your turn"—and stepped out, leaving me alone.

I stood at the spout and opened my mouth, water cascading down my chin and chest. What was going to happen next? It seemed, as the adult here, it was my job to start the necessary conversation, but I wanted none of it. When the hot ran out, I turned off the water and stepped into a puddle Tyler had left on the floor. I thought I heard the sound of a door opening and shutting and I wondered if he had let himself out. But when I stepped into the bedroom, following a trail of wet footprints, I found his towel in a heap next to the bed and him already in it—or on it; he was sprawled naked on top of the blanket. He was looking at his phone, leaning on one elbow, absent-mindedly running his hand through his hair, slicking it from his face.

"Oh, hi." He lowered his phone and smiled. "Is it okay if I stay here?"

I cut the lights and wiggled the covers from under him. I climbed in beside him, wrapping an arm around his waist and pulling him to me. I could smell the peppery fragrance of my soap on him and the scent of his scalp and its oils beneath that. Tyler's breathing deepened and slowed and he passed out almost instantly. We stayed like that, his body cradled to mine, until finally, I joined him in the darkness of sleep.

I woke in the morning to Tyler burrowing beneath the blanket and sheets, his hands and mouth crawling down the surface of me. Eddies of morning light pooled in the folds of the bedclothes, burnished and shifting. I reached down and found the side of his face. It bristled with sparse, new stubble. Tyler swatted me away and pulled me into his mouth. I hissed, jolted at the sudden burst of feeling as he sucked at me, rough tongue and wet lips. I dug the flat of my palm into my brow, pushing hard, to dull the pleasure and steady myself, as if I might careen off the bed. A low moan rolled up from my stomach, into my chest and out, and I finished in his mouth.

A moment later, he pulled the covers back and emerged, hair a wild tangle, a grin across his face, crusty with sleep or semen at the corner of his mouth. I felt the world around us fold in on itself and disappear into that grin. If only we could stay here, in this bed, forever, everything might be okay.

"Good morning," he said, still smiling. He sat cross-legged. The light caught the inside of his thigh and the memory of his taste rushed through me. I thought to pull him to me, to lie with me for a while, but he jumped up, springing to the floor. "Do you have anything to eat?" He turned into the bathroom. "I'm starving." He left the door open and I listened to the hard stream of his piss emptying into the toilet.

In the kitchen, I started coffee and checked my phone—last night's text from Stephen, I had forgotten it. I looked out the window to the street below, littered with trash from the fair. A truck pulled up and a moment later the driver leapt out. The side of the truck bore the name of the company that serviced the dining hall at Sawyer. A delivery for the restaurant next door. I didn't want to think about Sawyer; I didn't want to think about anything.

"What's going on in here?" I turned to see Tyler settling at the table. "Is that coffee?"

I passed him a mug. "There's milk and sugar." I pointed to where I had set them out. He poured the sugar right from the box, a ridiculous amount; it hurt my teeth to think of it. "I'll make some breakfast?"

"Yes, please."

I pulled some things out, eggs and bread and butter, and then said—an uptick in my voice as if it had only occurred to me—"I just remembered." I reached into the cabinet and grabbed the bottle of Adderall, passing it to him.

"Amazing," he said. "I was wondering what happened to this."

"It was in my car," I said, and then added, "I just found it."

"Could I have some water?"

I filled a glass. Tyler took it in one hand and unscrewed the bottle in the other, working it with his thumb. I dropped the bread in the toaster, cracked the eggs into a pan. "Can I ask you something?"

"Uh-oh, that sounds serious."

"No, it's not a big deal. Or it doesn't have to be." I paused a moment. "I noticed the prescription. It's not made out to you. They're Addison's?"

"Oh." Tyler laughed. "He just gets them for me." I set a plate in front of him, steam rising from the eggs. "This looks so good."

I grabbed the other plate and sat. "What do you mean? I'm not trying to press, I'm just curious."

He was already shoveling in forkfuls. "This is really hot," he said, and laughed, opening his mouth and fanning it so I could see the wet, yellow mash. He gulped some water and let out a satisfied sigh of relief. "That's better." He laughed again. "I've got the shitty campus health plan. They make you buy it if you don't have insurance from your parents. So you have to pay for it but it doesn't cover anything." He paused. "I know it's weird my parents don't have insurance."

"It's not weird."

"I don't want you to think they're bad parents. They're not."

"Of course not."

"Addison's family has this doctor that will basically write up anything, so he gets it for me. It's kind of sketchy but I wasn't sure what else to do."

I felt ashamed; I had been digging. I wanted something of Tyler's to hold on to. Something secret. And the explanation had been so obvious: He couldn't afford his medication.

I hadn't begun to eat and Tyler had already finished his eggs and was wiping the plate with the last of his toast. He folded it up and crammed it into his mouth. He had buttery grease on his chin and spoke through his chewing.

"Do you think I could have some more?"

In the weeks that followed, I gave myself over to this thing between us, whatever it was. *Affair* seemed inadequate, too thin. It was whatever you name an experience that subsumes you completely, animating each moment and every thought. I offered myself to it and it carried me through my days, which started and ended with both wild alertness and utter exhaustion. It reminded me of the final mile of a marathon when I used to run. And in a sense, I was running.

At some point in my life, sex became rote. I could be with someone and, by the following afternoon, find myself unable to recall the details of what we had done. The acts and scents and bodies bled together, sloughing distinction. But sex with Tyler had woken me up. He burned with excruciating specificity, the outline of our nights sharp and resonant. I had forgotten that sex could be like this and was brought back to my first times, furtive and confusing, each encounter electric with the mere fact of its happening. Even as Tyler and I fucked—my fingers stretching through him, the strain of his legs clamped around mine—I recalled the sex, the pleasure doubling upon itself, the act of it and the idea of it. These are our bodies, I thought, pushing myself into him. This is me.

In class, we acted as if nothing had changed. Tyler came and went as usual, silent and unobtrusive. This Tyler in class, my student, become a separate person from the other Tyler, the one who showed up at my apartment late at night, wired with shiny eyes, the one whose musky sweetness leaked from my pillows and sheets. Whose hair I would find in my shower, a light spark against white tile. Two Tylers for a reality I cleaved in two.

I resigned myself to the strange habits of this second Tyler, who disappeared in the middle of a text exchange only to resume hours later like no time had passed. While my head spun out with disbelief at the things we were doing, and that we were doing anything at all, Tyler seemed to enjoy the sex while it was happening and be completely untroubled at its completion. If anything about what we were doing startled him, he gave no sign. He would launch into a story as he cleaned himself off, sometimes requesting a glass of water or asking if I could check the internet because his phone was acting weird. I puzzled over his nonreactions and did my best to rein in my spiraling thoughts, frantic with desire and fear. At his age, I'd had sex just a handful of times; I would agree to disrobe only with every source of light extinguished, and even then I removed only the absolute necessities. Tyler, meanwhile, displayed an athletic capacity for sex and, it seemed to me, no shame about any of it (including things I had only discovered well into adult-hood, in the far reaches of the web). I felt both compelled and threatened by his comfort in his body; he seemed alien and dan-gerous, and I was terrified he would discover my own total lack of self-possession.

Nights Tyler stayed over, I found something comforting in his rambling way of talking. Topics would turn on a dime, with no clear thread connecting one to the other. One night, telling a story about a cousin who'd gotten arrested breaking into a neighbor's house on a dare, he interrupted his own monologue to ask—"Lausson. What kind of name is that?" I explained it was German-Jewish, or it used to be. It had been *Loewestein* when my grandfather's family came over, but it was changed at Ellis Island. "Huh, weird," he said, and moved on to something else. I let his stories flow around me, a wash of names from high school and Sawyer and cousins and other family members I couldn't possibly track. And stories about Addison—a joke Addison made, a party that ended with Tyler locked in a closet. I hated to admit the jealousy Addison sparked in me. I pushed the feeling down as swiftly as it appeared but I could feel it calcifying, a stone lodged in the coil of my guts.

He sometimes asked about my research, saying, "Tell me another scary story about your murderers." I'd share some finding I'd uncovered. That Jeffrey Dahmer's first teenage crush was a neighbor. From the bedroom window of his childhood home, Dahmer would watch the boy biking around; later, in the same room, he'd kill a hitchhiker he picked up, his first victim. Or Carl Panzram, who, confessing to twenty-one murders in 1928, proclaimed, "For all these things I am not the least bit sorry. I don't believe in man, God, nor devil. I hate the whole damned human race, including myself." Tyler would coo, asking for more until I begged off. "I'm going to give myself nightmares," I'd say. Outside work, and my last name, Tyler seemed to have little curiosity about me. And, in truth, I was fine with that; I worried if he started digging, he would realize there wasn't much there.

So he surprised me one night when he asked, "Does Stephen know about me?"

We were in bed, his head on my stomach, my hand drawing loops around his bare chest. He raised his eyes to catch mine.

"No. Of course not." I had never brought Stephen up. It proved an easy omission; I had been avoiding him since the night of the lecture. I wasn't sure what to do about him, and I wasn't ready to think about it. "I didn't realize you knew about him."

Tyler laughed. "Sawyer students know a lot more than you think."

As much as Tyler could talk, there was plenty I still didn't know about him, certainly nothing of his sex life apart from me. I almost asked about Addison, if anything had gone on between them. But I didn't want to know and maybe that was why I never mentioned Stephen. So I wouldn't start a conversation I couldn't get out of.

When time for sleep arrived, Tyler passed out cold in minutes, expanding across the mattress. I'd listen to his muffled snores and fight to hold on to my far wedge of the bed. He slept deeply and I would run my hand down the length of him—the fact that I could, a marvel. And the nights he didn't stay over, he took off immediately after we finished, mentioning an early practice or a class assignment. There was never any negotiation and the decision to stay or leave was his alone.

I sat at my kitchen table, trying to catch up on grading for my Comp course—I had fallen monstrously behind, the stack of papers growing week by week—when my phone buzzed with a text. I went to the counter and flipped it open—I had kept my old phone and given that number to Tyler. It felt safer, quarantining our communication from the rest of my life. And I liked it, too—this private thing just for us. I had deleted all my old texts and contacts and now there was only him. He was on campus, an evening film screening organized by a friend.

How is it? I asked.

Art films made by Sawyer undergrads. What do you think?

I laughed. *You're a good friend.*

Ha I don't know about that. . . . Can I come to yours when this is over?

I hesitated; we had seen each other the past two nights and the lack of sleep was undoing me. But his asking was all it took.

What time do you think?

I waited, but no reply. Had he sensed my hesitation?

I sat back down to work, unable to focus. An hour passed. Finally, the phone buzzed. I grabbed it.

Sorry got distracted. 10?

I brushed my teeth and ran some water through my hair. I looked at myself: the dark slashes of my heavy brows, the tilt of my crooked nose. What did Tyler see when he looked at me? I thought perhaps I caught it for a moment—the lines of my face interesting, handsome even—then the light wavered in the silvered surface of the mirror and it was gone. I wandered my apartment, unsure how to pass the time. I poured a whiskey to settle my nerves. I thought about Tyler every moment we were apart, a rumble beneath whatever else I was doing. And when we were together, I felt rattled by disbelief. I almost couldn't bear to be beside him; the fact of his presence was too much. I thought this unease would dull against its own rubbing but it hadn't yet. I poured another drink. Ten o'clock came and went. Then eleven. I turned on the TV, a movie about something or other. I kept my phone in view on the coffee table. If Tyler didn't reach out by twelve, I would go to bed. When midnight arrived, some degree of relief softened the edges of disappointment: I was released from the turmoil of waiting.

I was submerged in a cavernous sleep when a pounding at the front door woke me. I checked the bedside clock. After two. When I opened the door, Tyler spilled into my apartment, liquid. His glossy face shone, hair sweaty and damp. He mumbled a greeting and laughed, boozy breath soaking the air. He pulled at his jacket but was tangled in it somehow. I recognized the jacket, with its racing stripes. It was Addison's. It was enormous on Tyler. He yanked an arm out and wriggled free. The jacket fell in a pile to the floor.

"You know the door to your building doesn't lock," he said, laughing.

"I know." I kept meaning to get on the landlord about it. "It's really late."

"Did I wake you up?"

I led him to the couch. He dropped into the cushions with a spongy thud. I sat beside him.

"Are you okay?"

"I'm great. Fantastic." His pupils sank beneath heavy lids.

"I should get you some water."

I started to stand but Tyler seized my arm. "You don't have to be so serious all the time. Serious Professor Lausson." He laughed and leaned into me, mouth open, licking at my face.

I pulled back. "Seems like you had a big night."

"It was fine—it's hot in here." He struggled out of his shirt and tossed it over the couch, slumping back. "I don't know. Sawyer kids are pretty annoying, but I guess I had fun." He made no mention of being four hours late and shut his eyes. I thought he had passed out, but then he sat straight up, grabbing the bottle of whiskey I'd left on the coffee table. "Can I have some of this?"

"Are you sure you don't want some water?"

"Just a sip. Have a drink with me, Professor Lausson."

"Come on, Tyler. Don't call me that."

He picked up the empty glass and poured. The contents splashed over the side, pooling on the table. He pushed the glass toward me and knocked the bottle against it. "Cheers. Mark." He jerked the bottle to his mouth and took a deep swig. He closed his eyes, leaning back into the couch and then suddenly jumped to his feet. He wobbled and careened above me.

"I think I need to go to bed."

I pried the bottle from him and set it aside, following him as he wove his way into the other room. At the foot of the bed, he flung himself forward, facedown, feet dangling from the mattress edge. I waited but he didn't move. He moaned softly, his breathing slowed.

I untied his laces and loosened each sneaker, slipping them free. They looked brand-new: bright fluorescent white, impeccably clean. I remember when I put this together, when I was a TA for undergrad classes at NYU—the way rich kids dressed like slobs, and poor kids maintained the cleanest, most meticulous appearance.

"Tyler?" No response. He was out. I turned him over and held still, not wanting to wake him. I timed my breathing to his own. Carefully, slowly, I unbuttoned his jeans. I bent over him and placed a hand under the small of his back, arcing him so I could slide the jeans over the mounds of his ass and off. I folded them neatly and laid them on the chair. I peeled off one sock and then the other, tucking them into his shoes. I placed them against the wall.

I turned back to the bed. For months now, every time we'd been near, I had strangled my compulsion to stare. Even when I fucked Tyler on his back, his legs laced over my shoulders as I hovered above, I couldn't look directly at him. Now, safe from his scrutiny, I took all of him in. Prone, at a funny angle, he looked even younger. His mouth hung open, red tongue visible with each inhale. His calves and thighs were thick on his thin legs, built up from years of soccer. He had on the same black underwear he always wore, something synthetic that glistened.

My hand moved across the space between us, appearing in the low light of the room as if it were not attached to me. Like it might be someone else's hand. This hand floated down toward Tyler and tugged at the elastic of his briefs, the slightest pull. Just enough to reveal the line of dark hair. I watched the fingers of this hand move down, drawing small loops along the inside of his thigh, then up, across the front of the briefs and their soft flesh, and down again the other leg. My dick hardened and I pulled it out, stroking it slowly, up and down as my eyes followed this other hand tracing this body, unaware.

I cleaned myself up in the bathroom and climbed into bed. I pulled the blanket around us, slowly and carefully. But he stirred and rolled against me, face mashed into my arm.

"Mark?"

I froze, his breath steaming my skin. "What is it?"

I listened and waited but that was it.

CHAPTER 8

The door to the bar swung open. No Safie. A pack of suited men poured in. Ties loosened around unbuttoned collars below ruddy faces. Sweat bubbling at temples. This was not their first stop of the night. Hours later, they would crash into homes already pungent with the beginnings of tomorrow's Thanksgiving meals, wives lying stiff and awake in darkened bedrooms. The din of the men swallowed the room—voices raised to shouts, a hand thudding a back. They pressed past, toward the bartender. Instinctively, I drew myself in, eyes lowered. Safie and I had arranged to meet at the bar of the hotel restaurant, on her suggestion. I was nervous about returning after my night here with the Mitchells. If not the scene of the crime, it was where it had begun, the hours here now cast with a sense of inevitability by the events that followed. What could have happened that night except exactly what did?

I watched the bartender pour the group of men their drinks, tall glasses of beer, a tray of shots. She was middle-aged, probably close to fifty. Bright smears of makeup around the creased lines of her eyes. The group cleared to a back room. One stayed behind; he shouted as they left, "Someone get Mikey to drink that water. I don't want to hear about it tomorrow." He passed a card to the bartender and turned to me. "He's married to my sister. She likes to blame me for his hangovers."

"Oh," I said. "Okay."

"Lighten up." He scribbled on the receipt and crumpled his copy, leaving it on the bar. "You look like somebody died."

He left and the bartender waved a hand behind his back, shooing him along.

"Another?"

I nodded and drained my glass.

Hadn't somebody died, though? Somewhere, somebody had.

"Sorry," Safie said, grabbing the stool beside me. "The committee meeting ran over. They had to wring out the last of our blood before releasing us for the break." She surveyed the room. "This place is nice, right?"

"It is nice, yes." I hadn't mentioned I'd already been. "For Sawyer, definitely could be worse."

"Things could always be worse." She signaled to the bartender, eyeing my empties. "Looks like I have some catching up to do. You leave in the morning?"

I nodded. I had put off booking a flight until tickets were obscenely expensive, so I was taking the only cheap option left, early Thanksgiving morning. "My mother said the visit was so short she didn't know why I was bothering."

"That's just her way of saying she misses you." Our drinks arrived and we toasted. "It's nice to see you. You're looking good."

"Sorry I've been M.I.A.—this book is killing me."

"It must be. I haven't seen you on campus in weeks."

"I don't know, I can't focus when I'm there." I was being truthful—campus had become charged with too much possibility of crossing paths with Tyler outside of class. I couldn't handle the chance of it, not knowing how I would respond, not trusting my ability to hide my surprise and pleasure. But I also had been avoiding Safie. It wasn't that I didn't want to see her, but I was worried that she would sniff out my secret. I had fantasized about telling her everything—I wanted her to help me hold this burden. But it was too risky. I just needed to get through the semester, get Tyler out of my class, and then I could figure things out. "How are you?"

"Alright, I suppose. I met with Susan—" Safie cut herself off; something was ringing. "I think that's you. Want to get it?"

She pointed at my jacket, slung over the back of my barstool. It was my old phone. The one I used with Tyler; I'd forgotten it in the pocket.

I pulled it out—"T" flashed on the little window and the memory of our last night shot through me: Tyler facedown on the mattress, my hands pinning his wrists. His gasps muffled by the underwear I'd shoved into his mouth. My face flushed with heat and I hit the button to cancel the call.

"You're still using that thing?"

"Oh. I just . . . I haven't updated everyone."

"Okay, Mark Lausson, carrying around a burner phone. If I didn't know better, I'd think you were up to no good." She took a slow slip from her drink and then asked, "Who's T?"

"No one." Shit. "Just some guy from grad school—" I searched my brain, I could think of no name but Tyler, and then, "—Tom."

"Tom? I don't think you've mentioned him."

I hadn't; he didn't exist. "He's not important, I have no idea why he'd be calling. Probably a butt dial."

"Probably." She tipped her head, a gesture I didn't know how to decipher.

"Anyway," I said, desperate to change the topic, "what were you saying?"

"Just about Susan."

"What about her?"

A pause, a stutter in the air between us. Safie tilted her glass, considering something. "The tenure stuff."

Fuck. "Of course." What was wrong with me? I'd completely forgotten—since we'd talked about it at the lecture, I hadn't thought of it once. "I'm sorry, I've been meaning to ask. What did she tell you?"

She shrugged. "More of the same."

"I don't get it."

"Promotion and Tenure says I show *strong promise*. Which, frankly, is just insulting. I'm supposed to let them know by end of term if I want to withdraw my intent to file and take another year."

"Jesus. But you've done everything right."

"Believe me, I know. There's no leeway for me in a place like this. I've been killing myself for years, and for what? And you know who else they asked to withdraw?"

"I don't have a good feeling about this."

"Just one other case. Federico Garza, from Psychology. That's it. The only Mexican guy on faculty, and a Black woman."

"Sawyer is fucking awful."

"I don't know," Safie said. "It's just part of the world."

"What are you doing to do?"

"I'm not sure. But we are going to get drunk and talk about something else."

Hours later, we stood on the empty street, everything shuttered for the night. The air was frigid; there was no more denying winter's arrival. Safie hugged her coat against herself as we waited for the car she'd called. I closed my eyes and the ground beneath me wavered, dipping down then up. I tried counting my drinks but lost track. The alcohol had unraveled our night—it was all dangling threads I couldn't trace back; trying to only pulled them loose.

"Are you okay?"

I opened my eyes. The scene snapped into place: red brick, cracked asphalt, Safie's hands warming in her breath.

"I may regret that last one. But I'll survive." I shook my head to clear it. "Did you tell me what you're doing this weekend?"

"I'll eat with Loren and Eugene tomorrow," Safie said. "And I guess I have a date on Saturday."

"A date? And this is the first I'm hearing of it?"

"We're just hanging out."

"We who?"

"Maria from History," she said, and looked down and smiled. "I know, so obvious. But she's very sexy."

"Well done," I said. I had met Maria at some event last year. "She really is."

"Speaking of dates"—she paused—"Stephen says he hasn't seen you since Fall Fest."

I was aware all night that we were sidestepping the topic of him; she'd been letting me off easy. "Yeah, I guess we haven't really talked."

"What's going on there?"

"I don't know," I said, which felt in the moment both sad and honest. "Nothing?" And that seemed sadder. Blood pulsed behind my eyeballs. Tomorrow was going to be rough.

"Hmm," Safie hummed, and then—"You know I really like him."

"Well, I like him, too. You think I don't?"

"I'm not sure, actually." The stoplights had been switched to caution, blinking red and yellow overhead. "As is often the case, you've never really said how you feel."

"What is that supposed to mean?" I could hear the hard edge of my voice, and I saw Safie blanch. "Sorry, ignore me. I'm drunk."

Safie's eyes narrowed. "You're good." The cab arrived and she opened the door. "Drink some water when you get home."

I watched her leave and pulled out my phone to check the time. Behind me, the door to the bar crashed open.

"You again." It was the guy from the group, the one who told me to lighten up.

I forced a smile and asked, "How's it going?" but looked back at my phone.

"I have a question." He swayed into the air between us then caught his balance. He wiped at his face, rough down the length of it, and cleared something from his throat. "You teach at the college?"

"I do."

"I can tell. You and your friend. Did you move here for that job?"

"That's right."

"Where from?"

"New York," I said, and immediately regretted it. I should have said somewhere less worthy of interest, anywhere really. The wet cold of the night pressed into my bones. I was underdressed. "Listen, I need to get going."

"What's your hurry?" He surged toward me. I stepped back and smacked my head into the wall behind me—my phone knocked from my hand, landing on the sidewalk with a snap. He leaned in. His breath stank, sour from hours of drinking. "Do you think you're better than me?"

"What? No." My head throbbed.

"I think you do."

"I don't even know you."

He seemed to look through me, watery eyes unfocused.

"Would you want to?"

"Want to what?"

"Know me." He reached and grabbed my forearm and I flinched but didn't move away, there was nowhere to go. He gripped me tightly and held me there, against the wall.

"What?" I stammered, trying to figure out what he wanted me to say, what could make him leave. "I—"

And then he let go and laughed, his big mouth hanging slack. "I'm just fucking with you. Relax." He patted my cheek, two quick, dry slaps. He turned and walked off, laughing to himself. "Fucking Sawyer professors."

I waited until he was out of view and then counted down from one hundred. When I reached the end, I picked up my phone. A jagged crack along the back. But it still worked. I dialed without thinking. I felt foolish, or really, I felt like a child: needy and scared. I was about to hang up when the call clicked on from the other side.

Stephen's voice, groggy with sleep.

"Mark." Across the street, a car U-turned, tires screeching, headlights off. I tensed, but it kept going and disappeared around the corner. "Are you there?"

"Sorry." Why had I called? "I know it's late."

A pause. "Are you okay?"

"I'm fine. I don't know." I waited a moment and then . . . "Would you come over?"

"What's going on?" The gravelly underbelly of sleep in his voice was gone, cleared out with alarm.

"I'm just having a weird night." I flattened myself against the building. The brick pushed back, cold and ungiving. My head swam. "Never mind. I'm sorry I woke you up."

Nothing, and then, "I'll be there soon."

Stephen arrived at my apartment not long after me: low, soft knocks on the door.

I called out. "It's open."

I was splayed on the couch, thumbs pushed into the pocket of my brows to still the pounding. The door opened and Stephen stood still in the threshold. He reminded me of a scene from a movie, any movie: men standing in doorways, filling the space with their silence.

"Are you coming in?"

He took his time, hanging his jacket on the hook by the door, making his slow way around the couch. I moved my legs to make room for him but he perched at the edge of the coffee table, hands folded together. I sat up and a rush of air whooshed through me. Dizzy, disoriented.

"I do not feel great."

Stephen went to the kitchen and returned a moment later, glass of water in hand. I edged over, making room. "Come sit." He did. "I guess I'm drunk, it just hit me. It was Safie's idea." I drained the glass in one long swallow.

"I'm sure she had some help."

"We all played our parts." I smiled, and it made my face ache.

"Did something happen tonight?"

How to convey the strangeness of the man, my fear of him, my feeling that I had somehow brought it on myself? The ways it made me hate this town, and this job, and hate myself for thinking I could make something work here. What could I say about how he held my arm, the force of it expressing a desire to hurt me, but some other desire as well? It all seemed suddenly minor, not noteworthy, my recollection fuzzy.

"No," I said. "Nothing happened."

"Well—okay."

Stephen looked disheveled but still somehow dignified, his handsomeness pushing through. Hair messy with interrupted sleep, stubble like pinpoints of light across his cheeks and chin. I could see the uncertainty behind his eyes, the waiting. I'd been a horrible boyfriend, and truthfully, I hadn't been a great one before all this. And yet, Stephen was the one I called, and he came right over, in the middle of the night without asking a thing.

"I know I've been awful, disappearing on you," I said. "I'm sorry."

Stephen eased into the couch, releasing himself to it. "It's alright."

"It's really not. I'm sure it hasn't been fun for you."

"Not everything has to be fun, Mark."

"I know."

"I just don't like having no idea what's going on with you. You ditch out on your own drinks, no explanation. Acting like it's nothing. And then I don't hear from you for weeks. What am I supposed to do with that? It feels like—you've gone somewhere."

"I know, I'm sorry."

"Well, what is it? What's happening with you?"

"I'm not sure."

"Then let's figure it out."

We sat in quiet and a clammy sensation wrapped itself around my neck and I understood why I had called. Stephen deserved better, he always had. He reached for my hand and I pulled it back.

"I don't think we should do this anymore." And then, like he wouldn't have understood what I meant: "I need this to end." Stephen said nothing. The moment stretched on, the silence shattering. He made no sound. Tears pooled in his eyes and he clasped his hands, knuckles white with pressure. "Stephen."

And then he leapt from the couch, lifted, it seemed, by a sudden rage.

"You called me here in the middle of the night to break up with me?"

"No, I didn't. I mean—"

"You." His voice a growl, the word an insult. He was trembling all over. He raised his hand and I panicked in that instant he might strike me. And then the fear turned pliable, bending inside me, rubbery and soft, and I wished he would. But he stepped away, moving toward the door. "You drunk piece of shit. I've always known you weren't into this."

"That's not true. Sit down. Let's talk."

"What is there to say? I guess it's pretty pathetic, me sticking around. Hoping sooner or later you would see this could really work. I might be a fool, but I'm not an idiot. Something has changed. But you, you can't even look at me." At that I raised my head, of course; I wished I hadn't: Stephen's face was twisted, terrible. I had done this to him. "You're too shut down and scared of people to just tell me whatever the fuck is going on. I'd rather be a fool than a coward."

"Stephen, wait—"

But he was out the door. It slammed shut, rattling in its jamb. I listened to him bounding down the stairs. I thought I even heard a pause, halfway down. I imagined him realizing he had left his jacket—it hung on its hook, limp and gray—and then deciding it wasn't worth coming back for.

I woke with a vicious hangover, a lump on the back of my head where I'd struck the wall. Somehow I made it to the airport. The plane was mercifully uncrowded. I had a row to myself. We took off, rocking through pulpy clouds. I palmed some aspirin, forcing them down with a cup of lukewarm coffee. It tasted of plastic. When the flight attendant passed a second time, I asked for a beer. She hesitated—it was not yet eight in the morning—before smiling. "It's how we get through the holidays, isn't it?" I fell asleep and woke, a searing crick in my neck, to the announcement that we were landing.

I stepped onto the jet bridge and the eager humidity enveloped me. Even in late November, the South Florida air clung to you, a second skin you could not shed. It felt immediately and deeply familiar. I turned my Tyler phone back on and a moment later it sounded with a message. I opened it: a photo in bed, shirt off, wide grin. He had gone home to North Carolina at the start of the week. He said he argued with his mother about it; it seemed like a waste of money when he'd be back for winter break in just a few weeks. "But she's obsessed with Thanksgiving," he said. "Last year she asked me to do grace and when I said something about genocide, she started screaming about why can't she have just one nice day." He'd laughed as he told the story. I peered at the photo grainy on the small screen, trying to glean some detail about his life from his surroundings. But there was nothing but a blank wall behind him. I typed my reply—*miss you*—and hit SEND.

I moved out with the slow mix of other last-minute arrivals: retired snowbirds starting their winter seasons, struggling off-kilter with overstuffed suitcases; young couples, voices stretched with tension, wrangling children fussing to be set loose; a teenage girl traveling alone, head encased in gigantic earphones, the tinny sounds of thrashing guitars eking out. Curbside, families reunited, grandparents swooping those same fussing children into out-stretched arms as the parents hoisted luggage into trunks. Traffic was light but steady and I watched for the car, trying to remember my last trip down. Had it been a year? Or more? They were almost upon me when I spotted them, my father at the wheel, my mother pointing through the windshield in my direction. The car looked more weathered than I remembered, sun-bleached maroon, paint brindled and curling at the seam of the roof. I tossed my bag into the back and followed.

"You made it," my father said—he loved announcing the obvious.

"I did."

It was freezing inside; I'd forgotten how high they kept the AC. My father wore a baseball cap, thin wisps of white hair flying from the sides. My mother's hair, too, seemed grayer. And then I real-ized: She had stopped coloring it. She faced forward, watching the road, correcting my father's driving and asking questions about my classes, my book. Traffic picked up outside the airport, families headed to join other branches for the day. The battery of cars inched along in fits and starts. We exited the highway and rolled down a long stretch of road, blocks of parks and condo develop-ments and gas stations, medians crowned with palm trees, shop-ping centers with grocery stores as big as amphitheaters. Every other building new and unfamiliar.

We pulled into the driveway of my parents' house—our house, I suppose. One night, right before the start of ninth grade, toward the end of what I thought of as my mother's year of exile, we sat around watching some show none of us cared about. My mother grabbed the remote, shut off the TV, and announced, her voice shredded with exasperation, "I can't live in this house anymore." They sold that home, where I'd grown up, and we moved to this one, twenty miles away, closer to the center of the town. My father fretted about me changing school districts, but I didn't care. I didn't make friends at the new school, but I had so few at the old one anyway. I had learned to keep to myself, to avoid the trouble that inevitably came from being noticed; at least now, no one knew anything about me. I would eat lunch alone at a picnic table near the teacher's parking lot, picking at my sandwich until the bell rang and I went back inside to get through the rest of the afternoon.

"Do you need help with your luggage?" my mother asked.

My father answered for me. "He's hardly brought anything."

My mother busied herself in the kitchen, wiping down counters that already gleamed. My father tended to the plants on the back patio, green tendrils, vivid orange and yellow blossoms. I dropped my bag in my room. It was sparse, as if it had been cleared out when I left home, but I had never decorated; I always felt like I was visiting this house, on a stopover. I wandered down a narrow hallway that led to a small back wing with my parents' room. Framed photographs lined a wall. Though the photos were old, they only started appearing a few years ago. Cassie and I, I think at eight and three, in bathing suits, jumping through a sprinkler in the backyard. Cassie before a ballet recital, enormous smile, bangs curled tight against her forehead. Her fingers spread wide across layers of pink tulle. A photo from my first track meet—clasping my ribbon, mouth set in a tentative smile. A newborn me, hospital band enormous around my wrist, cradled in Cassie's arms as our father knelt; his own arms stretched behind, protecting us both. Next to that one, a photo I remembered from my mother's dressing table. Her high school graduation portrait, shot in black and white. Her luminescent face, unmarred by life or age, tipped toward some light, the source of which could not be seen.

A few years prior, my mother had decreed no more cooking for Thanksgiving. "It's too much fuss, just for us," she said. My father had made a reservation at a new Italian restaurant. When I said it seemed funny to eat pasta on Thanksgiving, my mother replied, "Italians are American, too."

We spent the afternoon on the beach. The pale bodies of holiday visitors, released from the bundled layers of their northern lives, were stark among the tanned and oiled bodies of locals, some young and muscled, others old—tawny skin soft and wrinkled. The sun burned warm and yellow. Only an occasional flat wisp of cloud smudged the chalky blue sky. My mother sat in a low chair, draped in a thin blanket. The blanket hung over the arm of the chair, billowing out around her when a light breeze brushed past. She read a book, one of her mystery novels, pausing every few pages to glance up and scan the crowds. Next to her, my father's book lay open across his legs as he dozed. After a while, my mother woke him, waving a bottle of sunscreen in front of his face. He obliged with a grunt, smoothing thick sheets of it across the dark hair of his arms.

I stretched beside them, letting the sun bake its heat into me, cells waking to the sensations of salty air and soft, gritty sand. I felt new in my body as I glanced down at my outstretched form. Sweat rose in bubbles across my chest, glossy with sunscreen. I looked different to myself, unfamiliar, as if the hungry fascination my eyes had for Tyler were turning to me as well: the sinews of my legs, the eddies of hair circling my abdomen, disappearing below the waistband of my trunks. This is me, I thought, and felt surprised, the way I often would with Tyler. The feeling had traveled with me.

"I'm going to take a swim. Want to come?"

My mother wiggled her fingers. "I'm too comfortable. You go."

At the water's edge, the ocean swelled, forward and back, concaving the sand beneath my feet. I drew a breath and plunged in. The brisk shock of it jolted. The ocean's volumes pushed against me, dampening the noise of its waves and the combative screams of teenagers. I sank slowly until my lungs ached. I twisted back up, breaking through the surface, the air pricking goose bumps along my arms. A lifeguard whistled at a group past the swim line. She stood in her raised station, the red sleeves of her windbreaker rippling as she motioned for them to come in.

I realized I was hungry; I hadn't eaten all day and my hangover had passed. I swam back to the shore. The current was stronger than I realized and I had been in the water for some time—I had drifted quite far. The sun had shifted, pulling itself farther into the sky. It took a moment to orient myself. I headed back and passed two guys together on a blanket, one in a blue speedo, one in green. The one in blue waved and called out—"Come say hi"—the one in green hiding his face behind his hand, laughing.

"I have to find my parents. Next time." I smiled and walked on—it felt good to be noticed. Maybe they could sense the new way I was feeling in my body, too.

I ate a sandwich my mother had packed and rubbed sunscreen on the back of her neck. I napped and woke to the beach clearing out. We had stayed longer than planned. There wasn't time to go home before dinner. We rinsed at the showers outside the bathrooms, brushing the sand from our calves, waiting our turns for the changing rooms. My father felt we would be underdressed for the restaurant. "We'll look like a bunch of beach bums."

"We're in Florida," my mother said. "We are beach bums."

The restaurant was in a part of town that was being aggressively developed. Glass towers, sea-green, loomed above an over-lit square bisected by a pedestrian-only street. The thick curved necks of enormous streetlamps swooped down at us, blasting with acidic light. Everything had been built at once so there was no variation, no uneven patina of wear. Storefronts and signage popped bright and loud. The whole scene looked as if it had been lifted from Disneyland, creating the uncanny effect of a town built to imitate an amusement park built in imitation of a town. (Somewhere, a first-year grad student hunched over a laptop writing a term paper about it, titled something like "Simulacrum by the Sea.")

My parents sat side by side. My mother leaned toward my father, their shoulders touching, her fingertip tracing lines of the menu he couldn't make out in the restaurant's faint lighting. They looked small there, together. As my mother read out loud from the list of wines, my father buttered a shiny dinner roll and placed it in front of her. I felt a quick and painful surge of love for them. The food was good, my mother kept commenting on it, repeating how glad she was to be there, her voice a little loud, giddy with her second glass of wine. When my father hesitated to join her, I offered to drive home and switched to water. I would let them enjoy the night.

We finished our meals and wandered back outside, the evening sticky after the air-conditioned restaurant. We did a slow loop up the promenade, stopping to look in the windows of shops, closed for the holiday. My mother *oohed* and *aahed*, pointing things out to me, my father a few steps ahead. We looped back, down the other side, waiting in front of the restaurant for the valet to bring the car.

"Evelyn! Michael!"

A small woman, my mother's age, waving and walking toward us.

"Joanne," my mother said, and then to me, "You remember Mrs. Landewehr."

Joanne Landewehr, my social studies teacher—sixth grade, seventh? My mother and she had been close, I couldn't remember how they'd met. Something at the school. Her son Jacob was in my year. Although I didn't understand it at the time, I had a terrible crush on him. Every once in a while he would come to mind and I would scour the internet for news of him. I'd once found photos of his wedding, which, absurdly, sent me into a depressive spiral for days. Some part of me had never let go of the idea we would be together, despite almost two decades of no contact and his enduring heterosexuality. Joanne's husband died some time ago—I remembered my mother mentioning it—and she had moved into one of the new condos crowding the sky above our heads.

"And this is your Mark?" she asked, opening her arms for a hug. She smelled of hairspray and breath mints. "Very good-looking," she said not to me, but my mother. "Are you still in New York?"

"No," I said. "Ohio, of all places."

My mother cut in. "He's an English professor. At Sawyer College."

Joanne hummed approval. "Very impressive."

"I don't know," I said. "They'll let anyone teach literature these days."

"He's just being modest," my mother said. "And he's writing a book."

"Really!"

"Well, I'm trying to. We'll see."

"That's wonderful," Joanne said. "I can't wait to read it."

I steered the car along the quiet roads. On either side, houses glowed with family gatherings lingering into the night. In the back seat, my father nodded in and out. His cottony snores kept harmony with the rumbling engine of the car.

"Do you want to put on the radio?"

My mother, seated beside me, made no move.

"I don't know why you do that," she said.

"Listen to music?"

"No." Her voice cut short and sharp. "With Joanne. The way you put yourself down."

The light ahead started to change. I pushed the gas, flying through.

"I wasn't putting myself down."

"You were. Dismissing your book like that. Saying anyone can teach. It's not true."

"I didn't mean anything by it."

"You worked so hard in school. All on your own. You never needed anything from us. You just did it. Most people don't even finish college, much less a PhD. And you have a great job. You get paid to think. It's insulting to act like it doesn't matter."

This story that I hadn't needed anything from them was one she repeated often. *Marky has always been independent,* she would say. *Marky doesn't like help, he likes to do things on his own.* Cassie was always the focus of their concern, and anger rose in me at the thought of it—that a child wouldn't want his parents' help. Of course I did, there just wasn't any left over for me.

"I was just joking. I didn't mean to upset you."

She turned from me and looked out the window, the headlights of passing cars streaking her face in white bands.

"Your life is not a joke."

We passed the next few days mostly in the house, venturing to the park a half mile away, to the outdoor mall for an early dinner and movie. The mall was built around a series of fake canals and after the movie we wandered over its bridges, eating small cups of ice cream going soft. I flew back to Ohio on Sunday. My mother was up early, as always. She poured us coffee and we sat in quiet around the kitchen table, sharing sections of the newspaper. My father joined us a bit later and when the hour of my flight drew near, they drove me to the airport. The highway was empty and still. We made good time and I found myself wishing we had left later, done more with the morning. They offered to park and come inside but I said it wasn't worth it; I was checked in, I'd head right to my gate. I stood at the curb with my bag and watched their car pull off and out of sight and then I turned and went inside.

CHAPTER 9

I guess sex always involves some degree of denial. If we really thought about what we were doing (the mashing of parts, exposing our most insecure and needful selves—our souls' misshapen moles and dry spots and singularly persistent, springy hairs), would we be able to do it? But it was also probably true that my situation involved a very high degree. I was risking my job at Sawyer, my entire career. Someone like Hal could get away with fucking his students; the academy was built on the backs of such couplings, complicitly overlooked. In my case, on the other hand, there was an entire cultural discourse ready to be mobilized against me: *rapacious gay man preys on innocent child*. If things with Tyler came to light, I'd be going the way of Annabelle Cleremont—*adieu*. Never mind what Tyler wanted. Never mind—even as our sex increasingly played with my dominance and his submission—that I felt entirely his supplicant, completely powerless in relation to him. (In calmer moments, I knew this was an illusion, but that knowledge did not make his grip on me dissolve.) None of this would matter if we were found out. I had done my best to box these fears. But as the end of term drew near—just a week of classes after Thanksgiving, the reading period, and then we were done—my fears grew, rattling around, going bump in the night. The menacing apprehension of an end in sight.

I spent the weekend after classes wrapped and the next few days largely with Safie, catching up on work; I was drowning in a backlog of ungraded assignments, and now all the final essays on top of that. I'd mumbled some apologies for the night at the bar, my sharp tone, my distance this semester; she'd graciously accepted. We fell into a rhythm like the old days. I'd show up at her house with my stack of papers and we worked sprawled across her living room, the easy quiet a balm.

One day we worked right into evening. We ordered food from this Chinese place that Safie had discovered. "Egg noodle cure," she called it. We sat on her floor, the paper wreckage of a semester surrounding us, eating right from the containers. "I forgot how good this is," I said. Safie hadn't decided what to do about tenure, to take another year or just forge ahead. I thought forge ahead, her case was so strong. But she wasn't sure and it cracked my heart to see her doubting and uncertain; it looked weird on her, like she'd been dressed in someone else's ill-fitting clothes.

I'd been holding off on bringing up Stephen; I'd heard nothing from him since the night in my apartment. Maybe it was the beer or the noodles or just the safety of being in this space with her again, but I asked Safie if she'd seen him.

She nodded.

"Is he okay?"

"He's okay. He's hurt, and a little humiliated, but he's okay."

"Okay." I fought the urge to dig for details, to cajole her into saying something I could feel wretched about, a sore spot to worry and inflame. I felt terrible about the way I'd ended things. But not that I had. Whether Stephen could see it or not, I was setting him free.

"Try this." Safie handed me a container—pork fried rice—and took mine. "You know you're allowed to want something different for yourself."

If she knew what that was, what I wanted, what I was taking, would she still think that?

Her phone rang—Maria from History. I kept an eye on Safie as they spoke, watching her face, radiant in the early throes of romance. It felt good to be here with her. And it even felt good to immerse myself in work. I'd fallen behind on everything—not just grading. I missed the deadline for summer grants and was being daily hounded by a journal editor to whom I owed revisions. It wasn't just the time I spent with Tyler, but the thought of him, the memories of a last encounter, the anticipation of the next—the fact of him consumed my days, burning through my hours so evening arrived with smoldering dismay; what had I done with the time?

I had been living in a kind of altered state. I could see that now, with a few days apart. And although I didn't want to admit it, it felt good to have a break.

Grades were due on Thursday, the last official day of fall semester. That night, with campus emptying out and to commence our six weeks of freedom, all the humanities programs in Walton Hall hosted a kind of building-wide open house. Each department set up snacks and drinks and faculty and staff wandered between the student-free rooms and floors. It had been known as Walton Walkabout until some junior faculty pointed out the name was indigenous appropriation; it was now called the Walton Walk. (The battle over renaming, with two senior colleagues years past retirement digging in their heels, had almost ended the event altogether; white men proving once again they would rather destroy a thing than not get their way.)

I was meeting the others on campus and as I got ready, I checked my phone again. No word from Tyler. I had texted the night before but heard nothing back, and then again that morning. Nothing. He was probably just caught up in the end of the semester, as I had been. But it was strange to go so long without contact, and an unsettling feeling about it had started to intrude into the relative calm of the past few days. What if something had happened? I had told him I needed the week to focus on work, and I worried now that he was upset about it. It had been hard enough to ask, maybe I shouldn't have. In a rush, I typed out a message—*Just thinking of you.* I hit SEND and immediately regretted it, embarrassed by my neediness. I saw myself all night long, sneaking peeks to see if he had replied, and then decided—I'll leave the phone behind. I was being ridiculous, everything was fine. No Tyler tonight.

We assembled at Safie's office—her, me, Colin, and Priya. When Colin called it pre-gaming, the rest of us booed. After a round of shots—or two rounds, actually—we went down the hall to get English out of the way. Previously English had a reputation as one of the rowdier stops on the Walk, but under Susan's miserly direction, provisions had been reduced to cheap boxed wine and a chemically pungent snack mix, handfuls of which Colin was currently chomping through. Priya and Safie had gone to fetch drinks and returned, distributing small waxed-paper cups meant for a child's birthday party.

"Susan went all out this year," Safie said.

"I'm getting notes of—" I sniffed at my drink—"budget cuts and quiet desperation."

"Anyway, all I'm saying," Colin said, "is you can't talk about the right wing turn in this country without accounting for the evisceration of working-class jobs." He dug his free hand back into the snack mix.

"What are you talking about?" Safie asked.

"The war on Christmas," I said. "Of course." There'd been an incident at the beginning of the week. The local elementary school was putting on its annual, recently rechristened "holiday" recital. Some parents had shown up carrying signs about the war on Christmas. One of them, who later claimed to be dressed as an angel, wore a white robe and hood. Police were called, the event shut down.

"He's obsessed," Priya said. "Lots of people lose their jobs and don't show up in Klan regalia at their kid's school."

"Sure," Colin said, "but what I'm saying is—"

"Take a night off," Safie said. And then, turning and raising her arm, instructed, "Everyone wave at Susan." Susan stood on the other side of the room, frowning about something. We all waved. "Great, we've shown our faces. Let's get walking."

"Where to?" Priya asked.

"I don't know," Safie said. "History?"

Colin lifted his cup. "I'm still working on my drink."

"Drink it or bring it," I said, tossing mine back. "We are marching forward with History."

Colin moaned assent and we headed out. He and Priya paired up and walked ahead. I wiggled a finger behind their backs and lowered my voice. "So there is something going on there?"

Safie nodded. "Priya said she's just testing the waters."

"I hate to say it, but I mean—I would test those waters." Colin's ass was looking particularly firm in his khakis.

"Gross," Safie said. "You seem like you're in a good mood."

"I am, as a matter of fact." I was happy to be with Safie and Priya, and Colin even. I'd been so disconnected, so caught up in Tyler, it felt nice to drop back into the rest of my life. I thought of the flip phone, sitting at home, pleasantly out of reach for the night. "And with Maria? It's going well?"

"I'm not taking any questions."

"Come on. It's nice to see you excited."

"I'm too old and jaded for that."

"But if you were younger, and less jaded?"

"Who knows? I might be excited."

A cluster of faculty clogged the doorway, flush with booze and the building's warmth. I didn't really know anybody but Safie knew them all, making introductions as we wedged through. The room was packed, way more crowded than English. Someone had brought a stereo, volume turned up, the conversations loud to match it. They'd cut the overhead fluorescents and set up lamps with low watts and blinking red Christmas lights.

"This almost feels like an actual party," I said.

Colin and Priya were already getting drinks. A table loaded with top-shelf liquor, wine in actual bottles. Next to a charcuterie board, a tray with a rainbow spread of macaroons.

"How does History have so much money?" Priya asked.

"This new budget model," Colin said. "Everything comes down to enrollment and tuition dollars."

Safie picked up a bottle of Scotch and whistled. "Their classes must be really popular. This stuff is not cheap."

I took the bottle and poured. "Drink up, little lambs."

"It tastes like," Priya grimaced and stuck out her tongue, "mulch?"

"It's the peaty resilience of being a viable major," I said.

"Let's make some rounds." Safie's gaze landed on Maria, who smiled and lifted her chin in hello.

We were about to move in Maria's direction when across the room, in stepped Tyler and Addison. They snaked through the crowd, heads low. I looked around to see if anyone else had noticed.

"I'll catch up," I said. "I skipped dinner—I'm going to graze off the fat of the land." Before anyone could protest, I grabbed a slice of something and shoved it in my mouth.

Tyler and Addison settled in a darkened corner near a bookcase, leaning in close and conspiratorial. Addison was acting something out, an impression or a scene, hands raised like claws beside his face. They exploded in deep laughs that bent them over. Tyler straightened and pulled something from his jacket—a bottle. With a quick glance to either side, he poured its contents into two cups and stashed it on a shelf.

"Mark! So wonderful to see you."

I turned. Elaine Friedman. "Elaine. Hi."

"And where's your better half?"

"Oh—" Apparently the rumor mill hadn't kicked in yet. "Stephen couldn't make it."

"Well, please say hello." A youngish guy I didn't recognize stood nearby and Elaine's hand fluttered, beckoning. "Paul, join us." He took a small step forward, sheepish look on his face. "Come, come. Paul is a doctoral candidate. At Michigan. Doing fascinating research in Mato Grosso. He's here on fellowship for the year."

"I was at your talk, at Fall Fest," Paul said. "I really enjoyed it."

"That's kind, thanks." I peeked across the room: Tyler lost in conversation with Addison. Had he not seen me? "I was glad to get it over with."

"It's always good to get it over with," said Elaine.

"No, it was brilliant," said Paul. It intersected with his own work, he explained, an ethnography of a farming village. They had suffered a series of brutal, unsolved murders a decade ago. It had deeply impacted the village and he was trying to track the stories they told to make sense of it, especially in terms of gender. The victims had all been young boys. "Americans think of Brazil as this violent, dangerous place, but this is a small community. Very isolated, very intimate. Things like that don't happen. It's not like here."

As Paul talked, I stole glances at Tyler and Addison, making quick work of the bottle. They were in constant physical contact: Addison's hand on Tyler's arm, Tyler pressing his forehead to Addison's shoulder, overcome. Something electric passing between them, sizzling and white.

And then Addison moved from the corner, handing his cup to Tyler. He headed for the door.

"Pardon me," I said, cutting off Paul. "I see someone I should say hello to."

"Sorry," said Paul, "I'm talking your ear off. But I would love to get together if you have time." He smiled. "To talk about your work."

"Wonderful, delightful," Elaine said. "I'm so pleased you made the connection. And Mark, Stephen and you must come for dinner. Robert's a little in love, I think." She laughed.

"Sure, sure," I said, not really listening. "That sounds great."

I crossed the room and Tyler acknowledged me with a slight dip of his head, the smallest gesture. There was something feline in the arc of him, lithe and disinterested.

"What are you doing here?" I spoke quietly, willing him not to draw attention our way.

"Nothing. Hanging out." I'd seen this look on his face before, nights when he showed up late at my apartment, damp and tingling with drink.

"This isn't really for students."

Tyler shrugged, but not even. Less than a shrug. "No one else seems to mind."

"What happened to Addison?"

"He went to the bathroom." Tyler slouched into the wall, examining his cup.

"Is something going on?"

"No. Why?"

"I haven't heard from you."

"Oh, yeah. Sorry. I got busy finishing up classes." He looked up at me. "Are you upset?"

"Of course not." There was an insistence in my voice I didn't like and I tried to soften it. "But is something bothering you?"

"Not at all."

"It's just—you seem a little off."

"I think I seem just like myself." He reached for the bottle. Vodka. More than half of it gone. He refilled his cup and I glanced around us.

"You should be careful with that. It'll be a mess if you get caught."

Tyler snorted.

"I'm not trying to hassle you," I said.

That half shrug again. "It's no hassle."

"Tyler, listen." Why were we fighting? "I didn't mean—"

And then Safie was beside us—I hadn't even noticed her approach.

"What's happening over here?" Her eyes passed from Tyler to me and back to him. "I'm not sure we've met. I'm Dr. Hartwell."

Tyler smirked. He raised his cup and emptied it in one long swallow.

"I was just wishing Professor Lausson happy holidays."

I followed Tyler's eyes across the room. Addison had returned— he stood by the doorway, watching. Tyler signaled for him to turn around.

"Well it's probably time to say goodnight," said Safie.

Tyler grinned, a tight smirk. "Goodnight." He reached his empty cup toward the shelf—he missed, and it clattered to the floor. I watched him weave across the room, limbs loose and swinging.

"What is he doing here?" Safie asked.

"I have no idea." My words had been coming out wrong and I'd upset Tyler and now I'd lost my chance to set it right.

"He'll get this whole thing shut down," Safie said. "Some of these kids are so spoiled." She bent to pick up the cup he'd left behind.

"It's not that big a deal."

"It kind of is," Safie said. My face felt hot and patchy, throat parched. The lights of the Christmas bulbs burned red and harsh. I wanted out of there, out of this conversation. "I think I saw him at your talk. Is he a student of yours?"

"What does that have to do with anything?"

Safie blinked and stepped back. "Excuse me?"

"I had a handle on things, you didn't have to interfere." Safie and her meddling, thinking she knew what was best for everyone else.

"I was just helping."

"I didn't need your help. That was humiliating."

"What?"

"I know you like to be in charge of everything, telling everyone what to do. But I was dealing with it—I'm not a child, I don't need a babysitter."

And then a voice interrupted—"Here you are." We both turned to look—it was Maria. "Oh sorry, I'm one short." She'd brought Safie a drink. "The infamous Mark. Hello."

Safie lifted the drink from Maria and looked directly at me. "Mark was actually just leaving." I stared back at her, her stony expression, like I could be anyone.

"That's right," I said. "I was."

And then I left.

I stalked my apartment in a storm of fury and shame. Why had the conversation with Tyler gone that way? I felt belittled, a nobody. As if nothing of these last weeks had happened.

How had I ended up here?

Hours later, the phone rang.

"What?"

A long pause.

"What are you doing?" Tyler's voice gauzy, distant.

"What am I doing?" I had finally calmed down but everything jerked back alive, kicking inside me. "What the fuck was going on tonight?"

"I'm really sorry."

"Is this a game for you?"

"No. I just—"

"You have fucked up my life, Tyler."

"Don't say that."

"You have. You have fucked it up completely." I was heaving, quick, sharp breaths. "This is such a mess."

Tyler's voice broke. "Please. Stop." And then he was crying, great, wracked sobs, deep and desolate.

"Tyler."

He said nothing, just kept crying.

"Tyler, come on. It's okay. I'm sorry. Don't cry."

I waited. A minute passed. His breathing slowed and evened out. A space opened and filled with quiet.

"Are you okay?"

"I'm okay." He sounded flat, spent.

"What's wrong?"

"I know I'm fucked up. I don't know why I act that way. I shouldn't drink. I'm such an asshole."

"You're not an asshole."

"I can't stand the idea that you're disappointed in me. I hate it."

"Tyler." Something released in me, a latch letting go. "You could never disappoint me."

I poured a whiskey and crouched to scan my record collection, untouched for months—a year? I needed something to help calm me down, even out the emotional upheaval of the night. I pulled an album and set it on the turntable. I lowered the needle; the comforting crackle. I stretched across the couch, the music cocooning around me.

Soon there was a tap at the door.

Tyler's eyes were swollen, his face puffy. He looked hollowed out, beautiful. I pulled him to me, holding him to my chest in the fold of my arms. He poured heat against me, pushing into me, burrowing. I kissed the top of his head, petting his hair and the back of his neck. I would have taken all of him into me if I could.

"You're going to be the death of me."

He pulled back, smiling. "I hope not."

"Did something happen tonight?"

"Yeah. It's stupid."

"Do you want to talk about it?"

"Not really." He laughed. "Is that okay?"

"It's okay." I noticed then he'd brought a duffel bag with him. It was packed full, heavy on the floor beside him. "What's with that?"

"I can't deal with the dorms right now. Could I stay here? Until I go home?"

I looked at him, his patchy face and bloodshot eyes.

"Of course."

He threw himself back at me, quick and ferocious, wiry arms wrapped tight. I kissed his head again—once, twice, and then once more.

He settled into the couch and I rummaged around in the kitchen, returning with a bowl of warmed-up pasta in each hand. We didn't really talk, just sat together, eating and listening to the music. Tyler ate with abandon, legs folded under himself, wiping tomato sauce from his face as he went. The record reached the end, the needle making a soft, swooping sound as it circled the vinyl edge.

"Should I play the other side?" I asked, getting up.

Tyler nodded and said through a mouthful, "I like it. What is it?" I flipped the record. An orchestral bloom filled the room. I passed him the album sleeve. "I've never heard of them," he said.

"Are you kidding me? This record saved my life in high school."

"What do you mean?"

"I just—I was so miserable."

"Why were you miserable?"

"It was high school. Weren't you?"

Tyler shook his head. "I mean, there was annoying shit. But high school was great. I kind of miss it."

I couldn't imagine what that would feel like—queers survived high school, we didn't miss it. "Sometimes I don't understand you at all." The track reached its chorus. I had listened to this so many times over so many years, I felt it in my bones. "This song is one of my favorites." We were finished eating and I lay back on the sofa, pulling him to me. He smelled of weed, muggy and sweet. We listened in silence, Tyler's weight pooled against me. Was this so bad? To offer some part of yourself and have it gently held and cherished? This is all I wanted. We stayed like that to the end of the album.

When the last song finished, I tapped him. "Let me up."

He peeled himself from me and I went to shut off the stereo. "I liked that," he said. "You should play music for me more often." He picked up the record sleeve again. He ran a finger across a piece of masking tape, faded letters scrawled in black sharpie, barely legible. "Who's Cassie?"

"Oh." I had forgotten the tape was there. Cassie labeled all her records—it had just become part of the cover to me. "My sister. This was hers. Lots of these were."

"I didn't know you had a sister. I'm so jealous, I always wanted one. Just like the idea of a sister seems so cool." He laughed.

"Cassie was always much cooler than me."

"Where is she now?"

I stumbled, caught off guard, and something must have shown on my face, I could see it reflected in Tyler's eyes. He grabbed my hand. I couldn't remember him ever doing that; it was always me reaching for him.

"I'm sorry. I didn't mean—"

"You didn't do anything wrong. I never talk about her."

"Why not?"

"I don't know, it's just—I'm not sure, really." I looked at him. A stillness around his eyes and mouth.

"What happened?"

By the middle of Cassie's senior year, she and our mother rarely occupied the same room at the same time. When they did, it ended in fights that got so vicious, both of them screaming at the top of their lungs, I thought it might bring the house down on all our heads—and part of me wished it would. Cassie lied about applying to colleges. She never mailed in the applications and had found some way to get the checks cashed, so she'd been stealing from them on top of it all. The night my parents found out, I worried someone might really get hurt. Something inside Cassie was burning. I could see it, convoluting her, the anguish unbearable. Her rage was a way to let it out, to release the heat from her. But through all those months of fighting, screeching curses and slammed doors and broken dishes, it kept burning.

Rumors about Cassie filtered down through the grades, making their way to me. Stories about a blow job in the boy's bathroom, a guy she was hanging out with who was almost forty. Stories about drugs, needles. I did everything I could to keep these accounts from reaching me, but my classmates seemed to take a sick pleasure in confronting me with them. Cassie's grades had fallen so much she almost didn't graduate. When she did, our mother said it was only because the school didn't want to deal with her anymore.

The night before graduation, Cassie disappeared. She didn't show up the next morning. The rest of us got dressed for the ceremony and waited in case she returned in time. When she didn't, my father suggested maybe she had gone with a friend to the school and thought we should go meet her. "I'm not going to waste my time," my mother said. She closed herself in for the rest of the day behind the shuttered door of their bedroom.

A few days later, Cassie returned. She had been disappearing on and off like that all year, a day or two every few weeks. As summer progressed, the stretches grew longer. We would hear nothing from her and then she would show up with no explanation, as if she had been gone an hour, doing errands. During her absences, I begged our mother to go easy on her, but Cassie's return only set off another brawl that sent her from us again.

Then, toward the end of July, Cassie disappeared for almost three weeks. When she came home, I could see it immediately: She was not well. The rings under her eyes had grown so deep and dark, I almost missed the bruise yellowing beneath one. She was defeated. The fire had burned itself out, leaving nothing behind. She would sleep half the day, only leaving her room to eat scraps of food she mostly pushed around the plate. She smelled sour, her skin sallow, she had nothing to say. I felt frightened of her, this shell, and didn't know how to ask what happened.

And also—I was relieved the fights had come to an end. And the waiting, the waiting for her to come home and then bracing for the explosion. I was glad this was over. I think this is what I felt most guilty for. That some part of me was grateful for Cassie's suffering, for whatever had broken her, so desperately did I want the semblance of calm that had returned to our home.

We were into August and nothing changed. Cassie had no plans for the fall, no job, but our parents had backed off. I think they, too, were willing to accept a tenuous peace. Soon, I would start eighth grade. I'd be thirteen in September and I'd been getting ready for my bar mitzvah, with no idea we would end up calling it off. I poured myself into preparing, the time at temple an escape from the pallor Cassie cast across the house, even locked up in her room. One night my parents picked me up—I'd been meeting with the rabbi to go through the prayers. It was dinnertime and we had leftovers at home, but it was a lovely night—frictionless, cool air. We wanted to linger in it. "Fuck it," my mother said, and then laughed, covering her mouth. "Cassie isn't going to eat anyway. Let's go out." They took me to a Japanese restaurant, a chain. We sat at a long table with two other families. The chef cooked right at the table, doing a hammy routine, rapid-fire dicing the cuts of meat and vegetables, showy flips of the blades at which we couldn't help but gasp. Later I understood that this place was tacky and the food not very good, but that night, we enjoyed ourselves. Everything else dropped away, just me and my parents, a normal family, making stupid jokes, sneaking bites from each other's plates, laughing at nothing.

We stayed out late, hours past my usual bedtime. When we got home, Cassie was not in her room. The bathroom door was locked. My mother knocked; no reply. A gentle whooshing hummed from the other side. I pointed to the crack of space at the bottom of the door. "There's water coming out." My mother started panting, repeating softly, "No. No." I didn't understand what was happening but my father was frantic, shouting Cassie's name, pounding at the door. He was scaring me. "What's going on?" He barked at me to step back but before I could move he barreled forward, the whole body of him crashing through, ripping the door from its hinges. My mother screamed.

My father rushed in, bathwater splashing up the front of his pants, spinning in tight circles, yelling into the empty room.

"Cassie! Cassie!"

My mother crumbled against the splintered threshold, pale-faced, eyes wide.

"Where is she?"

I told Tyler all this, more or less, sitting together on the couch, my eyes tracking the ceiling. It felt like the room had gotten darker but the lamplight had grown brighter, an orange glow cast about us, pulsing, holding us in place.

"Where was she?" Tyler asked.

"I don't know. We never found out."

"What do you mean?"

"Whatever she'd planned—she didn't follow through. She just . . . disappeared."

"She never came back?"

I shook my head. "We never heard from her again. And we didn't know her friends, or whoever she'd been hanging out with. Even this girl Meg, who she'd been so close with. Cassie had cut her off toward the end. So we never found out what had been going on. I know I was young, but still—"

"What?" I didn't answer and Tyler repeated himself, voice vibrant with urgency. "What?" He tugged at me, making me look at him.

"I don't know. For her to be so unhappy, to just leave. I should have tried to help. I could have done something."

I realized then that Tyler was crying, thin streams running down his cheeks.

"But you were just a kid. You must have missed her so much."

I realized then that Tyler was crying, thin streams running down his cheeks.

"Tyler, no. I'm okay. Please don't cry."

I pulled him to me. His face against me, wetness spreading across my shirt. "That's not fair," he said. "It's not fair." I stroked his hair as he clung to me, comforting him in a way no one had ever done for me. We stayed like that for a long time. We didn't speak and we didn't need to. We had gone somewhere else, crossed to something, and we could take our time coming back.

Eventually we got up and went to the bedroom.

"I have a plan for us." An idea had revealed itself to me and taken shape. "You're all packed for your trip home, right?"

"I thought I would just leave from here. Is that okay?"

"Let's go away this weekend."

"Really? Where?"

"I'll sort it in the morning. But are you game?"

He smiled. "For sure. I'm in."

In the dark of my room, we undressed each other, our clothes a tangle on the floor. Tyler lay on his side under the covers and pressed his back to me. I wrapped my arms around him, hands folded across his chest, breathing him in. We did not have sex. We lay still in the quiet and for the first and only time, I fell asleep before him.

* * *

I woke early and by the time Tyler got up, I had booked the trip: tickets to New York, a hotel on the Lower East Side.

"You're crazy," Tyler said.

"Have you ever been?"

He shook his head no.

"Are you excited?"

"Yes." He almost shouted it. "Was it expensive?"

"It was nothing." I had put it all on credit cards and would deal with it later. I didn't care. I loved the idea of spoiling him, taking him on a trip his family couldn't afford. "There's some breakfast in the kitchen and then we should get going."

I'd gotten flights from Akron, farther away; hopefully, anyone from Sawyer would be flying from Cleveland. But I was antsy in the airport as we crawled through security, scanning for familiar faces. I wanted to be in New York already, safe from this school and this town.

"Are you okay?"

We'd made it through security and were headed to the gate. "Sure," I said. "I just get anxious about flying."

He seemed satisfied with this answer. "Mom is scared of flying, too." He looked at me and smiled.

"What are you smiling about?"

"Nothing. You look really handsome."

And then I asked—I couldn't help it—"You think I'm handsome?"

"Duh." He laughed and looked away, back at his phone. "What are you, stupid?"

I once read a study that said unhappiness sprang from the gap between expectations and reality. The researchers focused on work and found that academia was among the unhappiest professions. The authors attributed this to the fact that the life we imagined as eager young graduate students—high on critical theory and the freedom from a nine-to-five status quo—was so far from the truth of what the job entailed. The article concluded that we might be happier if instead we expected the career of a midlevel accountant.

I remember thinking that summer, after my first year—I worked so many years for this; for *this*? I fantasized about quitting, but had no idea what else I could do. My dread grew as a dull ache inside me, thinking of a lifetime spent in this relentless rotation of weeks and semesters, of meetings and reviews, conferences and publications. Driving my same car to the same lot, to walk the same path to the same building to sit in the same office. Is this all the promise my future contained? What a cruelty, to have to work to live.

I often go back to that night before the trip, confiding in Tyler about Cassie. This is the memory of Tyler to which I most regularly return. I can lose myself in the sweetness of its recollection. How it felt to confess, the way he offered his body to be held like a child, when it was him holding me. And other times, I obsess over it, searching out some detail I missed, desperate for knowledge I will never have. Wondering what he was thinking as he listened to me. Wondering what he already knew that night, what he had already decided. I can make myself crazy trying to figure out what of that night was real—whether it was Tyler at his most loving or his most traitorous. Sometimes, I'm not sure there's a difference.

But what I do know is that, that second year, when Tyler appeared, the dread and despair that had haunted me my entire life, and which Sawyer had only compounded, began to fade, replaced by something like hope. Hope that my life could be more than I'd thought. And this I can say with certainty: Those few days with Tyler in New York were the happiest of my adult life. They were perhaps the happiest of my entire life, or least since Cassie left us. I had not been back to New York since coming to Sawyer. The moment the city came into view from the cab, it dazzled all over again, as if it were my first visit, too. The ambition of it: its towers spiraling into the upper reaches of the atmosphere, its avenues stretching for miles, bending beyond sight. Tyler's awe only amplified my own. I loved watching him take it in and, even more than that, I loved being the one who had brought him to the city. I'd had moments of rabid jealousy; his comfort in bed was something clearly earned, and the thought that he'd had sex without me could make me feel crazed, scraped out. I desired Tyler with an unsettling depth and persistence. But this, introducing him to New York, being with him the first time he walked across the Brooklyn Bridge, an icy wind leaving us alone at the crest; giving in to his insistence and taking him to Times Square, the glow of his eyes competing with the neon blast overhead, these firsts—no one could claim these but me.

We ate dim sum in Chinatown, stuffing our faces with dish after dish, sweet meats and bitter, soothing greens, staying in the restaurant until close. We wove the streets of Williamsburg, jockeying with frat boys and foreign tourists to stare across the feral waters of the East River at Manhattan, a mountain of glass and steel pushing itself to the very edge of the island. We went to my favorite bar, near Tompkins Square Park. I had discovered it on my first night in the city. A tiny chamber with black booths bathed in pink light, Patti and Nina and Nico crooning with longing as we bent over drinks gleaming and dark. Back at the hotel, we christened the room with our fucking, each surface and every corner an invitation to reach farther, push harder. As if the room itself begged us to fill it.

Our last afternoon, before heading to LaGuardia—he would fly to Charlotte and I back to Ohio—we visited the Met. We strolled through an exhibit of early fashion photography, the images growing sharper, both more complete and more abstract as the decades unfolded across the warren of rooms. Back downstairs, I led us past the throngs to my favorite part: ancient Egypt. Room upon room of pilfered goods, benevolent mummies greeting us with their hallowed silence. A glass case displayed tiny scarabs and we sought out the smallest among them to marvel that human hands could make something of such beauty, that could survive so long, defying time itself, to arrive in a future terrifying and unknown. At the end of the corridors, we found the temple, disassembled and rebuilt here, stone by stone. Outside the glass walls of the room, the bare trees of Central Park bowed over empty paths. We shared the space with few others, or maybe there were more and my memory has subtracted them. It felt as if we were alone, a hush stilling the room. We walked the perimeter of the temple, the path of water, the low afternoon sun glinting at us, leading us to the gate. I took Tyler's hand and held it in my own, marveling that a gesture so small could suffuse me with such expansive joy. It felt like everything was mine, all of it belonged to me: this city, this day, this museum, this room, this light, soft and yellow and breaking apart, the padding sound of our steps on the rose-gray stones of the floor, the sand-colored stones of the temple's gate, this boy, his hand in mine—it was mine, just for me: a universe of wanting, answered.

PART II

CHAPTER 10

Returning from New York, I saw my apartment for what it was: half-furnished, incomplete, a holding pattern in the shape of a few small rooms. I stood between the thin walls of its cramped kitchen and suddenly understood: the problem was Sawyer. In the bloodless air of the school and town, I was shrinking, fading away.

And then from this realization, a fantasy of another life bloomed. I would get a new job. If not in New York, in some other city, on one coast or the other, a place that met you with something unexpected, that kept you moving. Somewhere not hemmed in all sides by the rusted-out sprawl of the US collapsing on itself. And I wanted this with Tyler, what we'd had on the trip, something public and known. This alternate life of happiness, pleasure, and surprise felt not only possible, but like it had been there all along, just waiting for me to open my eyes.

When we'd left each other at LaGuardia, I waited with my luggage and watched Tyler weave through the security line toward the checkpoint. I followed the arc of his shoulders until he disappeared into the crowds; a murky dread that I might never see him again uncoiled within me. But now I realized the break was a gift. Six weeks to devote to my book. This project, which had felt like a leaden weight around my neck, now, I could see, was the key. I would finish the book, I would go on the job market, and Tyler and I would be free.

I rearranged my living room, clearing space to work—even my office on campus had been constraining me; who could think in that place? I piled towers of reference books against one wall and against another stacked my research documents, one for each chapter. I read through everything I had written up to that point: lectures and chapter fragments, notes squeezed in the margins of photocopies, flashes of insight scrawled across manila folders. Above the kitchen table—I had hauled it into the living room, it was now my desk—I tacked sheets of yellow legal paper, across which I worked out a map of the project: black ink for what I already had, green for what was missing. I had done more over the past years than I realized.

I dove in, swept up in the currents of the project. I felt like a first-year graduate student again, the thrill of thinking through writing, of discovering an idea as you were putting it down in words. The anxiety that had greeted me every morning for years, my loyal and persistent companion, gave way to a kind of electrified anticipation: nerves, raw-edged, alert and ready. I'd wake up and leap right from bed and by the time the coffee was ready, I was already deep in the work.

Tyler and I slipped into an easy groove without naming it, texting each night, and only at night. This granted me working hours free of distraction, but with something to look forward to, a promise at day's end. I would sink into the warm, cushiony bubble of our exchanges in satisfied exhaustion, worn out but not weary, grinning at his daily reports. Updates on high school friends, a story about his father setting an oven mitt on fire, his mother yelling as she doused the flames. He sent photos, close-ups of his face, blasted with light from a bedside lamp, goofy and unaware, as if he had surprised himself. He asked about the book always with the same

question: *How were your murderers today?* I sent thoughts on a letter from the archives, a grisly detail I'd uncovered in a coroner's
report. I told him my ambition—to have a draft, rough but complete,
by the end of break. But I didn't tell him why—that I was working
toward our escape. I would save that for his return. After we signed
off for the night, although it was late and the next day would begin
early, I would stay awake a while longer, basking in the feeling of
his company.

These weeks of work experienced just one interruption, once a day.
An intrusion I tried to hold off, but always, at some point, it
pushed through. Sometimes it happened without my realizing. I
would find myself not at the table but standing in my bedroom,
my hand holding my phone, which I hid in there during my working hours. The new phone. Every time, the same result: still no
word from Safie. We'd had no contact since the Walton Walk. I
would steady myself and start to compose a message—I had been
an unforgivable asshole; it was on me to reach out—but everything
sounded trite, insincere. I would vow to write later that night, with
a clearer head not muddled by my manuscript. I just needed to get
through this day. The weeks wore on and as the gap of communication widened, it felt even harder to imagine what to say: The
deepening silence demanded more words to fill it. Maybe the break
was good for us; Safie just needed some space. We would reunite
when the semester started, me unburdened and ready to be a better friend. We would sort things out. We always did.

I also set the next steps of my plan in motion. A few years earlier,
I'd met an editor from a university press who was excited about the
project. I tracked down her email and wrote. *I am not sure you*

remember me from the conference. We talked at the reception and somehow got into a long conversation about Tana French and reality TV. But I have made good progress on the book and would be eager to connect. I worried that too much time had passed, that I'd missed my opportunity, but she responded the next day. *Of course I remember. I'm so glad you reached out. Actually just last week I heard this story about a serial killer and thought of you. Ha, you must get that a lot!* We decided I would spend the semester revising and send her the manuscript by the end of the spring. With all going well, I would enter the fall job-hunting season with a book contract in hand—it was an ambitious plan, but doable.

And by the Saturday before classes resumed, I had done it: a draft of the entire thing. It was a mess, of course, but it was there, it was real, it had a beginning, a middle, and an end. I was one step closer to freedom.

I spent the rest of the day getting ready for Tyler's return. Table moved back to the kitchen, books tucked neatly on shelves. I took everything down from the wall. Alongside the map of the project—it had grown dense and convoluted over the weeks, the scratch of my handwriting almost illegible—I had tacked up grainy printouts, photos of my murderers, childhood portraits and mugshots. The blank wall glared, naked without them. I should get some art or hang up a poster, I thought, like a normal person.

Late in the afternoon, he called.

"Hello," I said. "You're back."

"I'm back." He raised his voice over a din of music and pitched conversation. "How are you?"

"Good. Great." More noise, the smack of something crashing to the ground. "What's going on over there?"

"Sorry, it's crazy in the dorms. Everyone is amped about being back. Hold on." Shouts, a door banging shut, and then quiet. "That's better."

"Where did you go?"

"I'm in the stairwell. Addison's in the room."

"How was the ride back?"

"You know," Tyler said, and laughed. "Dead cornfields and freeways." I had offered to pick him up but it turned out Addison's flight was getting in around the same time, so he gave Tyler a ride. "Addison left his car parked there the entire break. It cost like a thousand dollars."

"That's a lot of money to park a car." I laughed. "We're on for tonight?"

"Yes. I can't wait to see you."

"I'll pick you up at eight. At the usual spot?"

"Perfect."

I'd made a reservation two towns to the east, dinner at a restaurant in a converted mill. New York had settled something between us, but it made me greedy as well. I wanted more with Tyler than the confines of my apartment. Until I could get out of Sawyer, this is how we would manage. We would explore the surrounding towns—everyone kept insisting that Ohio had its rustic charms; we could discover them together. And we'd take trips farther afield, safe and anonymous. I'd been curious about Pittsburgh, and maybe Louisville, when the weather warmed up.

That evening, I drove to the doughnut shop. I pulled into the lot. No Tyler. Two figures bundled in winter coats stepped into the liquor store, but nobody else was around. I parked, idling, and checked my phone. No message. He would be here, in a minute or two. I double-checked directions to the restaurant. My stomach growled; I'd gotten so caught up in cleaning the apartment, I'd forgotten lunch.

And then the door to the liquor store swung open and the two figures reemerged: Tyler, with Addison. Tyler, spotting me through the windshield, waved. He had a pack of cigarettes in his hand and he pocketed them, pulling Addison toward the car. Tyler jumped in and a moment later the backdoor opened, Addison sliding in behind us.

"Good to see you again, Professor Lausson. Happy New Year."

Tyler didn't look at me, just pulled on his seat belt and said, "Sorry, we were just grabbing some things."

From the back seat: "Tyler invited me to join. I hope that's okay."

Tyler laughed. "He doesn't mind. Right?"

I couldn't breathe—it felt like someone had reached into my chest and grabbed my lungs, ringing them like a wet rag. The car's heat blasted at me. I swiped the air vent closed and stabbed at the door, searching out the button for the window. It swept down; cold air rushed in.

"What are you doing?" Tyler said. "It's freezing." He turned to the back. "Can I get some of that gum?"

Addison passed him a piece. "Do you want one?"

I could tell them to leave, throw them out. Or I could just get out and go. Abandon the car, come back for it tomorrow.

"Dr. Lausson? Some gum?"

Addison was talking to me.

"No. I'm fine."

"I heard about this party in Columbus," Tyler said. "I thought we could check it out."

"What?"

"One day back in Sawyer and I already feel suffocated. It's on Greenwood, near the Short North. I'll navigate." He pulled something up on his phone. "Can I put the heat back on? I'm losing feeling in my face."

"Calm down," Addison said. "You're so dramatic about everything."

What had I gotten myself into? Anything I could say would only draw attention to the fact that I shouldn't even be here. I had no idea what to do. So I put the car in reverse, pulled out of the lot, and listened as Tyler directed us out of town.

We'd exited the freeway and were coasting through Columbus, dark streets, slick with melted snow.

"This better not be some stupid frat party," Addison said.

"I wouldn't do that to us, these guys are cool. They're all graduated."

"How did you say you know them?"

"We met in the fall, when I was down here."

My trip to the archives. Tyler's lost hours.

"I don't remember hearing about that," Addison said.

"Oh, turn here!" Tyler waved his hand at the window. "Right!"

I cut the wheel, tires skidding beneath us.

"Give a man some warning," Addison said, laughing. He leaned forward, a hand on my shoulder. "Tyler sucks at directions."

"Please withhold your commentary," Tyler said. "It should be just a few blocks, another right."

The party was in a neighborhood south of the university campus. We turned onto a residential street, low brick apartment buildings giving way to houses set back from yards still laced in last week's snow.

"There's a spot." Tyler pointed to a gap behind a car.

"I think it's too tight," I said. "I'm going to block the driveway."

"You'll be fine. It's late, no one's going anywhere tonight."

I parked and we got out. The flash of a lighter and Tyler's face lit up, cigarette at his lips.

"I thought you were quitting this semester." Addison hoisted a plastic bag from the car, provisions from the liquor store.

"Semester starts on Monday."

The party was in an old house, sagging roof and dull chipped paint. Despite the weather, packs of partygoers huddled at the lawn's edge and on the porch. We wove between smokers sitting on the steps. The porch careened to one side, like it might detach itself from the house and slide away. Near the front door, a guy in a red ski cap waved, face shining, and he called out, "Tyler!"

Tyler shouted hello and Addison swooped right in, introducing himself and then me—he called me Mark, not Dr. Lausson, thank god.

"So glad you made it," the guy said—his name was Connor. "Get in here."

We walked smack into a wall of noise, dense clusters of people shouting over brash music turned up too loud for the cheap sound system, all punctuated and frizzy. A crooked lamp jammed into a corner glowed orange beneath a piece of fabric slung across the shade. A wide staircase led to a second floor. Guests crammed along the length of it, fiddling with phones, passing down a joint.

"Kitchen is this way," Connor shouted and took the bag from Addison.

A door beside the staircase opened and a group of girls spilled out, laughing.

I called, "We'll catch up with you." I grabbed Tyler's arm, pulling him into the room and shutting the door. It was small, lit by a bare bulb, meant to be an office perhaps, but used for storage. Rusted bikes stacked against the wall, a battered desk. The air reeked of perfume and weed.

Before I could speak, Tyler jumped in. "I'm sorry! I'm sorry! I didn't mean for this to happen, I swear."

"Well, what did happen? I'm trying to stay calm here."

"I know, I'm sorry. Addison was being super weird. He's been in this foul mood because of some stupid shit with Kennedy. And I don't know, he really wanted to hang out and kept asking what I was doing. He was like pressing and wouldn't let up. So finally I said I was going to this party. I just needed something to say. And then he asked if he could come and wouldn't drop it."

"Jesus, Tyler. You should have called me."

"I know. I'm really sorry. He was being so needy, I didn't know what to do."

"What did you tell him?"

"What do you mean?"

"About us. About me. About what I'm doing here."

"Nothing. Just—I said we're friends. That's it. It's fine. You don't have to worry about anything."

"I don't know about that, I'm pretty worried." I closed my eyes and leaned against the desk. From the other side of the door, a cackling laugh cut through the music.

Tyler tugged at my shirt. "Look at me." And then another tug, when I didn't. "Mark, look at me." I opened my eyes. "I'm so happy to see you. I just wanted tonight to be fun."

"I wanted that, too."

He placed a hand on either side of my face, holding it like a book, or a prayer.

"Then let's have fun." He kissed me, the cigarette fresh on his breath. He pulled away, smiling. "It's not so bad."

I smiled back, despite myself. "It's not." And maybe he was right, I was freaking out over what? We were in Columbus, we weren't even on a campus.

"Check it out." On the floor, beside the desk, a bottle of wine. "Those girls must have forgotten it." He took a long swig and coughed. "Wow that's sweet, even for me." He passed me the bottle. The pink label had a drawing of a cat—I felt a quick pang; Safie had once said *never drink wine with an animal on it.* I tipped it back—it was almost painfully sweet—and then drank again.

Tyler laughed. "So you're not mad."

"I'm not mad." I reached around and grabbed his ass, pulling him to me. "I missed you."

Tyler wiggled in my grip, rubbing himself against me. "I can't wait for you to fuck me tonight." He stretched on his toes and licked my chin.

The doorknob rattled again and then someone was banging on the door. It shook in the frame. A shout. "Who the hell is in there?"

Tyler pounded back, three hand punches. "Calm the fuck down!"

"We should go out there."

Tyler took another long drink and passed me the bottle. I did the same, the sugary sweetness making my mouth water. I licked my finger and slid it down the back of his pants, past his underwear. He groaned. I leaned down and kissed him again, tongue filling his mouth, finger reaching inside him.

Whoever was on the other side shouted something else, I couldn't make out the words.

"Fuck," Tyler said, and pulled back, giggling. "Let's go."

We left, pushing through the press of bodies down a short corridor to the kitchen, where we found Addison. "There you are," he grinned.

Tyler rooted around the countertop, crowded with bottles. He grabbed cups and poured, spilling some on his hand. He licked it off, red tongue darting. It was bright in the kitchen and the wine was already spreading its warmth, softening the space.

We threw back the tequila, chasing it with long gulps of beer. Addison laughed and coughed, spilling beer down the front of his shirt.

"You're already a mess," Tyler said. "I told you we would have fun. Let's get in there."

The other end of the kitchen opened onto the living room and we moved into it, humid and dense with dancing bodies. It was dark, no lights, and it took my eyes a moment to adjust. Groups in tight circles, facing each other and singing along. Girls with long hair swooping across their backs, bright fingernails clutching cups they raised above their heads, in triumph. Scattered throughout, pairs of guys and girls slid up and down, snakelike and urgent.

Tyler yelled over the noise. "God, Sawyer parties are so boring."

"Yo." It was Connor. He pulled a joint from his mouth and lifted it toward us.

"Yes, please." Tyler took a long drag, eyes narrowing, pink lips a slit beneath them. He released the smoke, a long, slow stream. "That's perfect." He passed the joint to Addison. Addison hesitated—his eyes shifting from me then back to Tyler. Tyler laughed. "It's fine."

Addison looked at me and I nodded. "Go ahead."

He took a drag, a smaller one, and then turned to me, eyebrow raised. I hesitated.

"Come on," Tyler said. "It's a party."

Addison smiled. "Just a puff?"

Fuck it, I thought. I'm here. Fuck Sawyer.

"Sure." They both whooped. I closed my eyes and inhaled the muggy, pleasant burn of it. I held it in then let the smoke spill from my mouth.

"There we go!" Addison said, and clapped me on the shoulder— an easy friendliness that flattered; I wanted him to like me. Tyler laughed, and then I did, too. The noise of the party swelled around us.

"This is awesome," Tyler said. "My two guys."

From the throngs, one of the long-haired girls spotted Tyler and shouted, waving him over.

"Of course you know everyone here," Addison said.

"Let's dance."

"You go ahead," I said. "I'm going to take a moment."

Addison charged into the crowd; Tyler lingered.

"This is okay?" he asked. "You're having fun?"

"I am," I said. "I like seeing you out in the world."

"You don't want to dance?"

"I'm happy just watching."

"Yeah?" he asked, smiling. "You like watching me?"

"Go," I said, laughing. "Dance."

Tyler dodged through the crowd, joining Addison. The song ended and as the next one kicked on, Tyler threw up his arms, head tilted back, and let out a whoop. The sounds of the party expanded and contracted around me. My hands tingled. I reached to touch my face and discovered I was smiling. I never went to parties like this in college, or after—or ever. But I liked it. Tyler and Addison's comfort in the space, in the world, maybe it was catching on. What had Tyler said that night at my apartment? *Serious Professor Lausson.* He was right. I'm allowed to have some fun.

My mouth had gone gummy. My bottle was empty. I needed a drink. I called Tyler's name. "I'll be right back." He answered but I couldn't make it out. He flashed a thumbs-up. I smiled and nodded. In the kitchen, I found an abandoned cup of something. I rinsed it and filled it from the tap. I gulped it down and poured another. I found a beer from the fridge and held it to my cheek, the cold soothing—I needed to go outside. I squeezed from the kitchen, back into the hallway we'd entered, and stepped onto the porch.

The night air washed over me, calming, perfect. This was a good idea. The porch was packed. More people had arrived. Tyler hadn't been wrong, it was a mix of ages. Columbus was a real city, part of the wider world. I wanted more than Ohio, but this was better than Sawyer.

There was an empty chair in a corner, against the half-wall encasing the porch. I sank into it.

"Are you okay?" someone asked.

"Yes. Thank you." I looked over. Two girls sat together, one with red curly hair that fell to her shoulders, the other, dirty blonde, pulled back. I realized they were on the back seat from a car—it had been dragged to the porch and propped against the wall.

The redhead noticed me looking and said, "I told her this was disgusting."

The blonde one introduced herself—"I'm Jessie, this is Rebecca"—then pulled a bottle of vodka from between her feet. "You want? Rebecca, where are those cups?"

"I'm okay," I said, raising my beer.

"Beer is just going to make you sleepy and cold," Rebecca said. Jessie filled a cup and passed it to me. They raised their drinks in a toast, and I followed. The vodka seared the back of my throat. It was cheap, I could feel it in my nose, but Rebecca was right. It warmed me.

"I haven't seen you at these before," Rebecca said. "How did you end up here?"

"Just tagging along," I said, "and you two?"

"We were all at OSU together," Rebecca said. "And now we're stuck in Columbus."

"Rebecca's brother lives here. Connor."

"Red cap?" They nodded. "We met."

"Don't hold that against me," said Rebecca. "He's a complete ogre."

"Well, he was a very friendly ogre."

"He and all these guys are disgusting. Present company excluded, of course." Rebecca raised her cup.

"Well, thank you." I tipped my own and took another drink.

"Actually, you know what the problem with men is?"

"Rebecca," Jessie said, "please don't antagonize our new friend."

"He can take it."

"I can," I said. "In fact, I want to know. It would probably be an immense help. What is the problem with men?"

"The problem with men is they hate themselves."

"That's it?"

"It's everything. Deep down in those bodies they stuff with beer and porn and all those stupid supplements they think will change something. They honestly, truly hate themselves."

"But don't you think a lot of women hate themselves?" Jessie asked.

"Fair point," I said, because I wanted to hear Rebecca go on.

"Some women. Sure. But I'm talking all men. Every single one. And women, what can we do about it? We just keep the hate inside, brooding and seething. But men. Because of the fucking patriarchy—"

"Fuck the patriarchy," Jessie said.

"Men can turn that hatred on the world. It's themselves they hate, but we all pay the fucking price."

The door to the house burst open. A guy, face washed of color, shirt half unbuttoned, lurched across the porch in wide swinging steps. A voice shouted out—"Hey!"—he'd knocked right into someone. The guy swerved and heaved down the steps, hitting the ground and jerking forward. A stream of vomit hurled across the lawn.

"Gross," Jessie said. "Jesus."

"See, this is exactly what I mean. You have to hate yourself to get like that. I almost feel bad for him." Rebecca tossed her cup, now empty. It clattered down the path, landing with a dull echo some feet from the guy. He was bent over, on his hands and knees. "Don't hate yourself so much," she shouted. "It's not working!"

Back in the house, throngs of bodies pushed together. The air had thickened, sticky and warm, music pulsing. The lamp was knocked over, unplugged or the bulb broken. I shoved my way back to the kitchen.

No Tyler. Addison was talking with a girl, standing close, his hand at her waist. I started to back away—maybe Tyler was still dancing—but stopped as Addison called out, "Come here."

He handed me a beer. What had happened to my last one? After this—water. I drew the bottle to my mouth and swallowed. Something malty, rich.

"Don't go anywhere," the girl said. She touched the swell of Addison's arm. As she exited the kitchen, she turned and waved, light sparking off her rings.

"She seems nice," I said.

Addison laughed. "How's the party going for you?"

"Fine. Great, actually. I'm having a nice time. And you?"

"The best," Addison said, broad face beaming. "My parents are obsessed with you, by the way."

I laughed. "I had a really nice time with them. You'll have to tell them I say hi. Although"—I swooped my hand in the air—"maybe don't mention all this."

He laughed again. "Okay, deal. And you know, Tyler thinks you're great."

"Oh." Was there something in his voice—had it shifted? I glanced at him—standing beside me, smiling, perfectly happy in the moment. There was nothing going on. He was a nice guy being nice. "You're a good friend to him."

"That guy is crazy, but I love him."

"It was cool you were able to bring him back from the airport today."

"What do you mean?"

"He said you gave him a ride?"

"Well, sure. We flew back together."

"You were in Charlotte?"

Shouts exploded from the other room, the crowd cheering something on. The music got louder, blaring.

"Tyler was in LA. He stayed with me after the holidays, after Malibu."

"Malibu?"

"They always do New Year's in Malibu with his grandmother."

On New Year's, I'd ended work early and ordered a pizza. I sat with it and a bottle of wine, texting back and forth with Tyler until midnight arrived. He said he'd gone to a party with some high school friends. He called it tragic and boring. Why would he lie about being in California?

"Ah, here he is—"

Addison shifted, making space for Tyler as he crossed the kitchen. Tyler's eyes were dark spinning disks, the lights of the kitchen swirling in his enormous pupils. He was with some guy—someone familiar. Where did I know him from?

"Where have you all been?" Tyler asked.

"Oh, hi," the guy said. He stuck out his hand. "It's Paul. From Sawyer. We met at the end of semester thing."

At the Walton Walk. Elaine's grad student.

"You all have met?" Tyler asked. I saw then that his hand was resting on Paul's shoulder and Paul's arm circled his waist, holding Tyler up, or pulling him close, or both. "That's so funny we're all here."

"Small world," Paul said, grinning.

Tyler peeled himself away and rummaged through the counter's debris, lifting bottles, finding them empty, putting them down. He grabbed one—still half full. "Let's go back and dance."

"Come with," Paul said, eyes lighting on mine. He turned and moved out of the kitchen. Tyler stepped to follow—I grabbed his wrist, holding him in place, letting Paul leave.

I lowered my voice and leaned in. "What is going on here?"

"It's a party. Relax." His eyes ricocheted around the room, looking at everything but me. "That hurts."

"What are you doing with Paul?"

"I thought we said we were having fun tonight."

"Just—come outside. I need to talk to you."

Paul stuck his head back in the doorway, eyes bright. "Get in here!" He stretched an arm toward Tyler.

Tyler yanked from my grip and disappeared into the crush of bodies. I started to yell after him and caught myself. I pushed from the kitchen toward the corridor.

"Hold on." Addison reached for me, but I pulled away, shoving through the crowd. As the hallway met the living room, I turned to look. Paul and Tyler dancing, closing the space between them. Paul's hands at Tyler's waist, Tyler's palms on his chest.

I flew down the porch, across the lawn, into the street. I turned left, then right. I needed to get out of here. Where was the fucking car? My keys slipped from my hand, clanging to the asphalt. I bent to pick them up and the street spun, out of balance and askew. I stood, the rush of blood through my brain an avalanche.

"Fuck."

"Hey, Dr. Lausson! Mark!" Addison was sprinting across the lawn toward me. "Wait up." He gasped and steadied himself, his breath steaming the air between us. "Are you leaving?"

"I am. You guys are going to have to find some other way home."

"Are you sure that's a good idea?"

I looked down at my hand. I must have knocked it against the ground. The knuckles were scraped, small dark bubbles of blood popping up.

"I think it's the best idea I've had in months."

I turned to leave—the car was down on the left, I could see its bumper—when I felt Addison's grip on my arm, firm.

"I'm sorry. I don't think I can let you drive."

"Back off." I yanked myself from him, stumbling then catching myself. I'd shouted, and my bark echoed down the street and Addison stepped back, startled. Behind him, a shuffling on the porch, as people rearranged to see what was happening.

"I didn't mean to upset you in the kitchen." His voice was low, calm. "I'm sure it's just some misunderstanding. Come back inside. I'll be fine in a little bit, I haven't had too much. And then I can drive us back."

Blood pounded in my ears. Across the street, a bare tree tilted and righted itself. I was in no shape to drive. But going back to the party, facing Tyler, seeing him with Paul—I couldn't bear it. At the end of the block, where the road hit the commercial street, a taxi passed, and then another.

I pointed that way. "I'll get a cab."

"Can I help you flag one down?"

I was already walking away. "Go back inside, Addison."

A cab pulled over as soon as I made it to the end of the street. I dropped into the seat and shut the door. I could see Addison standing in the middle of the road, waiting.

"I'm going to Sawyer."

"You sure?" The driver eyed me in the rearview mirror. I sat up straight and smiled. I didn't want him throwing me out; I wouldn't survive the disgrace. "That's going to be a hundred, a hundred and twenty."

"It's fine. Just get me out of here."

As we moved through the town, I closed my eyes and sank into the seat. What just happened? The lights of passing cars and stoplights played across the insides of my eyelids, red and white, red and white.

"Okay, buddy." The interior light flashed and I jolted up. I had passed out. "This is it."

I emptied my wallet and stumbled from the car.

I woke to dull afternoon light. My shirt and shoes in a heap at the foot of the bed. Pants and socks still on. My muscles seized in the frigid air. I'd fallen asleep on top of the covers, after apparently opening a window. I got up to close it. Bile rushed from my guts. I made it to the bathroom just before the sour heaving began. The floor's icy tiles dug into my knees. I stood and another round of nausea swelled up. I sat back down, head against the toilet, waiting for it to pass. Eventually, I made my way to the shower. I shed the last of my clothes and stepped into its scalding blast.

I dried off and dressed, muscles screaming at me. I couldn't find the flip phone, my Tyler phone. I ransacked the apartment. Where the fuck was it? I must have lost it at the party, with the evidence of everything between us on it. I checked the timetable for the bus that traveled between Sawyer and Columbus. I forced myself to eat a piece of toast and waited to see if I could keep it down. Enough time passed and I made my way to the station.

When we arrived in Columbus, the bus let out on a wide stretch near the empty downtown. It was a few miles from the party, a straight shot more or less. I started walking. Overhead, the gray shroud of the low January sky pressed down on the city. A bracing wind pummeled me, my feet ached with the cold, my head pounded. It felt good to push my body, to punish it. The distracting pain, a mercy. I wanted to empty myself of all thoughts.

I found the street and turned. Quiet and desolate in the day-time. Red cups, debris from the night before, scattered down the length of it. A scrap of bright orange flashed on my windshield. A ticket: blocking a driveway.

I turned the ignition and cranked the heat. My fingers had grown numb on the walk, the cuts where I scraped my knuckles pulsing. The phone was inside, on my seat. It still worked, on the last of its battery. But there was nothing. No message from Tyler. No calls.

I got lost on my way to the freeway and ended up beyond the outskirts of town, in the undeveloped county. As I tried to find my way back, I passed a sign announcing a fairground. A second sign was plastered across it: closed to the public. I turned anyway, fol-lowing the road as it carved through dormant fields, drained of color and life. A long-abandoned barn, a tree growing through a hole in the roof. At the intersection of a narrow road, another sign. No trespassing. I ignored it and turned in. After a mile or so, the road ended at a fence and a rusted gate, shoulder-high, thick metal chains looped around it, a strangling braid, padlocked shut. Beyond it, the fairgrounds. I pulled to the side and got out. The black and calloused trunks of stripped trees stood watch. I rested a foot on the lower rung of the gate, and it shifted under my weight. I paused, seeking the equilibrium then hoisted myself up and over, landing with a soft thud against the packed earth. I stepped forward and a thin sheet of ice, snow melted and then frozen again, cracked and splintered beneath me.

The fairgrounds spread out before me, great and ghostly. This place had been abandoned for some time. The rides were cloaked in torn tarps, small dirty pools of mushy snow gathered in the dips and folds. In the distance, a giant Ferris wheel loomed, naked to the battering abuses of the seasons. I walked in farther, passing a shuttered building. Across one of the boards planking its side someone had spray-painted AIDS FAG, and then underneath, a swastika—it's like they were expecting me. On the ground against the building, a pile of empty beer cans, the charred remnants of a campfire.

I walked a loop of trash-strewn paths. I found a bench missing most of its back slats and sat. The gnarled tracks of a roller coaster twisted against the sky. Cassie had been obsessed with roller coasters. She had this giant book about their history. At the back was a list of famous accidents from around the world. Senior year, in the weeks leading up to the annual county fair, it was all she could talk about. When it finally arrived, she told our parents we were going to a movie and took me. There was a new ride that year; it boasted the highest climb and the fastest fall. I was too short for the required height. But Cassie flirted with the zitty, pockmarked guy working the line and got me in.

"I could just watch," I said. "I'll wait by the exit."

"You can't be serious," she said. "You don't want to miss this."

The attendant snapped us into place. I gripped the metal guard, my arms locked. The volley of cars lurched forward and made the slow climb up. The noise of the crowds below fell away; the grind of wheels and gears all I could hear. I wanted to close my eyes but Cassie kept saying, "You have to watch, you have to watch." I wanted to be anywhere but there, in any life but my own. We edged toward the peak, slowing to a pause before for the drop. That's the last thing I remember, the vast void of air coming into view.

When we got home, I was still so shaken, Cassie had no choice but to tell my parents where we'd been. I brought it up again, years later, I don't remember why. After Cassie was gone. My mother insisted that I had gotten the story scrambled. It was Cassie's friend who had taken me on the ride, Cassie had nothing to do with it. I was completely worked up, screaming at her—I never got like that. "That's not true. It was Cassie. Why won't you listen to me?" Finally, exasperated, she shouted back, storming from the room. "Drop it, Mark, just drop it. What does it even matter?"

By the time I made it back to the gate, the sun had long disappeared below the flat skies. There were no lights out there and as my eyes adjusted to the black-gray of the night, my car emerged from the dark encasing it. Seeing it at the side of the road, knowing it would take me back to Sawyer, a murmur of grief opened within me. It grew as I rode along the side roads and onto the highway north, filling my body and then exceeding it—filling the car and spilling out to fill the freeway and the space beyond, so this grief surrounded me, engulfed me, and carried me home.

CHAPTER II

The alarm sounded. I threw back the covers and jumped out of bed. I pulled on my sweatshirt and running shorts, grabbed my headphones, and headed out. The dawn air held the overnight chill, a surprise against my skin, still waking. A soft white light bled out from the horizon, the sun just starting to emerge.

I jogged in place for a minute, warming myself up, blowing into my hands. I fiddled with the headphones, running the cord under my shirt. I clicked on the stopwatch and took off. The music kicked on, low but rising, encouraging me forward. I swooped through the still-deserted dawn streets of downtown Sawyer. The town was pretty in the empty silence, all potential and promise. At the western edge, I turned south, opposite campus. I flew beneath an underpass, the first spring buds of March pushing from a patch of dirt on the other side. The town fell away and I moved along fields. Some farmers were up, preparing for the growing season. I passed one I saw most mornings; our schedules had synced. I had invented an entire life story for him: parents who died young, leaving him the farm; a wife who toiled beside him; three kids they'd saved up to send to college. From his tractor, Harold (I had named him Harold) raised his arm in a still wave. I lifted my hand in reply and skimmed by. In the third mile, I picked up the pace, ignoring the pinch in my lungs. Sweat slicked my body, pouring down my face and sticking my clothes to me. I pressed on. Paved roads gave way to dirt.

I did not stop moving until I closed the loop, just over eight miles, arriving back at my building, bent forward, one hand against the wall, wracked and panting, my side split in two. Back in my apartment, in the small book I kept by the door, I made note of my time. Forty-seven seconds better than the day before. Six weeks of this daily run; I was getting close to the best time of my peak period in college, before grad school ate my life and I lost the discipline. I stripped and stepped into the shower. The shock of its icy force seized my body. In the kitchen, I made coffee. I scrambled some eggs, scooping them onto a piece of toast. I ate over the sink and when I finished, I washed the crumbs down the drain.

Each day began like this, exactly like this. I had whittled my life down to the bone of it. I slept, I ran, I ate, I worked, I ate, I slept. I was focused, purifying—a clarified light, everything else filtered out. This was it. My life at Sawyer had disassembled with so little effort, it was almost sad. But I did my best to keep ahead of such thoughts. When they surfaced and caught up with me—a memory of Tyler in bed; the impulse, when coming upon an unintentionally hilarious line in a student paper, to text Safie and share it—I dove back into work, or lengthened my running stride, or turned up the cold in the shower; those remainders of my previous life vanquished.

I wasn't exactly unhappy, though. While I used to find the monotony of academic life and the smallness of Sawyer stifling, now that constriction comforted. I took an inverse pleasure in my new ascetic existence and its lack of anything extraneous. Each day, an atonement. Each day, one more day without speaking to or seeing Tyler. Another twenty-four hours of distance between us. Almost the entirety of my existence unfolded inside my apartment. I worked on the book, revising and reorganizing, filling in gaps in arguments, checking back against source materials. I went to campus only when necessary. I would arrive just a minute before class, hold office hours in the hallway, and then return immediately home. I had skipped out on every meeting—the monthly departmental ones and a school-wide emergency assembly to address a growing "plagiarism epidemic." My no-show approach garnered increasingly incensed messages from Susan, her outrage escalating with each abstention. *Let me remind you,* read her most recent email, *participation in the life of the department is an obligation of your position and is weighted accordingly in the tenure review process. None of your colleagues approach it as a matter of whimsy.* The last bit struck me as homophobic—I couldn't see Susan accusing Colin, say, of engaging in whimsy. But I replied to this as I did to all the others. *Thank you for the message. I will keep this in mind. Mark.* While it is true that I took some satisfaction in imagining Susan unraveling upon receipt, I was not trying to stir the pot. Far from it. I just wanted to disappear. I knew I was tanking my chances at Sawyer, but I saw this as a kind of insurance policy: It meant I had no option but to land a new job. I was happy with the progress of the book, even excited about getting it to the editor to review. I reached out to anyone from grad school I thought might remember me to say I was going back on the job market in the fall. *If you hear of anything,* I'd copied and pasted from email to email, *I would be very grateful if you let me know.*

That evening, I prepared for a trip to campus. Each year the department rotated responsibility for supervising senior thesis projects, and this year the assignment landed with me. Susan had sent two or three messages checking up on me. I resented her attempts to micromanage and deleted the emails without replying, although I had been sitting with the students every week. We met in a study room I booked in the Chemistry building because I knew I would run into nobody there. I had been to my office only twice, at the start of the semester. The first time, on a deserted Sunday afternoon, to collect some books and whatever papers I needed for the term; and again the following Sunday, to guiltily retrieve the plant I had left to die on the windowsill.

I supervised nine students and we met together as a group. While this was to limit my trips to campus, I told them it was to "facilitate cross-fertilization." (I lifted that phrase from an email about a workshop offered by the Center for Teaching Excellence; I did not attend the workshop but I did read the email.) I didn't mind the meetings, though. The thesis was a requirement for honors and the students were earnest and hardworking. They trickled in and I listened as they talked among themselves. News about acceptances to grad programs, efforts to line up summer internships, complaints about unreliable internet in the dorms. Two students shared competing rumors about the lead in the spring play, who had abruptly withdrawn from classes and flown home. ("Her roommate says her parents made her because of an eating disorder, but I don't know, she's not even that skinny.") When the group had fully assembled, I had each give a status report on their projects and identify one issue they wanted to workshop with the group. We were approaching the midpoint of the semester, spring break almost upon us, and so they were starting to feel some pressure. The collective anxiety mounted as they took their turns, each feeling they were in worse shape than the student preceding them. Sometimes higher education seemed good for nothing besides multiplying insecurities and intensifying feelings of inadequacy. I did my best to reassure them. "This is why we're here," I said, "to get you where you want to be. We'll figure it out together." I wanted to add that, in the grand scheme of things, these projects didn't really matter. But they had invested so much of their young identities, I didn't want to minimize the experience.

We made our way back around, problem-solving each student's thesis. About halfway through, my phone dinged with a message. I didn't think to turn it off for these meetings; I never heard from anyone. I glanced and was taken aback—it was Stephen. We'd had no contact all these months. As I did with Safie, I'd looked up his teaching schedule on the registrar's website, so I could better avoid a run-in. I couldn't imagine why he'd reach out. An anxious loop of questions distracted me the rest of the session. I rushed the students through to the end, insisting they had no reasons to worry.

After the last of the students cleared the room, I opened the text:

Hi Mark, I hope you're doing okay. I know we didn't part on great terms but I was wondering if we could meet for coffee or something. I'd like to talk.

I read through it again and again, trying to glean some hidden meaning between the words. I'd thought of Stephen often enough that it surprised me. He had been a bigger part of my life than I realized; I was too caught up in the maelstrom of Tyler to see it. I found myself wondering how things might have turned out for us if I hadn't fucked it all up. But I couldn't imagine that after some time had passed without me, Stephen felt anything other than relief. I sat in the empty room for a while, twenty or thirty minutes, staring at the phone. Cassie had this trick for whenever I got overwhelmed by a decision. This had started happening when I was seven or eight, intense fits of worry bursting within me. I would panic about insignificant matters—which shirt to wear, what ice cream to choose from the endless array of bins. "Close your eyes and take a deep breath," Cassie would say. "Now open." Her face hovering above mine, placid and unmoving, she would ask, "Now what do you want?"

I hadn't thought of this in years and yet the memory arrived intact and immediate, as if it had been waiting for me. I shut my eyes and inhaled. I could almost feel Cassie's hand on my shoulder. I took another breath and opened my eyes. I picked up my phone and typed out my reply:

Yes, I'd like that. It's nice to hear from you. This weekend?

We arranged to meet at a café downtown. In this semester of exile, I'd had virtually no interactions with anyone other than my students. And those conversations were easy to navigate, drawing from scripts determined by distinct roles and the clear boundaries of our relationships (or at least, roles made distinct and boundaries reclarified by my transgressions). I was worried I'd forgotten how to conduct myself in a different kind of conversation and I fretted about what Stephen wanted to discuss—if he would berate me or beg me to take him back. I thought the first option most likely. Anything he could say, I deserved, and perhaps letting him have at me would release me from some of my guilt.

I arrived early. I didn't want to face the awkward negotiations of seeing one another for the first time while ordering drinks or considering where to sit. ("What's the difference again between a cappuccino and a latte?" "I fucking hate your guts.") The café had just opened, in a long-empty space formerly housing a pizzeria. The new owners hadn't really renovated. They just painted the walls a muddy blue and hung a poster of the Eiffel Tower. An attempt to transport us from Naples to Paris, I supposed. I stationed myself on the small patio in front. It was a warm enough day, at least for these hours of peak afternoon light. I needed the feeling of space around me.

A few tables over sat two older women, in their seventies, maybe even eighties. They were immediately recognizable as sisters, something in the line of their noses, handsome profiles of a different era. They sipped frothy drinks from giant brightly colored mugs—one yellow, one red. They cooed over a piece of cake, passing a fork back and forth. I could make out the gist of the conversation. An upcoming christening, someone's grandchild, not theirs. I wondered if they'd outlasted husbands or if it had always been just the two of them.

Stephen arrived, wearing this shirt that always looked great on him and a new jacket. (I still had the one he'd left at my apartment; I'd hung it neatly in a closet, thinking he might want it back someday.) I stood. We passed awkward greetings back and forth, arms at our sides. I asked if the table was okay or he'd rather be inside; he said outside was fine. He asked if I needed anything else to drink; I said I was fine. He left to order and I sat back down. Across from me, the women laughed and one said, "Well, I guess I don't pick my church based on how good-looking the pastor is."

Stephen was gone a while. Maybe he changed his mind and slipped out the back. I pictured him wrestling with a high window in the restroom, pulling his body up and through, anything to get away from me. I kept checking my phone. Finally, he returned.

"Sorry that took forever. I think they're still getting the hang of things."

"I should have picked somewhere else."

"No, this is great," he said. "It's warmed up today. It's nice to be outside."

He had a small dark freckle on his cheek that, I am not sure if you'd asked me to describe him I would have known it was there, but now, it felt like—oh, there it is, the freckle. Stephen's freckle. I asked how the semester was going.

"I can't complain," he said. "Classes have been fun. And actually, I got some good news last week."

"What's that?"

"That big grant I applied for? It came through."

"Stephen, that's amazing. If I'm remembering right, it was for a lot of money?"

He smiled. "You're remembering right. I almost feel guilty. It's going to buy me out of all my teaching next year."

"I think you'll get over it."

"And how's your semester? And the book?"

I said it was going well and explained what I was working on that week. I mentioned the editor and the press; Stephen said it sounded great. I asked about his plans for spring break. We had one more week of classes, and then Sawyer shut down completely. Admin made it mandatory that students leave, even staff got the week off. Stephen said he'd go visit his brother in Connecticut; I said I'd stay behind and work on the book. (Though I wouldn't even go to campus, just the thought that everyone else would be gone felt like a comfort.) We discussed the movie theater closing down, the college's fund-raising for the Health Sciences school. And then I started to wonder—is this it? When Stephen said he wanted to talk, did he mean just *talk*? The conversation went on long enough that the sisters finished their cake and left. Finally, Stephen shifted in his chair and I could sense the turn coming as he made it.

"Listen, there is something I wanted to discuss with you."

"Okay, sure," I said, bracing myself—here it comes. "But first—I just—I really am sorry for everything. I know I was a complete fucking asshole—"

He cut me off. "It's okay. It's in the past. I wanted to talk about some stuff going around campus."

"Oh. Okay. What kind of stuff?"

He paused, perhaps turning the words over, seeking the right way to begin. "There's some rumors circulating. About you."

"What about me?"

"I feel weird bringing this up. I'm not trying to accuse you of anything."

"Come on, Stephen. What are people saying?"

"Stories about socializing with students. Spending time together off campus. Parties."

There it was, laid out before me: an account of my own foolishness. My heart raced, fists clenched under the table. And this was just the start.

"That's absurd."

I don't know if he expected me to say more, because he didn't reply. I sat there, defiant in the silence. Finally, he spoke again.

"Mark, I don't need to know what's been going on. And, frankly, I don't want to know." He blinked, the slightest flicker. "But I thought you should be aware. You know this sort of thing can end a career. Especially for us."

"Why are you telling me this?"

"I just want you to be careful."

"Well, I appreciate your concern, but there's nothing going on. So there's nothing I need to be careful about."

Stephen opened his mouth as if to say something else, then changed his mind. "Alright. I'm glad to hear that."

"Was that all?"

"Yes, I guess that's it."

"Okay. Great. I guess we're done then."

Stephen had parked in the direction of my apartment. We walked without speaking. It was taking all my energy to push down a rising tide of panic. Each step felt like a weight had been bound to my ankle. We arrived at his car and stood there, neither making a move. A raft of clouds passed across the sun, casting shadows gray then gone.

"I didn't mean to snap at you."

"It's fine, Mark."

"I appreciate you looking out for me. There's nothing to worry about, you just caught me off guard. And it's good to see you. I don't want us to end on a bad note." I could hear how stupid that sounded. "I guess, on another bad note."

Stephen laughed, soft and gentle, like the good man he was.

"I'm glad to see you, too. At the risk of mucking things up, can I say something else?"

"Sure."

"I don't know what went on between you and Safie exactly, but I wish you would fix it. She could really use some support right now, with everything going on."

"The tenure stuff?" I had been wondering about it, but I'd cut myself off so completely from Sawyer, I had no way of finding out.

"Well, that. And then this student complaint."

"What are you talking about?"

"You haven't heard anything?" I shook my head. "A student from last semester filed a formal complaint against her. I don't think it has any teeth, but you know how schools are about these things. They set some whole process in motion at any peep of bias. Trying to protect themselves from a lawsuit."

"Bias?"

He grimaced. "A student claims Safie is unfair in her treatment of white students. White, heterosexual, female students, in particular."

"You're fucking kidding."

"I wish I were," he said. "You should call her."

I paced my living room, the conversation with Stephen running in loops. Who had talked? Tyler or Addison? Paul? And what else had they said? Gossip at Sawyer was resilient. In that shuttered environment, people latched onto anything with a whiff of the unseemly; they enlivened their tiresome days by relishing the suffering of others. And my absence from campus had left a vacuum for these stories to fill. Had I been showing up and playing my part, I could have countered the rumors, in deeds if not words, demonstrating my upstanding nature. Was everyone talking about this? I wished I had questioned Stephen, getting some sense of the rumor's reach. I was too caught off guard to think clearly, and now I'd blown my chance to figure out what was going on.

And Safie. I had thought of Safie every day, bargaining with myself to make contact. But the only way to explain my horrendous behavior would be to confess everything. I couldn't bear it, the thought of her seeing how pathetic and foolish I'd been. Losing my shit over a student. I didn't want to show her what I'd known all along: that I was undeserving of her friendship. And now, I'd lost her, and she'd know everything anyway.

I could call Tyler, to find out what he'd said, what he knew. Just one conversation—

I needed to get out of the apartment. Go somewhere else. Anywhere.

Just as I pulled to the off-ramp I realized—it was one exit too soon. I landed in a broad intersection. I crept along the frontage road, scanning for signs. In all directions, Cleveland sprawled, flat and endless. I had been up a number of times over the years, but still, the blocks of vacant and burned-out buildings surprised. These stretches of Cleveland contained the destitution of Detroit but without the folklore of apocalyptic glamour. This was just collapse. Every few blocks, some solitary structure showed signs of habitation—a single yellow light in an upstairs window, a couple sitting close on a porch.

It took me half an hour to get oriented and find my way. I'd chosen a club over a bar, thinking it would be easier to lose myself in the noise and crowds. The club was on a wide commercial road, a light industrial area; these outskirts of cities that harbor gay histories. Pockets of young people hung out on the corner, underdressed, calling out bawdy provocations to cars slowly cruising by.

I paid the cover and went in. I hadn't been out to a gay club in years. It was a cavernous space. Shiny black surfaces and mirrored walls volleyed the flashing strobes back and forth. On a dance floor a few steps down from the bar level, an already dense crowd moved to a remix of a top forty song, high-pitched and frenetic.

"What are we drinking tonight?" The bartender, a thick butch with close-cropped silver hair, cleared some empties and wiped at the bar top.

"I'm not sure." While I hadn't exactly given up alcohol, I hadn't had a drink since Columbus. I couldn't afford any foggy, hungover days: Getting my book together and getting out of Sawyer was too important.

The music swelled and the crowd called out. "A little something to wet your whistle?" she said.

I'd come all this way. Why not? It would help take the edge off.

Behind railings, two raised walkways ran along either side of the dance floor. I stationed myself in a corner, watching the activity just below. In New York, each subgenre of homosexual has its own bars and parties, even a slice of a borough. Here, the crowd varied in every possible way, nothing in common except being queer. As if gathering together mattered and could be enough. I'd been there a few songs when I noticed a guy, dancing in a small pack of friends. He was in conversation with his group but kept lifting his head, eyes in my direction. Finally, he smiled and waved at me to join. I shook my head no. He motioned again, mouthing *C'mon.* I shook my head again, more forcefully this time. Something in his insistence irritated me, like it underscored how out of place I was. How alone. I threw back the rest of my drink. Coming here had been a mistake.

I pushed through the crowd, looking for the exit. The layout felt obvious when I arrived but now the music seemed to grow louder with every beat and I felt disoriented, as if the sound were fucking with my sense of space. Just ahead, a sign pointed to the exit. The corridor was jammed with people coming in; I tried to maneuver through.

Behind me, I heard a voice—"Relax, I'm just trying to catch up to my friend." I felt a hand on my arm and turned. It was the guy from the dance floor. He was sweaty, soft cheeks rosy red.

"I'm sorry if that was obnoxious. I didn't mean to be annoying."

"No, you were fine."

"My friend told me—you just drove another man away." He laughed. "You're not leaving, are you?"

"I have an early day."

"You sure you don't want to stay a little longer? Let me buy you a drink."

"Sorry—" I felt suddenly light-headed. The crowds, or the noise, or the liquor. "I think I need some air."

"I'll get my jacket from coat check. I'll join you. I'm Andres!" He laughed again. "Don't go anywhere."

I stepped outside, the cold air calming my nerves. Some moments later, Andres appeared, bundled in a thick parka. "Where's your coat? You must be freezing."

"I left it in my car. I parked just across the street."

"You parked on the street? In this neighborhood?" He made a sound of disbelief.

"Where do you live?"

"Tremont."

I'd been to that neighborhood once. Old Polish restaurants, some new cafés. A park. Before I could think it through I blurted out—"Let's go."

"Now?" His eyebrow shot up. "To my place?"

"Yes."

"Alright then." He smiled. "We're going."

We waited for the attendant to bring his car from the lot. Andres asked where I lived; I explained I was up from Sawyer. He had been born and raised in Cleveland. His parents came to the US from Guatemala, landing in Queens but then moving to Ohio to join his mother's cousin. "She married a white guy with a construction company, so they got my dad a job." Andres had no plans to leave Cleveland. He liked his work, he liked his friends. He'd bought a house last year. "Why not be happy?" A million reasons, I thought. "And what do you do down in Sawyer?"

"I'm a teacher."

"So cool. What grade? My sister teaches middle school."

"I'm at the college."

Andres whistled through his teeth.

"I could not handle if you were my professor. All your students must have crushes on you."

I followed Andres in my car. We left the industrial neighborhood and entered neat, dense blocks of modest Victorians. He pulled into the driveway of one and I parked at the curb.

"Please excuse this mess," he said, waving at the house. One side was blocked in small squares in different shades of blue. "I'm painting it myself. I started in September but couldn't make up my mind, and then it got too cold. I don't know what my problem is." He laughed. We went in and he showed me around, explaining the process for refinishing the woodwork, the story of the kitchen tiles. He was doing everything himself.

"It's gorgeous," I said. And it really was.

"You're gorgeous." He laughed. "Sorry, I'm so cheesy." He took my face and pulled it to his, kissing me, quick flicks of his tongue. I pulled back. "You alright?" he asked.

He had a lovely face, open eyes framed in a thick curtain of lashes, neat mustache cut to a perfect line.

"Yes. Sorry."

"Don't say sorry. Let's go to the bedroom."

I followed him up the stairs. He undressed all at once, so I did the same. "So beautiful," he kept repeating. "So handsome." He asked me to fuck him.

"Maybe we can just keep it simple tonight?"

"Simple is great," he said. "Whatever you want."

He got down on his knees, cupping me in his hands, mouth all over me. I looked up at the ceiling and closed my eyes and felt the part of me in the room with him split from myself and separate, like a sheet of ice.

It was the first sex I'd had since Tyler, and I thought of nothing but Tyler on the drive home. Back inside, I went right for my computer. I had been good—no snooping at all. I had even deactivated my Facebook account to make it harder. I tried to reopen the account but my password wouldn't work. I was prompted to reset it.

I opened my email to get the password link. There was an unread message, from a Gabrielle Lopez. The subject said, *interested to talk?* I couldn't place the name but as I clicked open the message, I remembered—from NYU, she was some years ahead of me. There'd been a drinks thing when she defended her dissertation. She'd landed a job, somewhere in the south.

Hi Mark, this is Gabrielle. I hope you're doing well! First of all, I want to say that I love your article from SAQ last year. I taught it in my Gothic Fictions seminar and the students went crazy for it. I hope you're expanding this with a book!

I heard from Peter Fleiss (who says hello by the way) that you were looking to move schools. We've had a last-minute opening in my department for the fall (long story, a forced retirement of a colleague who's been sexually harassing literally all of us for years, a battle to keep the line—the bureaucrats who run this place don't want to put money

*into anything except STEM and the business school, same
story as everywhere). Anyway, we are looking for someone
in contemporary American lit, with a preference for work
in gender and sexuality—so, of course, you came to mind.
Despite everything I just said, the department is lovely.
We've done a bunch of new hires in the past few years, lots
of smart and ambitious junior folks but no backstabbers.
And I don't know if you've spent time in New Orleans, but
it's magical. I cannot believe what we put up with in New
York! I would love to talk. Our timeline for reviewing applications is tight because the search has been underway for
a bit, and I'm sure you're buried in your semester, but do
let me know if the position sounds interesting to you. I sin-
cerely hope it might.*

Cheers,
Gabrielle

I read through the email again, looking for something I'd
missed. It was far from a job offer, but it was a chance. It would mean
getting out of Sawyer without having to slog through another year,
without being consumed with anxiety about the rumors of Tyler
catching up to me. I started to reply but then saw the time—almost
two. I would write back first thing in the morning.

Just before I shut the computer, I noticed at the top of my
inbox, the link to reopen my Facebook account. I checked the little
box beside it and hit DELETE.

CHAPTER 12

Things moved quickly. I wrote Gabrielle in the morning and we spoke that afternoon. I dove into getting my application materials together, working into the night: updating my research statement, pulling syllabi and assignments for my teaching portfolio. I sent everything over late on Monday. By the end of the week I had a first-round phone interview with the search committee. The next Monday, the first day of spring break, the department chair called. Would I make the trip out for a campus interview? Itineraries were settled, flights were arranged, and on Thursday, I left for New Orleans.

Ohio to Louisiana, it turns out, is not a bustling route, so I flew through Dallas and waited a few hours for my connection. The Dallas airport was a city unto itself, compacted down to its capitalist heart: a giant shopping mall. I picked through the limp, wet leaves of a $20 salad and reviewed the notes for my research talk. I would present from my Fall Fest lecture, along with some sections drawn from the book's introduction. I boarded the next plane and by the time we landed in New Orleans in the blue-black of mid-evening—one of those frictionless touchdowns, the wheels meeting tarmac with no snag, just matter returning to itself—I had a version of the talk that felt right.

I had offered to take a cab but Gabrielle insisted on picking me up. She chattered the entire drive, effusive and friendly, pointing out landmarks and offering history lessons. We passed buildings abandoned and untouched since Katrina. Gabrielle told me about a new city council candidate, young and razor-sharp. Everyone was getting excited she might have a real shot at winning a seat, and Gabrielle had just joined her door-knocking team. Off the freeway, we drove through wide, lush roads, windows down, the thick swampy air, familiar from home, washing over us.

"That's right, you're from Florida," Gabrielle said. "This climate will suit you, then. Some of my colleagues complain about the heat, but after all those winters in New York, I love it. A little sweat is good for you."

"These houses are incredible." Weighty beasts set back in expansive lawns, the buildings celebrated themselves, ostentatious and grand. Even the smaller ones puffed out their chests.

"This area is really rich. And white. Beautiful but dull. The administration will only pay to put people up at the campus hotel. Which is fine for a few nights. But you'd want to live closer to me, other side of town."

"You've been happy here?"

"I can find things to quibble over, but it's a great job. The students are eager. And New Orleans just chills you out. It's like you can't help but find a work-life balance because we're here. It's the South. It's Louisiana."

"Sounds pretty great."

"And Sawyer?"

I hesitated. "Sawyer's been good to me."

"Yes?"

"I've learned a lot and my teaching has improved. I just want to see what's out there."

"I know it's stressful being on these visits. And, god willing, I'll never go on another one. Nightmare. When I interviewed at

Cornell, the chair insisted I get a drink with him after the dinner. Just the two of us, this creepy guy old enough to be my grandfather. He downed three frozen margaritas—keep in mind this was February—and then had his divorce lawyer meet us so he could sign some papers."

"Oh my god. What is wrong with academics?"

"Anyway, I appreciate the stress of these interviews. But I'm not trying to assess you. I already know I'd love having you in the department."

"You're very kind."

"No, it's selfish. I want fun, smart people here. You can ask me about anything, I'm not going to bullshit you."

"Okay. Deal."

"And, no offense, but you don't have to bullshit me." She switched to an appeasing, sing-songy voice. "*Sawyer has been a wonderful place for me to develop as a scholar and teacher, and I'm excited to bring those experiences to the next phase of my career. Blah, blah, blah.*"

I laughed. "That is what I sounded like, isn't it?"

"No judgment. It's how you have to be on these things. But don't feel like you have to be that way with me."

I thought of what my non-bullshit answer might be: Well, I've been lonely and depressed for a long time, maybe my entire life, but Sawyer only compounded things. I dated a guy from the Math department I'm not sure I was even interested in, though I should have been. And then I tanked everything for a nineteen-year-old boy who upended my life and ruined me for sex, which I am certain will never be that thrilling again. Did I mention he was my student?

As we neared the campus, the streets narrowed, and we passed through some blocks of bars and restaurants. "For students,"

Gabrielle said, "Lots of chain imports from the suburbs. But there are some good spots, too." The sidewalks swarmed with groups of people coming, going, hanging out.

"This feels like a real place."

"I know tomorrow is epic, but after all the official stuff is done, we'll hang out, a few of us. So you don't think campus is all we have to offer. It'll be me, obviously. And Tommy Pak, he's amazing, our experimental poet, you'll like him. Desiree Lamar—she's on the committee, so you've talked with her. Brilliant, born and raised here. Her book of essays on post-Katrina New Orleans is coming out this summer. It's going to be huge. And Claire Albers. She's working on this crazy project, I don't really understand it. Something about cybernetics and modernist lit. She's great. Anyway, we'll sneak you out of the hotel after everything is done. We can just chill and answer any questions you've got."

"That's really great. Thank you."

"Well, we're trying to convince you that you could be happy here."

Happy sounded nice. And as we pulled up to the handsome hotel, buttery yellow clapboard and stately brick, grand, exuberant trees framing the cobblestone driveway, I thought it might even be possible.

In the profession, the academic job interview is referred to as a "campus visit"—as in (whispered with a mix of envy and skepticism), *She got four campus visits before even filing her dissertation.* While it sounds pastoral, in fact the campus visit is a treacherous terrain of land mines and booby traps: a day or two of nonstop meetings, with department chairs and the search committee, with various deans of bizarrely specific subdivisions of bureaucratized authority (none of whom, if you land the job, you will ever see again). Teaching demos, lunch with students. The so-called "job talk," the presentation of your research—you must appear smart but not intimidatingly so; nothing to threaten any fragile egos. Dinner with faculty at which you order a meal you barely touch, since you are performing and don't want to talk with your mouth full or splash curry down the front of your interview shirt. The advice given to terrified grad students prepping for their first campus visit is "Be yourself," which is, of course, the opposite of what you should do.

I woke quite early, wired and alert, and went for a quick run, just a few miles, to burn off some energy. Back at the hotel, I showered and dressed; I'd laid out and ironed my clothes the night before. Because of the tight timeline—I was the third of three candidates they were seeing in just a few weeks—they had compressed the schedule down to a single day. I double-checked I had my notes and my backup file and followed Gabrielle's directions to my first appointment, a breakfast meeting with the dean of the college at eight-thirty. It was fine, really, a pleasant enough start. From there I met with the search committee, and then two more deans. As the day went on—really, just a series of conversations—a strange feeling grew inside me. Not a bad one, but something I couldn't quite place. In the afternoon, I did a teaching demo. They had me visit a Comp class, which many programs treat as grunt work. But the new department chair, Sam—an affable guy with a mop of wild curly hair and bright blue eyes that actually sparkled—explained they were trying to reinvigorate the curriculum, encouraging faculty to experiment. The students were humble and engaged, the conversation easy, and I felt a tremendous gratitude—they were making this easy. As they set up lunch for me to chat with the majors, I waited with Sam in his office. It was hoarder-level packed with books and papers and boxes. I said the students seemed really smart, and he concurred. "You did a great job in there," he said. "That's what education should be. A way to play."

And then I understood the odd and unsettling feeling: I was enjoying myself. The realization that things were going well made the rest of the day go even better. The department was, as Gabrielle had promised, a warm and friendly bunch, free of the typical academic pathologies of narcissistic self-loathing. This seemed to be a group that genuinely, impossibly, liked what they were doing. The day would end with the job talk and then dinner. Before the talk, they gave me a half hour of solo time, stationed in a side room. I spent it looking out a window at the lawn beyond, watching the patterns of Southern light shimmer and shift. When the time drew close, Gabrielle came to fetch me.

"How are we feeling?"

"I think okay, actually," I said. "This has been weirdly enjoyable."

She smiled. "Everyone is buzzing about you."

"Really?"

"I shouldn't say any of this. Famous last words, right? But things are not looking great for the other two candidates. The first guy we brought out, people liked, but no one was obsessed with him. We knew he'd be solid and he was. But word is he's up for a job at Northwestern and is probably looking for a counteroffer for leverage. And I don't think anyone wants to waste our time getting drawn into that. The second candidate was great, really smart, but she blew the visit and just kind of fell apart. She's green. She'll be ready in another year or two. Please do not tell anyone I said any of this," she laughed, "or I'll be looking for a job. But things are going exceptionally well for you. I think this last part will be fun."

And it was. The lecture went off without a hiccup. The questions were generous and interested, none of that performative nonsense from the audience. I'd been so deeply immersed in the book project it was easy to discuss. I could feel it, the way I used to be about this work, I was getting it back. Knowledge that would have ordinarily sent me into terrified hiding—I wanted this job, I really did—even that felt good. It felt good to want something that was right to want, and that could truly be mine.

Dinner wrapped and I thanked the committee members, all vigorous handshakes and big smiles. Sam said they would be meeting soon and he'd be in touch. He reminded me to send him receipts for cabs or anything else. Desiree, who was as brilliant as Gabrielle had said—I'd asked about her book at dinner and could have listened to her talk all night—said she'd get me back to the hotel. Once in her car, though, she said, "Gabrielle did warn you that we're kidnapping you for the night?"

"She did."

"Fabulous. We're getting together at her place. I know you must be wiped out, but you can relax. This part is just for hanging out. A group did this for me when I interviewed."

"Sounds great," I said. "I'm all yours."

"Careful," she said, and then gunned it through the light.

Gabrielle lived with her boyfriend, an architect named Eric from Minneapolis who Desiree described as a "creamy vanilla milkshake." We were on the northern edge of the French Quarter; Desiree lived just around the corner. She parked on a narrow cobbled street, sliding into a space that seemed impossibly tight. An inch maybe on either side. It was a Friday night and the streets teemed with crowds shouting and laughing, drinks in hand. We entered a gate from the sidewalk and squeezed down a narrow passageway, the brick wall to our side laced in vines. We emerged into a courtyard, dozens of potted plants and votive candles crowding the ground. Strings of soft lights crisscrossed overhead.

"You made it!" Gabrielle clapped her hands together. "Welcome!" She waved us into a circle of low chairs where the rest of the group was already assembled. "Eric!" she yelled into the house; the door was propped open. "Grab that next bottle."

"We got a head start," Tommy said. I'd chatted with him and Claire, siting to his left, after the talk.

"This is where you live?" I said. "This is incredible."

"The place is really small, and it's kind of falling apart. But it's dreamy. The owners live in the front house. The wife's family has been here for generations. Amazing characters."

"Every time we're here," Claire said, "her landlord claims some other lineage. Who was it last time?"

"Something about Wynton Marsalis?" Tommy said.

"Right," Gabrielle said. "That her mother was a cousin of Wynton Marsalis's mother. Or her mother's cousin was?"

Eric emerged from the doorway—he was tall and thick, vanilla milkshake was right—a bottle of red in one hand and a pizza box in the other.

"You must be the guest of honor. Gabrielle says today went great."

"Don't embarrass him, Eric. You know academics can't handle praise."

"I think all we want is validation," Claire said. "But we picked a miserly profession that metes out the tiniest portions of affirmation, just one thimble-full every few years. So we're desperate for it, but ashamed of the need."

"Please," Tommy whined, "tell me I'm worthy."

Gabrielle opened the pizza box, pointing it toward me. "We figured you'd be starving after the dinner." I took a slice and she waved an empty glass in the air. "You want?"

"Yes, please." I hadn't had a drink since just that one in Cleveland—but I had done good work today. I would let myself enjoy the night.

"Have you been to New Orleans before?" asked Tommy.

"My first time. But I think I'm already in love."

"It does that to you," said Gabrielle.

"I'm meeting my boyfriend and some gays at a bar after this, if you want to come along," Tommy said. "See the Crescent City's seedy underbelly."

"So," Claire said, "how did it go?"

"Honestly, it was a really good day."

"What do you need to know?" Gabrielle asked. "We want to be helpful."

"Looking out for our other others," Desiree said.

"Desiree," Tommy said, "no," but everyone laughed.

"What's the 'other others'?" I asked.

"It was this whole thing a few years ago," Gabrielle said. "Desiree, you tell it best."

"Wait, I need a full glass for this," Desiree said, letting Gabrielle top her off, and then explained: A few years ago, in an effort to retain queers and faculty of color, the provost's office put some discretionary funds into social events to help foster community, though, Gabrielle interjected, they would have preferred the money itself. At the inaugural event, the provost, a white guy well into his sixties, made some opening remarks. "Because an old white man is exactly who you want welcoming you to the diversity luncheon, right?" Everyone laughed. "And he starts with something like, *We want you to know that the university supports its diverse faculty. Women, minorities*"—and Tommy cut in, "Minorities, like it's the 1950s"—and Desiree continued, "He goes, *and the LGBs*, tripping over the letters like he's learning the alphabet. And then says, with like this air of triumph, *and others*. Minorities, LGBs, and others." We all laughed again and Tommy raised his glass—"To other others!"

Another bottle was opened and passed around and I asked how long they'd all be in New Orleans. Desiree said she'd spent almost her entire life there. She left for grad school but got through her coursework and exams in just three years, and then came right back to write her diss.

"That's the way to do it," I said. "Where were you technically enrolled?"

"Berkeley," she said. "Oh as a matter of fact—someone from a few cohorts ahead of me is at Sawyer. Safie Hartwell? You must know her."

"I do." My voice caught, my throat suddenly dry—could she hear it? "Safie's wonderful."

"I haven't read her book yet, but I just got it. I can't wait."

"Yes—" it had come out and I hadn't even realized "—it's amazing."

"Please tell her I say hello. We didn't know each other, not really. She was done with classes when I started. But this woman was very cool."

"Mark, of course, was intimidatingly cool in grad school," Gabrielle said.

"I'm sorry, who was?" I asked, surprised, but grateful for the change of topic.

"You know everyone was a little obsessed with you."

"I have no idea what you're talking about."

"False modesty does not suit you," Tommy said. "It's not a good look."

Gabrielle turned to the others. "You know, NYU was great. But, god, people were so insecure they weren't at Columbia. It was like this inferiority complex that just bred a competitive vibe. And then Mark shows up. Twenty-two. Straight from undergrad, right?"

"That's right."

"And, no offense Mark—I mean I went to San Antonio—but he rolls up from some Florida school, and in seminars, he's running rings around all these people who'd gone to Yale and Brown. With MAs from Chicago. Like, seriously pedigreed. But he didn't care about any of that elite nonsense, or the politics of the department. Like he was actually there to learn."

"That is very novel," Claire said. "And as a person of serious pedigree"—we laughed at this—"it checks that people would be obsessed with you, and also unwilling to show it."

When Gabrielle had emailed about the job, I was shocked she even remembered me. I always believed people would forget me— the moment I left a room, someone might ask, *Was anybody here?* In grad school I felt perpetually out of the loop, like there was a secret way to be that everyone else somehow knew. If I'd been as focused and studious as Gabrielle claimed, it was only because I had so little else going on. But now I wondered, all these years, feeling forever on the outside of something, uncertain of how to get in—had I already been inside?

We talked about a TV show that everyone was hate-watching. A restaurant, not far away, that had closed after the celebrity chef's pastimes had been exposed. "Not just your regular white nonsense," Desiree said. "Grand Dragon–level nonsense." Eric joined us, told us about a new project his firm was working on. A housing complex for formerly homeless people in a neighborhood going through an intense wave of gentrification. The wealthy new residents had organized a campaign to stop the project, claiming it didn't fit with the historical nature of the neighborhood. "What do they know about the history of the Seventh Ward? They've lived there six months." We worked through another bottle and a second pizza.

Eventually, Claire said she needed to beg off and called a cab. Desiree walked her out. Gabrielle once more insisted she should drive me to the airport in the morning. I declined again but swore to be in touch if any questions came up after I got home. "About anything," she said. "Don't be shy."

I tagged along with Tommy and we headed deeper into the French Quarter. Street after street of restaurants and bars, no signs of the night slowing down despite the late hour. Balconies ran along the second floors, revelers draped over the rails, smoking, shouting down to friends gathered below, drinking on corners.

"You can just walk around with alcohol?"

"Literally you get them to go."

"What is this place? I feel like I've left America."

A drag queen in thigh-high patent leather boots, towering above the crowd, overheard and turned. She raised her arms as if balancing the world itself above her head. "Darling, you have. Welcome!"

We laughed. "I hate to be one of those people who shits on Ohio," I said. "It's beautiful in its way, it really is. But wow—I did not realize what I've been missing."

We arrived at a bar, rainbow flag whipping from the balcony, men everywhere.

"Tommy!"

A few of his friends were sharing a smoke out front. Tommy asked after his boyfriend, "Where's Brian?" but didn't wait for a reply. He grabbed the cigarette, took a small puff, and passed it back. "That's it! I quit!"

"Brian's inside," one of the guys said.

Another said, "Tommy"—but looked at me as he spoke— "you've been holding out on us."

I smiled. "I'm just in town for the night."

"A lot can happen in a night," Tommy said. "Join us for a drink."

"You go ahead. I think I might walk a bit more." Everyone protested, as if I were their best friend, shipping to sea the next day. "Tonight's been great, really. But I'm spent."

"Okay," Tommy said. "I'll allow it. But you had fun, yes?"

"I don't know if this is sad to admit, but this is the best night I've had in a very long time."

I wandered in no direction, letting myself get lost. It was warm out and humid. I liked it. The air clung to me, like it, too, was trying to convince me to stay. After an hour or so, exhaustion set in. It had been a very long day. I flagged a cab and gave the driver the address.

"My granddaughter graduated from there last year."

"You must be proud."

"She's got a lot of opinions, and is not afraid to express them. But she's got the brains to back it up. You're visiting?"

"I am."

"Did New Orleans treat you right?"

"Absolutely."

"Good, good. That's what we like to hear." He had the radio on low and the deejay announced the next track. "Ah, mind if I turn it up?"

"Please. Play me out."

He raised the volume and sang along as he drove. He had a sweet voice, low rich timbres. I watched the city roll by, logging each street, each corner, each person we passed. I wanted to remember it all.

The next morning, Saturday, I reversed my trip, flying to Dallas to connect for Cleveland. I thought to work but decided I had earned some time off. I got a coffee and beignet at the airport and then, passing a newsstand, spotted a paperback propped on display. A gothic murder set in the South. It had been a huge deal when it came out. They'd made a movie and everything. Claire had said something about it the night before. "You haven't read it?" she asked. "But it's about psychopathic gays, exactly your thing." I bought it. I read on the first flight, stared out the window. The second flight was delayed for hours, some kind of mechanical issue, and it was late afternoon by the time we left. When we finally boarded, I fell almost immediately into a deep sleep, before we even took off. I dreamt I was at my high school, but then in the dream I realized, it was not my high school at all. It was Cassie's. The halls were empty. I had the sense that the school was on break. I couldn't tell if it was winter or summer. The ceiling lights reflected against the glossy linoleum tiles as I walked up and down each hallway, as if I were surveying the building. I had something to do, but couldn't grasp what. I stopped at a wide set of double doors. Somehow I knew it was the cafeteria. I pushed the doors open. I stood outside in the bright afternoon light. Rows of tables on a kind of patio, thick green vines hanging from above. I heard a sound—not my name, but some other word that had to do with me. I turned to look. There at a table, smiling: Safie.

I woke from the dream and knew exactly what it meant. I couldn't leave things a mess with Safie any longer. I pulled out my phone. There was no service of course, but I wanted to draft a message right then, the glowy feeling of the dream still strong. I pulled up our text thread. The last message, sent from her, in December. The night of the Walton Walk, telling me to meet at her office.

Safie, I've missed you so much. I'm ashamed of my behavior. The night we broke up, Stephen called me a coward and he was right. I understand if you don't want to speak with me, but if you're open to it, I would love to see you. Please know the only thing as deep as my regret is my affection for you.

I slid the phone back into my bag and resolved, when I got home, I would send it.

I drove from the Cleveland airport back to Sawyer. It was a gray and dismal evening after the vibrance of New Orleans and I wondered how that place and this place could exist in the same reality. It felt like all of northeast Ohio had been wrapped in a shroud, blotting out color and life. A rainstorm broke out, battering the windshield with a hard torrent. I turned up the wipers. Visibility was shot. Traffic slowed and we crept along.

The storm did not ease up. The potholed parking lot behind my apartment was full of soupy brown puddles. I dashed out, fat drops of rain pelting me. I was drenched by the time I made it around the corner and into the building's foyer. I stood dripping onto the floor and couldn't help but laugh. What a welcome home. Fucking Ohio. I climbed the stairs, rewriting the text to Safie in my head. I wanted to make sure I got it right. I reached my apartment and dug around for my keys and noticed—in front of my door, a small puddle. I searched the ceiling—there had been a leak the year before. But there was nothing. It must be the rainwater dripping off me.

I grabbed the doorknob—it shifted under my hand and the door edged open. Had I forgotten to lock it when I left? I waited a moment and listened. Nothing, just silence. "Hello?" No reply. I eased in and turned on the lights.

There on the couch, folded over and unmoving, soaked through. "Tyler?"

He turned his head but said nothing. His eyes were swollen and though his face was wet with rain I could see he'd been crying.

"What are you doing here? How did you get in?"

He seemed smaller than I remembered, drawn in on himself. I took a breath and imagined myself cemented in place. The space between us was the one thing I could control: I can maintain this distance; I can keep myself from crossing this threshold.

"I didn't know where else to go. I had to leave. I didn't know what to do." His face crumpled and he started to cry. "I'm sorry."

I pressed my heels to the floor.

"You can't just show up like this."

"I know, I know." The words stuttered, caught in his throat. He looked small, tender, broken. His body shook, all of it at once. I had fantasized about this moment so many times, his return to me. In these many weeks of silence, all I wanted was to know he missed me more than he could bear. And now here he was.

"Get out."

He recoiled, like I'd raised a fist.

"What?"

"Leave, Tyler. Go away. Leave me alone."

"Please. It's Addison."

"Addison?" Rage swelled in me. "Your shit with Addison isn't my problem anymore. I'm done with this. I'm done with Sawyer—"

"Please."

"You're not going to fuck this up for me, Tyler. Get out."

"Mark, please." He was trembling, face frantic, searching the room like someone else might be there, someone who would help.

"Tyler—"

He cried out—"Addison's dead."

"You—wait, what?"

I dropped my bag and went to him. He buried his face, sobbing. He was sopping wet; he must be freezing. I thought back to the last time I'd seen Addison. We'd run into each once after Columbus. I was headed to a parking lot and saw him, walking alone. I froze in place. I'm not sure what I was afraid of, what I thought he might do. He stopped; across the distance, he raised a hand and nodded. A salute, a reprieve. What could have happened to him? I ran my fingers through the back of Tyler's hair, soft under the wet layers. His breathing slowed. He raised his face, eyes ringed in red, irises twisting green and yellow coils beneath the scrim of tears. He looked rubbed raw, like his skin would be sore to the touch.

"Tell me what happened."

"I'm not sure—I . . . We were in our room, hanging out. Things were okay. They were great . . . And then we got in this fight. It was stupid, I don't even understand how it started."

He trailed off and a dull pressure expanded from my gut and up.

"What?"

"I didn't mean for anything to happen. It just . . . I was so upset."

He burst into tears, a horrible rending sound. My heart slammed against my chest.

"Tyler, what are you talking about?"

"I killed him, Mark. He's dead. Please, can you help me? I killed Addison."

CHAPTER 13

I shut the engine and cut the lights. Black night and silence. "You're sure there are no security cameras?"

"I'm sure. They keep saying they're going to install them but never do it. It's been this whole thing."

The rain had finally stopped. We got out of the car. Students would return when campus reopened tomorrow, and Monday classes resumed. We crossed to a small path, avoiding puddles, weaving between a cluster of low buildings. They looked like they'd been built in the fifties, white brick and narrow windows. A sign above the entrance to each building christened it with a word, emblazoned on a bronze plaque: FAITH. GRACE. SALVATION.

Tyler noticed me looking. "They named all the dorms from the Bible. It's kind of weird, I think."

"I see." Before the school's secularization. How strange that I ended up here—although there was something Jewish about it, finding myself in a place I didn't belong.

"Nobody uses the names, we just say the letter." Tyler went quiet and stopped walking. He pointed, barely raising a hand. "This is it. P Building." I turned and looked. Over the entrance: PROVIDENCE.

I followed him around a corner to a side door. He pulled an ID from his pocket. I caught a flash of the photo—a girl's face, a sweep of red hair.

"Who is that?"

"Nobody."

"What do you mean?"

"Literally no one. My friend works in the ID office. He figured out a way to make fake bar codes. We found some random photo online."

Tyler swiped and the door popped unlocked. We pushed in. A light flashed on—"Fuck!"—I jumped—"Sorry." There was no one there. The lights were set to a motion detector.

We climbed the stairs. A light blinked on at the next landing, boomeranging off the thick glossy paint of the walls. At the third floor, another light flashed on and we exited onto a hallway. It smelled of mildew, cigarettes, weedy sweat. Worn industrial carpeting ran the length of it. No signs of life. Tyler led us down the hall. We stopped at a door, a small dry-erase board with Tyler's and Addison's names on top. A marker hung tied to a string. Across the faded remnants of old notes, someone had drawn a cock and balls reading a book. The book—*Das Kapital*—was upside down. Beneath the cartoon in blocky print: College is Hard. Tyler fished for his keys and found them. He pushed in and I followed.

He shut the door behind us and we stood still in the unlit room. A moment passed, and then another, as we waited perhaps for some intervention, divine or otherwise, that would set us down a different path. As my eyes adjusted, I could just make out Tyler in front of me, arms at his sides, white fingertips glowing. I wanted to reach toward him and brush my hand against his, as if to say, *Everything will be okay.*

Earlier at my apartment, after Tyler calmed down, I coaxed the story from him.

A group of friends had organized a ski trip for spring break. A family's house in Colorado. The trip had been in the works for months. Tyler and Addison were going, and Kennedy. She and Addison had been hooking up on and off all year. She'd pull away and then go back to him. But in December, just before the break, Kennedy ended things for good. She had been nice about it, Tyler said, but offered no explanation. She just wasn't into it. As more time passed, rather than getting over it, Addison had grown fixated on the idea there must be some reason. If he knew why, he could change things, make her understand that they could work. "I'd never seen him like that, probably because he's never been rejected. He has this spell he casts over girls," Tyler said. "Over everyone."

The day before they were set to fly, Addison backed out of the trip. Tyler tried to convince him to change his mind, pushing every line of argument: The others would think it was weird; the change of scenery would be good, he and Tyler could go off, do their own thing. Nothing worked. Addison was adamant. He asked the RA to let him stay behind, even though the dorms were closed. She wasn't sure; she might get in trouble. But, eventually, she agreed; everyone knew she had a crush on him. Addison swore not to tell a soul.

Tyler passed the days sulking in the house. He didn't care about skiing, he had only agreed to come along to spend time with Addison. In the bored and aimless hours, he started to worry. It seemed it would make things worse, being alone in the empty dorms. They were all meant to fly back together on Sunday but on Thursday Tyler made up some excuse. He packed and left.

He arrived on the deserted campus that evening. He hadn't told Addison he was returning, it would be a surprise. He got to their room but Addison wasn't there. Hours passed. He texted— something innocuous, *Hey what's up*—nothing to reveal he was back.

Tyler woke Friday morning to Addison's return. He had been hanging out with this girl from Kent State; he'd stayed the night. "I thought he'd be miserable, but he was fine, of course." They started drinking early, using Tyler's counterfeit ID to roam; it opened every building on campus, and they had it all to themselves. They'd hung out on the roof of the music building, wandered the creek that ran through the woods on the east side. They finished off a joint and a second six-pack in the auditorium. Addison had done community theater as a kid and tried to summon his monologue from a summer play. He stalked the stage, waving his hands and reciting the mangled lines, Tyler in the front row, egging him on.

Evening fell and they returned to their room. They opened a bottle of vodka and Addison ordered a pizza. And then he got a call, from the girl at Kent. She and some friends were going to a party. She gave the address, someone's house. Addison said he would meet them. Tyler was annoyed—"That's it, you're going out?" Addison said he could join them if he wanted. "Why would I want to hang out with a bunch of random girls in Akron?" Addison didn't think it was fair for Tyler to be pissed. The plans had been proposed the night before; Addison didn't even know Tyler would be around. "It's one night," he said. "It's not a big deal." He said he was going to shower to sober up. Tyler saw an opening and took it: They'd been drinking all day, it wasn't safe to drive. Addison was growing impatient with Tyler's insistence. On his way to the bathroom he said he appreciated Tyler's concern. "But you're not my mother. Or my girlfriend."

Tyler sat and fumed. He'd flown all the way back to check up on him and Addison wasn't even grateful. Suddenly, not even aware he'd gotten up, Tyler was crossing to the bathroom. "We never locked the door." Addison called out from behind the shower curtain. Tyler said nothing, just stood there. After a moment, Addison pulled back the curtain.

Tyler's arm snapped forward—"It just happened. I didn't know I was going to do it." The flat of his palm struck Addison square in the chest. Addison's feet sailed from under him and he flew back. There was a terrible crack as his head smacked against the tiled wall. And another sound, a snap. Tyler thought it was the curtain rod; Addison had pulled it down as he fell. "I picked up the rod. It was really awkward and heavy, like from the weight of the curtain. Water was spraying at me and I was just looking at the rod, trying to figure out where it had broken." He wasn't sure how much time passed before he realized the tub was filling up. Addison was covering the drain, the water rising around him. Tyler shut it off and for the first time looked at Addison, tucked into the corner as if someone had pressed him to it. His head was twisted at an impossible angle. His eyes stared, open wide, like he'd seen something he couldn't believe.

Tyler stepped forward and clicked on a small desk lamp. It tossed a cone of light across the room, angling over a bed abutting the desk. My breath caught. Addison's body was stretched across the mattress.

"You moved him from the shower?" Tyler had not mentioned this. He nodded, eyes cast toward the floor. I pictured him struggling with the heft and shook off the image. There would be traces of Addison's skin across the carpet, but that was fine. He lived in the room, there was nothing out of the ordinary about that. There was no external wound, so no bleeding, so no trail of blood. There might be carpet fibers in his skin, down the length of him, but it shouldn't be a problem.

"It's cold in here."

"They cut the heat to the whole building during the break. Addison was using this little space heater. But I didn't want, you know—"

"You did the right thing."

Tyler said nothing, just a snuffling sound.

"Are you going to be okay?" No response. "This is why you came to me. For help. So let me help."

He looked up. "Okay."

"Good. We need to dress him."

"What do you mean?"

"We need him in clothes. Pick something out. Something he'd normally wear. Actually—no. Where are his clothes from last night?"

"In the bathroom, I think."

"Get those." While I hoped for no trace evidence, any signs of how Addison had spent his last hours—drinking, smoking weed— could be helpful. "But cover your hands first." I had grabbed a box of sandwich baggies from my kitchen; they would have to do.

Tyler left for the bathroom and I pinched my eyes shut. No more thinking. I just had to follow the steps of the plan. Thinking could come later.

Tyler returned, Addison's clothes carefully folded. He held them in a stack away from his body. "I can't."

"Can't what?"

"Dress him. I don't know, I just don't think I can." He shook his head.

"I can do it." I took the clothes. "You'll be able to get into the basement?"

"It's open. I went down there when I got back. I thought maybe Addison was doing laundry."

"Okay. Go now."

He left and I looked around. I had often wondered about this room. I had even looked up the dorms on the college website. For photos, so I could better picture Tyler's life. His side was perfectly ordered, everything on his desk just so, a neat line of shoes at the closet. There was one poster, some soccer player suspended in air. And that was it; no other sign of who he was. It could have been anyone's room.

I crossed the narrow gap between their beds. Tyler had arranged Addison neatly along the mattress. He'd closed his eyelids and folded Addison's hands over his bare chest. A dark oval around the body marked the blanket; it had gotten wet and was still damp. Even in death, Addison was a thing of beauty. Perhaps more beautiful. The stillness brought out the sharp nose and straight brow. A small bruise bloomed on his cheek, marbled violet against the white skin. He must have hit something on his way down, a spigot or a knob. The light from the desk lamp traced the tight round curves of muscle. Under his hands, across the arc of his chest, a light patch of hair. It narrowed to a line down his torso, leading to a darker, thicker patch. Tucked beneath it, his penis and balls curled into one another, like soft pieces of candy. I bent in close. A powdery smell wafted off him, soap from the shower perhaps. It would still be some time before he started to reek, his insides breaking down. I noticed then, beside him, a pillow and a creased fold down the length of the blanket, and I understood immediately: This is where Tyler had spent the night.

I grabbed the plastic baggies, slipping one onto each of my hands. Addison's body had passed the peak of rigor mortis; the muscles were softening again, releasing the calcium that had started building up at death. I looped a foot through each opening of the underwear and then lifted his legs. Purple splotches like exploded flowers ran up and down the back of his calves and thighs. Gravity's pull on the blood cells. I got his jeans on and cupped his head. It was a heavy, somber thing. I slid my hand down to balance him and I felt the push of a bone against my fingers. A snapped vertebra. I shuddered at the thought that something so small could end a life. I pulled his sweatshirt around his face. I raised one arm then the other into the sleeves. A pair of shoes sat at the foot of the bed. I picked one up, turning it over, and brought it slowly to my face. I held it there, warm with his loamy scent. Imperceptible remnants of Addison—flakes of shed skin he'd never miss—flowed into me. I knelt on the floor at his feet and pulled on his socks and then the shoes. I tied the laces, two small, neat bows.

I was still on the floor when Tyler returned from the laundry room with a deep bin on wheels. He had explained they had them for move-in days, for carting things up from cars and into their rooms.

I stood. "Where's the sleeping bag?"

He pointed to a closet. "It should be on the top shelf. He never used it."

"Okay. Pack your change of clothes and I'll get it ready."

Across Addison's desk were the scattered remains of their day. Two plastic cups and a half-finished bottle of vodka. An open pizza box, a pile of crusts, abandoned slices congealing in their own grease.

"When Addison ordered the pizza, did the delivery guy come up?"

"No, he met him downstairs, outside."

"Just Addison?"

He nodded. I looked back at the desk. Something glinted and I bent closer. A smudged mirror, a rolled-up bill on top, and next to it, an orange prescription bottle. The Adderall.

Tyler stood watching me. "We crushed up some pills and snorted them."

"Clean this all up. Bag it all. And anything else from last night." I passed Tyler a trash bag I had brought from home. He picked up the bottle of pills. "Not that. Give it to me."

I put them in a baggie and into my pocket. I unrolled the sleeping bag across the strip of floor between their beds and folded it open.

"You're going to have to help with this part."

I stood at the head of the bed, Tyler at the foot. We slipped our hands under Addison. Tyler looked past me, eyes on the ceiling.

"Lift." Tyler's arms shook. We lowered Addison to the floor. "Where's his phone?"

"There." Tyler pointed to the desk. I picked it up and stared at it in the flat of my palm.

"What is it?"

"Nothing." I lowered the phone. "Is he right- or left-handed?"

"Left."

I slid the phone into the left pocket of his jeans. I zipped the sleeping bag around him. There was a small opening at the top. I stopped, watching for some movement, some change that would not come. I pulled the bag up over his face and pulled the drawstring closed. We lifted again. Tyler seemed calmer this time, with Addison's face hidden from view. He took the top half and I the bottom. I tucked his legs as we lowered him into the cart.

"Did you pack a pair of shoes for yourself?"

"Yes."

"And the bag of trash?"

He passed it to me. I set the bag into the cart, nudged into a corner, beneath Addison's feet. We stayed there for a while, long enough that Tyler finally asked, "What's next?"

I looked up from the bin. Tyler's face—frightened, waiting.

"Did you love him?"

"What?"

"Did you love Addison?"

He looked away, down at the floor, and mumbled his reply. Just my name—"Mark"—a softly whispered plea.

I'd thought we could haul the cart down the stairwell, but it was too heavy, the weight unwieldy. We would have to take the elevator. My heart raced as its doors opened to a small lobby, glass-fronted. But there was only us. We retraced our path to the car, less than a minute. I opened the trunk. We reached in and took hold. We had gotten a sense of the weight and positioned ourselves for leverage; it's amazing, really, how quickly a body can learn to do a thing. We hoisted Addison up and into the trunk. He made a soft thud and the car sunk under his weight. I shut the trunk and grabbed the bag of trash.

"I'll wait in the car. You take the bin back."

"Can't we just ditch it here?"

"The last thing we want is to be leaving evidence behind."

"It's just a cart."

"But it's not," I said. "You have to do exactly as I say. That's the only way this works." Tyler agreed, wordlessly, and headed back. I watched until he disappeared and got in the car to wait.

Earlier in the room, when Tyler left for the basement, after I dressed Addison, I had thought of running. I pictured myself going to my car, driving home, and getting into bed. I would pretend none of this had happened, that Tyler had never come to me. I would just let things unfold however they would.

But I didn't run. The thought of Tyler returning to the room and finding me gone, realizing he'd been abandoned—the idea of Tyler going through this alone was more than I could bear. I thought that when Tyler got back to the car, I could tell him this story. So he would understand I had chosen to stay. Through all this, I would be with him. And I thought of the other things I might say. That when I picked up Addison's phone from the desk, there had been two missed calls from his mother. That on our last night in New York, I had almost told Tyler I loved him. But I didn't, because I was too scared he wouldn't say it back. Now I wished I had said it anyway. And I hoped he had told Addison and that Addison had said the same to him. What were we protecting? What was there to lose? Everything, it seemed, and nothing.

But when Tyler emerged from the dark and slid into the car, all I said was, "Ready?" and started the engine and pulled into the night.

I drove us to an enormous, forested park, forty minutes outside of Sawyer. I had been there once with Stephen last summer, our early days. I'd forgotten until Tyler mentioned it—I had asked him about places off-campus Sawyer students might hang out. There were clearings in the woods and he said they'd gather for small parties, usually a few times over a semester. In the fall when the weather was still good, at the end of spring. "It's stupid," he said, "just another place to get wasted."

A small road ran along the eastern edge of the park and I followed it until we arrived at a parking lot. Tyler pointed. "Pull in here." I cut my headlights and rolled forward. There were tennis courts ahead. The tall towers of lights were out. We were well into the park, shielded from the road by the dark, enclosed on all sides by evergreen woods.

"Where are the trails?"

"They start behind the tennis courts, and go up that way." He motioned deeper into the forest. "Now what?"

"We'll get him out and take him that way."

"We have to carry him?" I nodded, and he protested. "It's wide at the start of the trails. You can drive up part of the way."

"We can't chance it." I'd checked the weather. Temperatures were supposed to keep rising, and the next few days should bring more rain. I was hoping it would wash away any trace of us but I didn't want to push our luck. "It's bad enough there'll be footprints. We don't want to leave any tire tracks, too."

"We could just put him here. We're nowhere near campus." A vibrato crack of desperation cut Tyler's voice. I didn't like it; I needed him calm.

"Tyler, we went through this."

I gave him a moment and then opened my door and got out. He followed. The air was cold, we were well into the middle of the night, past one in the morning. If anyone was there, there would be no way to see them. We would move as quickly as we could and be done with it.

As I popped the truck, I had an absurd wish—that we would find it empty. It wasn't, of course. The body was there, encased in the sleeping bag, just where we'd put it. We hauled it out and carried him past the courts toward the trailhead. The path ascended sharply, Addison weighty and burdensome in our arms. The outer fabric of the sleeping bag was a slick nylon and I had to dig in to keep it from slipping. I walked backward and Tyler navigated. His pale face glowed against the dark of the woods. The path crested and continued up to the right. A smaller path forked to the left. Tyler nodded his head. "That way."

We were deep in the park now, enclosed in a thicket of massive hemlocks blackened by the night. In their terrible reach, the trees blotted out the sky. As we moved in, I strained to listen and could hear the sound of it growing louder: the rushing waters of the river below. The path emptied onto a clearing and Tyler stopped. Remnants from past gatherings littered the ground, plastic trash bags weighted down with melted snow, a pile of cans and bottles.

"This is it."

We lowered Addison and as the body touched the ground Tyler leapt back, as if surprised. We paused a minute, catching our breath, and then Tyler led me past some trees, to a smaller clearing. My arms ached in the absence of the body's weight. We stood at the edge of an embankment, a sheer drop of twenty feet, maybe thirty, down to the river below.

Tyler leaned to look. The lines of his body stretched before me and then out of nowhere, in a flash, I thought: with just one, quick shove, all of this would be over, I'd be free. I swayed—a sudden rush of vertigo—and grabbed Tyler's shoulder to steady myself. He jerked back, out of my hold, and I saw it in his eyes: He had been thinking it, too.

We returned to the sleeping bag and I unzipped it so we could take Addison out. I could feel Tyler at my side, watching. Stretched out before us, you could imagine Addison had simply lain down in the woods to rest. I heard a sound, some murmur and turned to look. Tyler held himself, weeping—soft moans, a plaintive cry. I waited a moment, then called him forward. We lifted Addison a final time. We carried him to the ledge. I rooted down, pressing my weight, and told Tyler to do the same. We were anchored in place, Addison hanging between us, like he'd passed out, like we were carrying him to bed.

"We need to make sure he clears it. Do you understand? We lift and throw on three." Tyler nodded. With the early spring melt, the river was swollen, whiteheads rushing past. I counted, my voice low. "One . . . two . . . *three*—"

We swung Addison out over the edge and released him to the air. Tyler gasped and turned away but I stood watching. Addison blinked from view and then a crash sounded as he hit the water. He landed close to midstream, away from the shallow edges and any branches gathered there on which he might get snagged; we'd done well. In an instant, he was gone from view, riding the currents below.

We walked back to the clearing. If needed, I wanted a plausible story of how Addison had ended up in the river. A night partying in the woods, a slip and fall. And hopefully, if he was found, it would be after enough time had passed that decay would hide the fact that he was dead before he entered the water. I dragged his sleeping bag through a small opening between a tangle of growth. I took the bottle of Adderall from my pocket, opened the baggie, and tossed it. It landed on the bag with the quietest thud. I returned to Tyler and we left the way we came.

I drove back to campus, returning to the spot I parked in just a few hours ago. Those few hours a split in time: before and after. From the back seat, I grabbed a trash bag.

"Okay, get out of those clothes."

Tyler wriggled in the passenger seat, pulling off each item and passing it to me. I placed the clothes in the garbage bag. I would do the same with my own when I got home, and then tomorrow, I would find somewhere to dispose of it all. When Tyler got down to his underwear, he stopped.

"Everything," I said. I turned my face as he slid from them. I knew I was being overly cautious, but I wanted no trace left on us of where we'd been left. He passed the underwear to me and then his shoes and socks. He looked small in the seat, naked, hands pinched between his knees, waiting. "Go ahead and get dressed."

When he was done, I reviewed our next steps. Tyler should clean the room thoroughly. In the morning, he was to text Addison's phone, ask where he was. Students would be returning to the dorms. To those who knew Addison had stayed behind—the group from the ski trip, the RA—Tyler would mention that he hasn't seen him. And then Monday he would talk to the RA again: He hasn't heard from Addison and is getting worried. "That's it. Don't say anything more. And don't put too much stress on it. Don't act more worried than you should be."

"Alright." He sounded far away.

"You have to put all of this out of your mind. It's the only way to get through these next days. You have to believe the story you tell—that Addison wasn't here when you got back. And that's it. And then you need to let me know as soon as you're contacted by any administrators or the police—"

"Police?"

"There's going to be an investigation. Addison is a missing person. Or he will be. That's why we can't stir up too much concern too quickly. Once things get going, that's it. These first moments are the only ones we can control. Do you understand?"

"I understand."

"Okay."

He sat for a moment. "I guess I should go now."

"Can I ask you something?" He nodded. "Why did you lie about the Adderall?"

"I didn't. I told you, we did some lines of it."

"Not tonight. Months ago. That story about not having health insurance and Addison getting the prescription for you. You made that up. And about your family, about not having money." He said nothing, so I continued. "Addison told me, in Columbus. That you'd spent the break with your grandparents in Malibu."

"I know. He felt really bad."

"Addison knew about us?"

Tyler nodded again.

"Why did you lie about all these things?"

"I don't know, it just sort of happened. You assumed I didn't have money, and I let you believe it."

"What do you mean?"

"Remember when I told you about my soccer scholarship?"

"Yes." Of course I did—I remembered everything.

"It's true, I am on one. Not because I need it, just 'cause I'm good at soccer. But I could see it in your face—it changed what you thought of me."

"What are you talking about?"

"Like it made me different from what you assumed. Different from all the other rich kids at Sawyer. And I could tell you liked it."

"Liked what?"

"That I was some poor kid you were going to rescue."

"That's ridiculous. You didn't have to tell me all those stories."

"I think it's something about me," he said. "Like people are into some idea of me, but it's not really me. It's something they make up in their heads. So I was just, I don't know—trying to be the Tyler you had in your head."

We sat in quiet for a while, neither wanting to move. I didn't like what I'd heard, but I knew he was right. I wanted him to need me, I wanted to believe I could look after him. And all this time, he'd seen right through me.

"Okay," I said, finally. "Go in. Clean up and get some rest."

Tyler reached for the door but stopped.

"I did love him. I didn't want to, but I couldn't help it. And he loved me, too—I know he did. But he kind of loved everyone, I think. We hooked up once, last year, drunk after some party back at the room. I couldn't believe it was happening. It's like, I know it's just sex. It's not a big deal. But I had thought about it so much. What it would be like if it ever happened. We were kind of wasted and we passed out and when we woke up the next morning, my head was killing me but I was so happy. I felt so good. Like everything that usually stressed me out, soccer or my parents or grades, it didn't matter. It would be fine. That's what I thought—now everything will be fine. And I was just watching him while he slept—we were crammed together in my bed. And he opened his eyes and do you know what he said? He said—*Don't look at me like that, I don't want anything to change*. I felt so stupid. I just said I'm not looking at anything, or something like that. And then he goes, *What a funny night* and jumps up and gets dressed like it was nothing." Tyler paused, staring ahead, not looking at anything. "The ski trip was supposed to be special. For us. I really wanted him there—"

"I get it."

"He was supposed to be there. It was my birthday. I'm twenty now."

I moved through my apartment with the lights off. I stripped and stuffed my clothes into the plastic bag with Tyler's. I placed that bag in another, knotted at the top, to be safe. I showered, the heat as high as I could bear, and dressed. In the kitchen, I found a bottle of whiskey, untouched all these months. I poured, the amber liquid pooling in the dark. I pressed the kitchen window open. Cold air rushed in. I sat on the sill. There was nothing to see, just a great blank world. A half-smoked cigarette was tucked into a corner of the window's outer ledge. One of Tyler's from the fall, left to be finished later and forgotten. It was soggy from months of snow and rain, spongy between my finger and thumb. I brought the stub toward my mouth and touched my tongue to it. It tasted dirty but also like nothing.

In the silence and stillness, I finally felt the full weight of what I had done. What I had willingly, willfully gotten myself into. There was no turning back. Not for me, not for Tyler. It was the right thing to do, it had to be. If Tyler had called 911 right away, he could have passed it off as an accident. Addison had been drinking, a slip and fall was entirely plausible. But he had waited an entire night. And then came to me. When he needed help, he chose me. What choice did I have? Addison's life was over. It was cruel and unfair—but nothing could change that. What justice was served by Tyler's life being over as well?

I thought about Tyler, in the cold of that room, lying with Addison's body an entire night. Pathetic to be jealous of a dead boy, I know, but Addison had gotten what I wanted, what I knew all along could never be mine: Tyler's true affection, the heart of him. These past months—Stephen wanting me, me wanting Tyler, Tyler wanting Addison, Addison wanting Kennedy . . . is this all the world was? A chain of misplaced longings, never met?

But now, in some twisted, unbreakable way, I had gotten what I wanted. Now Tyler and I shared something no one else could or ever would. Something undoable. Finally, Tyler belonged to me and I belonged to him. And for this, I only had to sacrifice everything. I pinched the cigarette stub and flicked it into the void. A small price to pay.

I stayed in the kitchen the rest of the night and let my limbs grow tired and sore pushed against the window frame until the weak white sun climbed into a gray dawn.

CHAPTER 14

The next morning, Sunday, I drove west. I passed miles of shuttered shopping plazas, peeling billboards, strips of ribboned paper flapping in the wind. A barn folded in on itself like a collapsed lung. Forgotten towns and towns that were never known by anyone outside their borders. After fifty miles or so, feeling far enough out of Sawyer, I found a gas station. No one was there, no cars coming or going. I parked in back next to the dumpster, out of view of the street and anyone in the station office. I moved slowly, without urgency. I didn't see a security camera and there was nothing suspicious about what I was doing, but I wanted to appear relaxed and unconcerned. I pulled out the garbage bag with our clothes from the night before. I tossed it in.

I looped through the town. Most businesses were closed—if not permanently, for Sunday church. Signs announced homes repossessed by banks. Taken back for what? Families pushed from houses that would remain empty, unoccupied. No life would return here. I moved onto the next town, and then found what I was looking for: a giant orange sign announced a car wash. I cut the wheel and pulled in. A man rose from a metal folding chair and ambled in my direction. He was stick-thin, blue jumper hanging off him. I rolled down my window.

"What's your full service?"

"Prestige cleaning," he said, and motioned to a placard behind him. "Inside and out."

"Great." I passed him the keys and steadied my voice. "Would you take care of the trunk, too?" Would he be able to guess, just from looking in, its contents from the night before?

"Inside and out means inside and out."

In the office, I found a self-serve coffee station. I poured myself a cup and dumped in a plastic pod of half-and-half, and then another. Yellowish liquid pooled on the oily surface. I waited in the folding chair. A younger guy had joined the attendant and they shouted back and forth as they worked, jokey and light. "Darryl is crazy. I don't know why someone would listen to anything he says. Especially not her." They both laughed.

I was convinced some trace of Addison had been left behind. For Tyler, this was not a problem, they shared a room. But I didn't want any DNA linking me to him. I'd brought a towel in a plastic bag that I held in my lap as the attendants worked. When they finished and I'd paid, I smoothed the towel across the front seat. In case anything was still on me, I didn't want to taint the now-clean car. Back at home, I repeated my ritual from the day before, stripping and bagging my clothes and the towel. I would dump this in some other town, in another direction, tomorrow. I scrubbed myself in the shower under a burning spray. I emerged with raised, red skin. I filled a bucket with soap and scalding water, scouring every surface of each room of my apartment, digging into untouched corners, sweating in nothing but shorts. It felt good to work, to focus on just the square foot in front of me and then the next. I needed it all—my body, my clothes, the car, this apartment—to be renewed. Reset from what we had done.

Late Sunday afternoon. By now, campus would be filling up: the hallway of Tyler's dorm resonating with the exuberant shouts of return. I imagined friends asking after Addison, Tyler's face as he lied. I don't know if you could call it praying, but I repeated silently to myself in loops, *Please let him stay calm, please let him keep it together.*

Finally, that evening, my phone rang.

"I did it."

"Turn on some music, point it toward your door." He did as I said, the sound bursting across the line and then shifting, fading as he moved from it. "Do this any time you call me, okay?"

"Okay. Yes."

"Go on."

"I saw the RA. I told her Addison wasn't around. That I hadn't heard from him."

"And what did she say?"

"She kind of played it off at first, said I was worrying about nothing. I said it probably was nothing, but it seemed kind of strange. I asked if she knew anything. She acted weird, like why was I asking that."

"And what did you say?"

"I told her I knew she had let Addison stay in the dorms. That he'd been here all break."

"How did she react?"

"She got kind of jumpy and defensive. I think she's stressed about getting caught. She asked if I had told anyone, or Addison had told anyone else."

"Good." Eventually, she would have to admit that she had broken the rules and left Addison in the dorms. Her agitated energy would be a good distraction; it would pull the focus to her, away from Tyler. "Did she say what she was going to do?"

"She said she'd check with me in the morning. If he was still not around, she'd call his parents."

She had done us a favor. Once Addison's parents knew, wheels would be set in motion. But she was so concerned about getting in trouble she would slow things down to protect herself.

"What about everyone else? Your friends?"

"Honestly everyone is so self-absorbed. They just want to talk about stupid shit from their trips. They don't even care."

"Good. It will help things stay calm. You did well, Tyler."

"I'm really scared."

"I know you are. We just stick with the plan. Take each piece as it comes. Once they realize he's actually missing, they'll access his phone records, which will lead them to that girl from Kent. She'll tell them where they were supposed to meet that night and they'll go looking in that direction."

"Okay."

"And you're sure he didn't say he was with you when she called?"

"He didn't say anything about me at all."

I could hear it in his voice: He was still hurt. "That's good, Tyler. Get some sleep tonight. Talk to the RA again and just go about your day. You have class?"

"Yes."

"Great. Go to class. Act like your friends—be self-absorbed. You did what you were supposed to, you let the person in charge know. Let it be her problem. When you hear anything more, call me."

Time warped and slowed, dragging out the hours. I kept a small radio in the kitchen tuned to a local station that broadcast news, listening for anything about the park we'd gone to, the river, a body. Nothing. I watched my phone, waiting for Tyler. I made myself eat, small dry bits of tasteless food I forced down.

When my phone rang, I jumped and grabbed it before my mind registered the name on the screen.

"Mark, sweetie?" I almost hung up. "Are you there?"

"Mom, hi. You caught me by surprise."

"Is this a bad time? I just wanted to say hello. We haven't heard from you." She asked about my book and told some story about the neighbors and their lawn mower, complained about the new self-checkout stations at the grocery store that never worked. I stared at the window, mumbling replies. She said they were planning a weekend in Chicago, for a friend's birthday, but she was scared of the cold.

And then on the table in front of me, the other phone buzzed. Tyler's phone.

"Sorry, Mom, I have to go. I'll call you later."

"You're alright, though?"

"I'm fine. Just busy. I'll call you later."

"Okay, Marky. Don't disappear on us."

I hung up and flipped open the other phone.

"The dean of campus life called me in." Music hummed in the background. Good, he was listening, doing as I said.

"What happened? Don't leave anything out."

When Addison had not appeared by morning, the RA reached out to his parents. They were livid; they didn't know he had been in the dorms, they thought he'd gone on the trip. They called the administration immediately. When the RA came to tell all this to Tyler, she was shaken—she'd been reamed for letting Addison stay behind. The dean wanted to talk with Tyler. It was just him and the director of residence life, Tyler couldn't remember her name. "Melissa Something. Michelle." I said it didn't matter, keep going. The dean had asked some standard questions. When had Tyler talked to Addison last? Did he know why Addison stayed behind? Had Addison mentioned anything, about being unhappy, feeling depressed? Tyler answered all the questions, stayed with our story.

"It was short. I wasn't there long. He told me to be in touch if I heard anything from Addison, or from anyone. And that was it."

"Okay. This sounds fine."

"It's getting easier."

"What is?"

"Pretending I don't know where Addison is. Like he's just missing. It's like I'm starting to believe that he really could be anywhere."

The next few days passed without incident. Tyler heard nothing more from admin. The story had made the local news, but in just a few days it had been relegated to a short column of text, buried. The feeling of dread was fading. Like Tyler, I was beginning to believe the world of our lies.

I headed to campus to teach. I went a bit early, which I never did, but I needed to make copies of a poem for a class activity. I tried to think of what else we could do with the time but my brain went blank. It should be fine—campus was still; it was before the morning rush.

As I walked toward Walton Hall, I saw the first poster. On a board alongside outdated announcements for spring break trips and a flyer for graduation gowns. Addison's sharp, handsome face, grinning. The rest of the photo had been cropped, but you could see a stretch of blue cloudless sky behind him. Addison had one arm raised, across someone's shoulder cut from the frame. His father, perhaps. This Addison knew nothing of what lay ahead. This Addison's life opened to endless possibility, clear and infinite like the surrounding sky. Across the top of the poster: *Missing.* A number to call with information. A note about a reward.

The posters plastered every surface I passed—windows, walls, columns. Addison's face was everywhere. When Walton Hall finally came into view, I quickened my pace, willing myself not to break into a run. I slid into a side door, up two sets of stairs. I just had to make the copies, get to the classroom, get through class, and get out. I stepped into the copy room. I saw the bag, sitting on a table piled with boxes of copy paper, before I noticed someone with their back to me standing over the machine. That bag. Without thinking, I said her name.

"Safie."

She turned. Blinked once, and then again. "I see you've come out of hiding."

I was shaking all over, trying to contain it. "I needed a break from this place," I said.

She lifted her eyebrows, two perfect lines—how had I let that face out of my life? "Don't we all." Next to her, on a bulletin board: Addison's poster. I looked away, but not before she caught me. "Do you know him?"

I shook my head. "No. You?"

"No. His parents must be really important, even for Sawyer. They've practically enlisted the Air Force."

And then, because I didn't know what else to say, I asked if she was done with the copier. She looked surprised by the question, which made sense. Not because it was surprising that I was there to make copies but because it was a stupid and thoughtless thing to say.

"Sure." She grabbed her papers from the machine. They had gotten shuffled on their way out. It was a messy stack and she was trying to be quick about it, but it only made it messier.

"I heard from Stephen," I said. "Something about a bias investigation?"

She looked up from the papers and her face said something like *We should have stuck to photocopies.* "It's a nightmare."

"Well, I mean they can't really do anything can they? I mean, not really—"

"I don't want to talk about it. I just want it to be over. I want this year over and Kennedy out of my life."

"Kennedy?"

"Do you know her?"

"Safie, listen." I said, then stumbled. "Safie, I'm really sorry. I wanted to call. I didn't know—"

She sliced her palm flat through the air, cleaving the space between us.

"Let's not do this." She slid past me, to the door. "Take care of yourself."

I stood still in the empty room. The overhead light shut off and there in the dark, for the first time in these weeks, for the first time in years—how many, I don't know—I cried, a great torrent pouring from me, my body a cracked shell that could no longer contain the raft of my despair.

I went right to my car. I would email the class when I got home, cancel it. And then a buzzing ring. I jumped at the sudden noise. Tyler. I answered.

"I got called back to the dean's office. The police were there."

It was starting.

"Are you alright?"

"I think so. Can I come over?"

This will all be okay. This will all be okay.

"Yes. Come."

Tyler said I was making him nervous, pacing around. I sat.

"Okay. Go on."

"There were two cops there, and the dean. And this time, instead of the res life person, someone they said was a lawyer. She just sat there. She didn't say anything."

"They're trying to protect themselves, so they don't get sued. What happened next?"

"At first the dean just asked me to go back over what we talked about. And then the cops asked questions. Well, just one. One just sat there. The other one, his name was Detective Laurence I think. He gave me his card, I can check. He asked all the questions."

"Questions about Addison or about you?"

"Just Addison mostly. I said I would tell them whatever I could, whatever they needed."

"Good."

"They started out asking when I had last spoken to him, if anything seemed strange. That sort of thing."

"And what did you say?"

"Same as before. We hadn't talked since I'd left for Colorado. We texted a few times at the start, but then I didn't hear back from him. They asked to see my phone."

"Did they take it?"

"No, I just showed them the screen. The one who wasn't talking scribbled some things down and asked me to tell him the dates and times. That was all."

"Okay."

"They wanted to know why Addison hadn't gone on the trip. I said I wasn't sure. And they asked about what had gone on between him and Kennedy."

"What did you say?"

"I said it was hookups, that's all. I was surprised when he decided to stay in the dorms, it seemed random. I said he'd told me he wanted to catch up on some work and they asked if I thought that was the real reason. I said I thought it was a little strange and I had wondered if there was something else. Or some other person."

"Good." This is what I had instructed him to say. I wanted to create some mystery around Addison's decision to remain behind. "Did they mention anything about the girl from Akron?"

"No."

"Okay." Sooner or later, they would find their way to her. "What else?"

"They asked some questions about his family. I said they were great, that I was worried about them. And then they asked a bunch of questions about the trip. Who was there, what we did. Stuff like that."

They were trying to paint a picture of Addison's life, and maybe see if there was anyone on the trip he'd had conflict with. "Anything else?"

"Not really." He hesitated. "Well, they asked about Charlotte."

"What do you mean?"

"I guess they must have already talked to someone else from the trip. I don't know who."

"Why would anyone have something to say about Charlotte?"

"When I left Colorado, I didn't want everyone to know I was coming back here. I was worried they would think it was weird. It's like, when I brought up Addison on the trip they started ragging on me. Kennedy called me overprotective."

"So?"

"So I told them I was going home. I said some stuff was going on with my mom. And I guess someone, Kennedy maybe, must have mentioned it to the police."

"What did you tell them?"

"I said the same thing. That I went home for a few days."

"You told the cops you were in Charlotte?"

"Yeah. I figured I should just stick to what they already knew. It doesn't have anything to do with Addison."

Fuck. "Jesus, Tyler." How had I let this slip? I had gone through every detail of our plan again and again. But I had never asked what Tyler told his friends when he left Colorado. I just assumed they knew he came back to Sawyer. "They're going to find out you weren't there."

"How will they know I didn't go home?"

"When they talk to your parents."

"Why would the police talk to my parents?"

"Are you serious? Addison is missing. There's no evidence. And you're his roommate. They're going to check out your story."

"I didn't know what else to say." Tyler started crying, voice shaking. "Did I fuck everything up?"

"Shit." I stood up. "Fuck."

"Mark, please don't be mad. What should I do?"

"Let me think." We needed to come up with a believable story about where Tyler had been. And a reason he had lied.

And then it came to me—it was so obvious.

"You said the cop gave you a card. Do you have it on you?"

"I think so." He fished around in his pocket and passed it to me. Detective Daniel Laurence. Sawyer Police Department.

"Go back to the dorms. Stay there. If anyone comes by, don't answer. If anyone calls, don't pick up. Lie low until you hear from me."

"What are you going to do?"

"I'll call you later."

Behind me, the doors to the station banged open. Two uniformed cops pushed in, gripping the arms of a woman they pulled between them. She was in her forties, maybe fifties. Bloodshot eyes and sallow skin. Her hands were bound behind her back and she was yelling.

"These fucking cuffs are too tight. You're cutting off my circulation."

"The cuffs are fine." The cop who spoke was short, bulldoggish. She yanked on the woman's arm, making her yelp. "You need to quit jerking around."

"My fucking hands are gonna fall off."

The cop sitting behind the front desk, a young guy with a small face, pinched in the middle, nodded at the crew. "Good to see you, Stacey. Nice of you to pay us another visit."

"Fuck off." They pulled her down a hall and out of view. Her shouts echoed against the low ceiling tiles, muffled and useless. I approached the front desk. It smelled like microwaved food and disinfectant. The pinch-faced cop busied himself with paperwork, ignoring me. Finally, he looked up.

"Is there something you need?"

"I'm looking for Daniel Laurence?"

"Detective Laurence?"

Fucking cops. "Yes," I said. "That's right, Detective Laurence."

"Does he know you're coming in?"

"No. Is he here?"

"Slow down. Why don't you let me know what you need, and then we can take it from there."

"I'm here about the missing persons case. From the college."

A pause. "You work at the college?" I nodded. "Has Detective Laurence spoken with you?"

"No."

"And why not?"

"He didn't know he needed to."

He said nothing in response, just pushed his feet and rolled back. He got up and moved to a desk behind a low wall and conferred with someone there. A moment passed. He took his time walking back to me. He exited the booth and started walking down the hall. "Come this way." I followed him to a small windowless room. He motioned to a chair. "The detective will join you in minute."

I looked around the office. Gray hulking metal desk, a bank of filing cabinets against the wall. There was nothing of note, no personal touches other than a framed photo of a kid in a baseball uniform, holding a bat. I rehearsed what I would say, playing it over in my head to look for any gaps. This fuckup with Tyler had thrown me. I was drumming my hand against my thigh, quick staccato slaps; I made a fist to stop myself.

Someone stepped into the room, already talking.

"Don't get up." He stood over me, looming in a gray suit. "Daniel Laurence. Sorry to keep you waiting."

I nodded. "Mark Lausson."

He sat and leaned back behind his desk, spilling into the space behind him.

"What brings you in tonight, Mr. Lausson? Or is it Dr. Lausson? My colleague says you're from Sawyer?"

"Yes, I teach there. Either is fine."

"We don't deal with the school very much. They have their own police force now. I guess the parents figure they're paying enough."

"I guess so."

"But they do us the courtesy of calling us in for the bigger matters."

"That's why I'm here. About the missing student. Addison Mitchell."

Laurence bobbed his head, once, twice, like he was thinking it over.

"I understand you came in asking for me by name?"

"That's right. I got your card from Addison's roommate."

Laurence tipped forward. He flipped through a small notebook. He landed on a page and scanned it, or seemed to, humming to himself.

"Got it," he said. "Tyler Cunningham. Soccer player, right?"

"Yes. He's on the team."

"Tyler suggested you come in?"

"Not exactly. No."

"Alright. What then?"

I took a breath. This was it, it was the right next move—we had no better choice. "Tyler told you he went home to North Carolina to see his parents. That he left the ski trip early for that."

"That's right."

"Well, it isn't true."

"No?" Laurence paused, but I could tell it was not my turn to speak. He flipped around in the notebook and looked up at me. "Where was he then?"

"Tyler came right back to Sawyer."

"But that's not what he told his friends."

"I know. He lied."

"Why would he do that?"

"Because he was covering for me." Another breath, and then— "He was with me. We've been having an affair."

Laurence stretched back, looking past me. You could almost wonder if he was paying attention, he seemed so unbothered. Eventually, he lowered his head and spoke.

"I see. He's a student of yours?"

"Yes. Or he was, last semester. That's when we met. We started seeing each other in November. We stopped in January, but we started up again last week, during the break."

"Tyler seems like a good kid."

"He is."

"He did get a little skittish when we asked about leaving for Charlotte. I thought maybe he didn't want to talk about whatever trouble at home. But if I'm understanding, he didn't want to get you in trouble. I guess particularly not with some administrator there."

"That's right. But when he told me, I thought—I don't know. It would create unnecessary confusion."

"What kind of confusion?"

"About where Addison had been. Or who he'd seen."

"Seems like the two of them are pretty close."

"Tyler is really worried about him."

"Was Addison your student, too?"

"No, I've never had him in class."

"Look," Laurence said. "I understand it must have felt like a risk coming in here. I appreciate that. Whatever your relationship with Tyler, your personal business, that's not my concern. Tyler's an adult, you've broken no laws. And you're right. We would have sorted the details eventually, but you saved us that time."

"Tyler wants to be helpful. He just—he got scared."

"Understandable. Anything else?"

"No. That's it."

"Alright then. I think that's probably all we'll need. But let me know how to reach you if something comes up." He turned to a blank page and pushed the notepad toward me.

"Of course." I scribbled out my name and number and handed it back.

"One sec," Laurence said. He pulled out a stack of printouts and scanned. He flipped a page and I caught it—a phone log.

He looked up. "Tyler's records. I don't see your number, though, even back here in November, December."

They were already looking at Tyler. It was a good decision, coming in.

"I used a different phone with him. An old number."

"I see." He looked back at the records, running a finger down the page. "646 area code?"

I nodded. "That's right."

"Sawyer must seem really small after New York."

"Sometimes," I said. "Sure."

"We moved here from Philly at the start of the year. My wife's family is out here. It's pretty quiet, comparatively. Though not this week." He smiled and stood and so I did the same, confused by the abrupt end to our meeting. He grabbed my hand to shake it and then—"Oh, one more question."

"Sure."

"Has Tyler mentioned anything about a girl Addison was spending time with? From Kent State?"

They had traced the calls.

"No. I don't think so. Why?"

He shrugged. "Seems like Addison just picked up with her during the break. I guess he's a bit of a ladies' man."

When I left the station, I sat in my car and waited until my hands stopped shaking enough to get the key to the ignition. I drove home, eyes on my rearview mirror the entire way.

Tyler was still in my apartment, on the couch where I'd left him.

"What are you doing here?"

"I needed to know what happened. Where did you go?"

"I don't know how many times I have to repeat this. This only works if you do what I tell you. When I say go home, go home."

"I tried to, I swear. I just couldn't. I don't mean to upset you. I got up and then sat down again. Like three or four times. My feet wouldn't move."

I closed my eyes. The story had gone over well. The affair was just what we needed all along—a secret to distract from the true secret. And the news about tracking down the girl at Kent was good. A trail of breadcrumbs leading nowhere. Akron was forty miles away, in the opposite direction as the park. They would scour the roads and stops between here and there, searching camera footage, chasing a scent that never was. Everything was still okay.

"I didn't mean to snap at you." I sat next to him. "I met with the detective. I said you lied about Charlotte because you didn't want the school to know about us. And that you had been with me since you got back. That you didn't want to get me in trouble, and that's why you lied."

Tyler's face opened in surprise.

"You didn't have to do that. Get involved like that."

"I am involved. I don't have a choice anymore. You know that, right? I've helped cover up a murder."

His eyes narrowed and he yanked back.

"I'm not a murderer."

"Tyler—I didn't—"

"I'm not a murderer."

"I'm sorry, I know. Of course not. But I need you to understand how serious this is."

"You think I don't? I'm not a child. And I'm not a murderer. It was an accident. I was upset about the ski trip. I'd been looking forward to it all semester." He was getting worked up, face flush, eyes glowing. "I was really angry. But I didn't want this to happen."

"Okay, Tyler. I'm sorry. Listen. I fucked up. I should have thought this all through. But it's good, it's better. They know about the girl at Kent. They're going to be tracing those leads. And you have a perfect cover now. Us. We're the perfect cover. We just need to make sure our stories line up. If they talk to you again, you've been having an affair with me since November. We stopped it in January. You left the ski trip to come here, to start again. You came back to surprise me, not Addison. You stayed with me until Sunday morning. You went back to the dorms and your room was empty. Got it?"

He nodded but said nothing.

"We can't afford any more slips in the story. We get one chance to change it, and we've used it. They need to believe you."

"Well, if anything, we know I'm a good liar."

"What do you mean?"

"You bought it all, right? About my family. About the Adderall. I had you convinced."

"You did." He was mad at me, I could see it. He wanted to hurt me.

"So don't worry. I know how to get people to trust me."

"Okay, then. No more lies. Did you have something to do with Kennedy filing a complaint against Safie?"

He blinked and that was it—the smallest tell. If I hadn't been looking for it, I wouldn't have noticed.

"Kennedy was really struggling in her class. I mean, I love Kennedy, but she won't do anything she doesn't want to, and the class became one of those things. And she was complaining all the time, just bitching about the readings and like, why did everything have to be about race. And I was fucking around, but I was like—you should file a complaint."

"What were you trying to do?"

"I just—I was pissed. Addison had gotten obsessed. Kennedy was all he talked about."

"So what? You thought she'd get in trouble? Or kicked out?"

"I don't know, I just said it. I thought it would blow up in her face and that would be it. And I was mad about that night at the party."

"What party?"

"When Addison and I crashed that thing on campus, the holiday thing. And I was talking to you and she was like lecturing me."

And then suddenly I understood when Safie had confronted him at the Walton Walk.

"You mean you were trying to get back at Safie, too?"

He shrugged. "It was just a joke."

"A joke?" I deserved what had become of my life, but Safie? I jumped up, filled with an instant rage. "That is so fucked, Tyler. So fucked. You've put Safie's career on the line."

"She'll be fine."

From the moment we'd met, he'd brought nothing but ruin. I hated him. I hated everything about him.

"You fucking brat."

Tyler looked up and just leaned into the couch, an almost-smirk on his face.

"Are you going to hit me?"

"What? No."

"But you want to, don't you?"

"Tyler, stop. Go home."

He got up and stepped toward me, closing the space between us.

"You can."

"I can what?"

"Hit me. I want you to."

"No, you don't."

"I do. I want you to hurt me. Look what I've done." He stared up at me, face gone blank. That face had been my undoing.

And then he raised a finger and jabbed me at my collarbone, quick and sharp.

"Shit." I jerked back. "That hurt."

"Good."

He lifted his hand again but I swatted it from me. He stumbled and caught his footing, never taking his eyes from mine.

"Leave."

He moved his head side to side. "No."

My body clenched; a jolt shot through me.

"Get the fuck out, Tyler."

"No." Again, he shook his head.

And then my hand flew into the air and whipped down across his face. He reeled back and hit the floor. He looked up at me, eyes wet and wide.

"Get up."

He started to stand and I swooped toward him, yanking him to his feet.

"Fuck—"

I seized the back of his neck, twisting his head and hissing. "Is this what you want?"

"Yes—" I tossed him backward and he slammed into a side table. Books crashed to the ground and his leg caught the lamp by the cord—it flew to the floor and shattered. I grabbed the collar of his shirt and dragged him, whimpering, to the bedroom.

"Stand up."

He stood, cowering, terrified, electric. The side of his face was bright pink from my hand. I slapped it again, a sharp whack. He yelped. His lower lip had split, a bubble of blood darkening.

"Take off your pants."

His hands scrambled to his jeans. He had them just to his ankles when I picked him up and threw him onto the bed. I flipped him over and yanked down his underwear. I climbed behind him and pushed his face into the mattress. I held it there and undid my belt.

"This is what you want?"

He moaned. "Yes."

I hit him across the back of the head and gripped his neck, the tendons pushing pack.

The rest took a minute, no more. After, I sat at the edge of the mattress looking away while Tyler dressed and let himself out. Only when he was gone did I realize what he had been saying, just barely audible, prone and unresisting beneath me.

"Thank you," he said. "Thank you. Thank you. Thank you."

CHAPTER 15

I woke up the next morning with a desperate urge to get out of Sawyer. I found a late flight and booked it and drove to the airport in the evening. On my way through security, I called my mother. "I'm coming to Chicago to meet you and Dad." She was surprised, of course. I made an excuse, said there was an archive at the university I needed to visit. A quick trip, but we could spend Saturday together, before their party.

It was a short flight, just over an hour, and I found myself hoping it would last longer. The claustrophobic hug of the plane soothed me. If only we could stay there, suspended in space, circling the Earth forever. At some point, I nodded off and came to as we approached for landing into a rain-shrouded city, the lights dull and fuzzed out below us. Chicago's vastness always shocked me, spread out across disappeared plains, comfortable and at ease with its own reach. I checked into a hotel a mile or so from where my parents were staying; I'd meet them in the morning. I scanned the room service menu but didn't have the energy to make decisions. Down in the lobby, in a mirrored corner, I found the bar.

I had a view of the entrance and, as the bartender fixed my drink, two women appeared through the revolving doors, bodies arced toward one another as they strode along. I recognized the intimacy at once: they were lovers. One seemed to be trying to convince the other of something, tugging playfully at her sleeve.

As they approached I could hear her coaxing. "One more. We're celebrating. It's too early for bed." She flashed a smile and I watched as the other shed the last of her resistance. She smiled back. "Just one."

The coaxing one pulled the other toward her, into the fold of her arm. She pointed beside me at the empty stools. "May we?"

"Of course." I shifted, making room.

"Don't move. You're perfect." She waved down the bartender and ordered two beers and then added, "And two shots of whiskey—" she looked at me "—no, three. Three shots."

"You don't have to do that."

"We're in this together. I'm Justine. This is Clara."

Clara reached across Justine and took my hand. "You'll never be rid of us now."

"Why would he want to be rid of us?" Justine asked. "He's been waiting for us, haven't you?"

"I guess I have."

Justine passed out the shots. Clara raised hers. "I'm a little tipsy. Did you tell us your name?"

"I didn't." I wanted to stay unknown to them. Someone other than who I was. "I'm Mark."

They were beautiful, both of them. Justine had dark cropped hair, the wide bridge of her nose jutting, eyes black and deep set. Clara's face was placid, almost plain. Lovely and still.

"Where are you in from?" I asked.

"New York," Clara said.

Justine laughed. "Have you noticed how nobody in Chicago cares about New York?"

"That young girl tonight—"

"What did she say? *I went to New York once. It was okay.*"

"It's kind of refreshing," Clara said. "What about you?"

"Ohio," I said. "But I used to live in New York, does that count for something?"

"Ohio," Clara said. "That must be interesting. Which part?"

I told them Sawyer and Justine's face lit up. "Do you teach at the college?" I nodded. "My sister went there. She's the smart one."

"What brought you to Chicago?" I asked.

"This woman," Justine said—and she rested a hand on Clara's arm; for all her bravado, she was gentle, and affection for Clara rolled off her—"just had a solo show open at the Art Institute."

"Amazing. What do you make?"

"She's a photographer. But that doesn't really do it justice. What did the review say?"

"Stop," Clara said, but she was smiling. She enjoyed it, basking in Justine's adoration.

Justine cleared her throat and glanced up, recalling. "*The play of light almost extends from the frame, dissolving the barrier between the photograph and the world it does not so much capture as . . . *Wait, what does it do?"

"Shut up."

"Expose?"

"Reveal." Clara shook her head. "Now stop."

"The world it reveals!" Justine grinned, triumphant.

"Enough of that," Clara said. "What are you doing in Chicago?"

"My parents are in town, for a friend's seventieth. I came to meet them."

"Look who's a good son," Justine said.

And then it clicked it into place. "I just realized who you look a little like," I said to Clara.

"Who's that?" she asked.

"My sister Cassie."

"Cassie." She rolled her mouth around the word, tasting the sound of it. "A lovely name." It was something in her eyes. And the bend of her lips. A sly lift that let you know she was thinking more than she said. "Is she staying here, too?" At the question, I felt a knot tighten in my chest.

"Text her to come have a drink." Justine swiveled in her stool, one hand cupped at her mouth. "Cassie!" she called out. "We're down here."

I pictured it: The elevator doors slide open, Cassie steps out and crosses the room toward us. Pushing the hair from her face with the back of her hand. Would she recognize herself in Clara? Would she recognize me?

"Sadly, she's not here," I said.

"That's a shame. Why not?"

"Well—" I hesitated. "She couldn't get away from work. But I think she'd really like both of you."

"Of course she would," Justine said. "Next time."

"Yes," I agreed, and smiled. "Next time."

Some noise on repeat pulled me from sleep and as I came into consciousness I recognized it: the yap of a barking dog, shrill and insistent. From behind the wall against the bed. I pictured a small wiry thing, weaseled into the hotel by an overbearing owner. My gummy tongue filled my mouth, my head pounded. I peered at the clock on the bedstand. Just after six. I pulled open the curtains, woozy with the head rush of standing up too fast. Dim morning light eked through the window. Muffled sounds of the city waking—the hum of traffic, a sharp horn—rose up from below. I showered, choked down some aspirin. I dressed and headed out.

A hard cold hit me, but I liked it. I offered my body to it. The streets were opening to life, the day beginning. Couples and packs of tourists and food carts and buses and taxis and bike messengers. After the emptiness of Sawyer, Chicago's streets surged. A young kid walked between his parents, holding a hand of each one. The mother nodded along to his story, the father scrolled through his phone.

Twenty minutes later, I was warmed up, even sweating a little. My parents' hotel came into view, a behemoth of stone and glass. I stepped into the lobby, vast and ornate. The ceiling soared and the grandiosity of the room unmoored me: the shock of human creation—that we had learned to carve the space of the world into volumes such as this. I felt myself almost lift from the ground . . .

"Mark?"

The sound of my mother's voice brought me crashing down. The lobby erupted in noise—a motorcycle screeching from the street, a man barking into a cell phone, two children arguing. I spun around, searching her out.

"Marky."

She was there in front of me, wrapped in a heavy coat despite the warmth of the room.

"Mom." I could hear the small child in my voice and I stepped forward into her arms.

We pulled back and she looked me up and down. "You're so skinny. Are you eating?"

"Of course I'm eating, Mom. You can't sustain life without food. Where's Dad?"

"Talking to the concierge." She waved behind her; he stood at the desk. "About god knows what. This could take forever." She laughed. "I just can't believe you came all this way for such a quick trip."

My father joined us, greeting me with a barrage of questions: the length of my flight, what airport did I land in, which hotel, how did I get there. These were the mundane details in which he dwelled, the mechanics of infrastructure, the certainty of driving directions. When I was young, these interrogations annoyed me. How did any of it matter? Now I found comfort in it, the questions a kind of loving attention.

I had mapped the day. Breakfast nearby and then to one of the city's oldest department stores. My mother had been there once, in her twenties, her only trip to Chicago; she wanted something for the evening's party, but kept insisting it wasn't necessary. She pulled her coat tighter across her so she disappeared into its puffs and folds. It must have been thirty degrees colder than Florida. We walked to the restaurant, my father announcing the streets as we passed. Michigan. Lake Street. Huron. At breakfast, they asked about work, about Stephen and Safie—they didn't know I'd lost them both. I made up details; I was getting good at that. I asked them to remind me of the friend they were seeing. "You remember him," my mother said. "They visited us. I don't know, you must have been five? Cassie said his breath smelled like feet."

It was rare for my mother to speak of Cassie and the scene came back immediately.

"I remember. You got so mad at her."

My mother blinked, her mouth set in a straight line. "I did not." I'd upset her without meaning to. She looked down and reached for a menu, opening it across the table, although we had already ordered.

We got in a cab after breakfast, my father arguing with me when I paid. The department store was housed in an art deco building, untouched by time. My mother dazzled at the facade, trying to piece together her recollection from so many decades ago. "Nothing in Florida is old," she said. "Well, besides the people." She laughed at herself and touched my father's arm. "We're old."

We deposited my father at a restaurant on the ground level; he claimed to be allergic to shopping, a joke he'd made a hundred times. He stationed himself at the bar, surrounded by other men whose wives and girlfriends had claimed some temporary freedom. My mother and I rode the elevator a few floors up—brass doors, mirrored ceiling. She trailed through the racks of clothes, pulling at items, commenting and asking what I thought. It was nice to see her worrying a bit about what she would wear. After Cassie, she had adopted a utilitarian approach to almost everything. Life, for my mother, became something to get through. But as I watched I saw she had softened over these years. There was a sweetness I'd forgotten about.

She found a dress, deep blue, simple but for a web of beadwork around the neck and shoulders. She swept her fingers across it.

"Gorgeous, isn't it?"

"It is. Try it on."

"I'm not sure I could pull this off." She hummed softly to herself. There was something in it I recognized: she wanted the dress, but didn't think she could have it.

"Come on, Mom." I grabbed her hand and pulled her through the aisles, searching out the dressing rooms.

"This will be lovely on you, I can already tell," the girl at the changing room said. My mother brushed away the compliment.

"I'll wait here." I sat on a bench. "Come show me when it's on." I couldn't recall when we had last done something together, just the two of us. She and my father were such a unit. They had each other; that was the one unchanging fact of their lives.

My mother's voice rose from the other side. "I don't know," she said. "Is it too much?"

The salesgirl waved me in. My mother stood in the wide corridor, facing a mirrored wall, eyes lowered to meet her reflection. She shifted at slight angles, holding herself in serious regard. The dress shimmered against skin browned from afternoons at the pool. Since retiring, she had taken to doing daily laps at the nearby rec center. Swimming had brought a youthfulness forward in her face, even as the lines of age deepened, crinkling her eyes and smile. I thought about her previous visit here, a young woman in her twenties, in the first months of dating my father; they'd be engaged in less than a year, no sense of what their lives would bring. There was so much about that time of her life I didn't know. It was the arrogance of the child, to presume the mother's life only begins with your arrival. She ran a hand across the soft swell at the middle of the dress where her belly pressed out, just barely. Her shoulders lifted and fell and her hand dropped away.

"You look beautiful, Mom."

She turned from the mirror, looking young and shy, and smiled. She paid for the dress and we made our way back through the mall, the shopping bag in my hand, hers resting in the crook of my arm. We'd gone in the wrong direction and were turned around. "They want you to get lost so you'll keep shopping," she said. We made our best guess and continued on. "I hope your father's not gotten too bored."

"He's probably made friends with half the patrons at the bar."

"He's like that, isn't he? I'm perfectly happy with a day on my own, but he likes to be social. I think you're more like me." She patted my arm, gentle puffs of cottony air. "But this was fun. I'm glad you came."

"I'm glad you got the dress. It's perfect on you."

"I wouldn't have bought it without you."

"I am always happy to help other people spend money."

She laughed. "Your sister was always so thrifty. I suppose she got that from me."

Cassie, again. I was surprised, but of course, I, too, never spoke of her—not to Stephen, not even with Safie. No one but Tyler knew Cassie had ever existed. And there was something in that—*your sister*. The words a gift, making Cassie mine.

"Was Cassie thrifty? I don't remember that about her." It's not something I would have noticed. I was too young, I wouldn't have known to recognize something like that.

"Of course. I remember taking her dress shopping for her bat mitzvah. Do you remember that dress? The pale green one, with the long skirt?"

I strained to pull the image forward. There were photos of the day, and though I could remember those, I tried to locate an actual memory of Cassie and the dress. "I think I do."

"She was a nightmare to shop with. Not you, you were always easy. But you think I'm difficult. Cassie would get so stressed about spending any money. It wasn't even her money. I said—it's one dress, it's your bat mitzvah. Let yourself enjoy this. And of course she thought everything looked just horrible on her. Teenage girls are so hard on themselves. All that beauty, and they have no idea." My mother's voice trailed off. "She was practically in tears, trying on the dresses. And I'm sure I didn't help. I would get so impatient with her. I remember being so frustrated she couldn't see what she looked like, and I thought I could convince her."

"I always thought she looked amazing. Even in that ugly army jacket."

"That jacket drove your father insane."

"She never took it off," I said. "—ah, we're here." We'd made it back without realizing. The bar was across from us. My father was talking with a man, somewhere near his age, also sitting alone. The man pointed at the television screen. A flash of uniforms.

My mother stood beside me, small and quiet and calm.

"I'm sorry we never did your bar mitzvah. I just—I couldn't. That year."

"Mom—" I grabbed her hand. "You know Cassie wasn't your fault." She flinched and turned her face from me. "She wasn't. I missed her so much. I couldn't believe she would leave me like that. I thought—if she loved me, if she really loved me . . . I was too young to understand. I'm sorry if I blamed you—"

"Mark, no—"

"I am. You didn't deserve that. Cassie was . . ." I stopped, searching the words. My mother's hand trembled in my own. "Cassie lived on her own plane of existence. She didn't belong with us no matter how much we wanted her to. I know she was hard. But you were a good mother. You gave her your love. It wasn't your fault if she couldn't take it. You offered it. That's all we can do."

My mother looked at me and then away, milky eyes shining. Music played from a speaker overhead, the percussion mixing with the thrum of the crowd. She started to speak then turned toward the restaurant.

"We should go find your father," she said, "before he loses his mind wondering where we are."

We couldn't decide what to do with the rest of the afternoon. My mother was too cold to wander outside and my father bristled at the idea of a museum. I would usually get irritated by his silent inflexibility, her refusal to just say what she wanted. But I didn't mind. I was happy to be with them. And then I spotted one of those covered double-decker tour buses. "Come on," I said, already crossing the street.

I paid for our tickets and we climbed the narrow steps to the second level. The driver, deep voice rolling and showy, pointed out landmarks as we circled Chicago's blocks, telling tales of mobsters and the Great Fire. Lake Michigan bloomed into view—massive, still, steel blue. I thought of Stephen and his childhood on the Michigan side. I thought of the next person he would date, how happy they would be on their trips there together.

"Look!" My mother pointed out the window. A crowd gathered in the grassy fold of a small park, watching a young woman balancing in place on a unicycle. A rod perched on her head, a plate spinning on top. Next to her, a man on a stepladder added a second rod and then lowered another plate. He gave it a spin, setting it in motion. My mother turned to me, her face wide and glowing. "Can you even imagine?"

I dropped them back at the hotel before their party.

"What will you do tonight?" my mother asked.

"Just dinner and sleep. I have a morning appointment at the archives," I lied, "and then I fly home."

"I don't know how you do these quick trips. You must be exhausted."

"Dad, don't forget to take photos. I want to see Mom in that dress."

Back at my hotel, I ordered up food. My flight was early; I would just get up and go. I packed and showered and then sat awake in bed, playing through the conversation from the department store with my mother. Had we ever spoken so truthfully with each other? About

Cassie, or anything? And then I was thinking about the last time I'd seen Cassie, and what might have changed if I'd told my mother about it. Then, or now. That night in December when Tyler and I talked about Cassie—it wasn't true that I never saw her again. The next spring, almost a year had passed since she disappeared. I woke up in the middle of a night. There was a noise in the hall. When I went to see, a light shone from Cassie's room. I thought maybe it was my mother but when I craned to look, it was Cassie. An ash-gray apparition, gaunt in the yellow glow of her bedside lamp. She tore through her bureau with a manic energy, searching for something. Her shoulder blades like dislocated wings, almost slicing through the worn-thin fabric of her T-shirt. My heart was pounding and I hurried back to my room, springing on the balls of my feet, desperate to make no sound. I lay still in the dark, clenching my body, straining to listen until I heard the front door open and close. In the morning, there was no sign that she'd been there. I told myself—as I kept it from my parents, my mother tortured by unknowing—that I'd imagined the entire thing and Cassie had never come back. I hadn't thought of that night in years.

I grabbed my phone from the bedside table. I opened the browser, searching—and then found it. It was Saturday night, no one would be there. I dialed the number. The voice mail came on and then a beep.

"Hi, Susan," I said. "This is Mark. I'd like to meet with you. To talk about this complaint against Safie. It's important. I can explain everything."

CHAPTER 16

I had learned a lot over the years working on my book. Those stories had shown me the banal underside of murder, so that gruesome and unimaginable acts could be held close and understood. The research had prepped me to love Tyler no matter what he had done. (And, of course, the reverse was also true: My love for Tyler meant I would accept whatever he brought me.) I knew inside and out the machinations of these men's acts, including the ways they had hidden their deeds. The moment we left my apartment and returned to the dorms, and each step since, I calculated against what my research had shown me. The fake text from Tyler to Addison, how we moved Addison's body, what we told the police. I had been taught how to do this by those I'd studied. And we had done well, covering our tracks. An odd thing to take pride in, I suppose.

I understood one more crucial thing. I had hidden this from Tyler and did my best to hide it from myself. It was a necessary obfuscation that allowed me to keep going, to get through the days without losing my mind to second-guessing and paranoia. I pocketed it away but it was there all along, pressing duly, then sharp against my side. This knowledge I possessed but did not want: I knew that we would, in all likelihood, be caught.

I flew back in the morning and when I walked up to my building, the cops were there. Detective Laurence was on his phone. Next to him stood a shorter man stuffed into a blue suit. He looked familiar, probably from the station. In any case, he recognized me and said something to get Laurence's attention.

Well, I thought, there goes any chance for tenure.

Laurence spoke some last words into his phone and put it away. "Dr. Lausson," he said. "Good to see you again. This is my colleague, Detective Mike Hoffer."

"Nice building," Hoffer said. "My cousin used to live here."

"That idiot cousin? What's his name?"

"Not Patrick. Anne, on my mother's side."

"Go figure," Laurence said. His eyes lingered on my overnight bag. "Have a good trip?"

The two of them stood thickly planted in place, smug and certain of themselves and their belonging to the moral order of the universe.

"What can I do for you?" I asked.

"We were hoping you might come over to the station to talk."

I tried to stay calm, and spoke slowly. "Alright. My car is in back. I can meet you there."

"If you don't mind," Laurence said, "we'll give you a ride."

"Oh." My heart jumped, my breath caught, my throat went dry. Was I under arrest?

Laurence smiled, maybe guessing at my thought, maybe satisfied with himself at putting it there. "It's just to talk." He pointed at a gray sedan parked at the curb. "Shall we?"

I got into the back seat. We pulled away, my face turned to the window. The building I'd lived in for almost two years—Hoffer was right, it was beautiful, how had I never noticed?—shrank and disappeared from view.

*   *   *

They brought me to an over-lit room: faded linoleum floors, yellowed walls slapped with cheap, shiny paint.

"Go ahead and grab a seat." Laurence pointed to one side of a metal table and sat opposite. There was a low cabinet against the wall and Hoffer hopped on top, as if he were just hanging out, curious to watch what might unfold. Laurence picked up a small device from the table and turned it on. He gave his name and badge number, the precinct and date. He referred to me as the interview subject and asked me to state my name. I did.

"I'll be recording this. That's okay with you?"

I nodded.

"I'll need a verbal 'yes,' if you don't mind."

I should say no. I should ask for a phone call. I should stand up and walk away from this room and never come back.

"Okay," I said. "Yes."

"Great." He set down the recorder. "We had a couple questions for you."

"What about?"

"We're just trying to piece together the days before Addison disappeared."

"Okay."

"Was there anything else you remembered about Addison that you thought we should know?"

"I don't think so. He was majoring in economics? But I'm sure you know that."

"He probably inherited an interest in money from his parents. That family is pretty well-off. Although I guess that's not unusual at the college, is it?"

"No, it's not."

"Anything else?"

"Not that I can think of."

"I see." Laurence looked over at Hoffer and Hoffer gave a small frown in reply. "When we spoke, I asked if you knew Addison. And you said no, isn't that right?"

"I said he wasn't my student. But I'd seen him around. It's a small campus."

"It is. Feeling smaller every day, to be honest with you. But we heard you spent some time together. With his parents in fact. And Tyler. Back in November."

"Oh," I said. "Yes. I ran into them after an event at school."

"Right. A bartender remembered you. We confirmed with his parents. They had nothing but nice things to say about you." A beat. "And then after that, there was a party in January. Down in Columbus. Did that take place as well?"

I nodded.

"Sorry to be a pest," Laurence said, "but again, can I get a verbal reply?"

"Yes."

"So you did spend time with Addison. But when you came to see me the other day, offering your help, you implied you hadn't."

"I guess that's right."

"How come?"

"I don't know, I'm not sure."

"We were able to get over to Columbus and find a few kids who were at that party. Talked to a couple girls who recalled speaking with you. Met you on the porch?"

"I remember them."

"They said they had a good time with you."

"Actually," Hoffer cut in, "they said they really enjoyed talking to someone who wasn't a brain-dead meathead."

"That's right," Laurence said. "But then they saw you again, later in the night. Out in the street, having some argument with Addison. They said it got pretty heated. Do you remember that?"

"I do."

"Do you remember what you fought about?"

"It was nothing."

"It was enough to draw some attention."

"I decided to leave and Addison didn't want me to drive. He said I needed to sober up."

"Did you drive home that night?"

"No. I took a cab. I came back for my car the next day."

Laurence raised an eyebrow. "Good on Addison." A pause, and then, "I'm sure you're wondering how we came upon this information in the first place."

"No," I said, "I'm not."

"Come on, now. You must be a little intrigued."

"Not really."

"Fine, then indulge me. We saw your friend Tyler again."

"Okay."

"He's a real talker once you get him going, isn't he? Anyway, we just wanted to follow up with him. Since you tipped us off that he'd been in town after all. See if he remembered hearing anything about this girl from Kent State. Or anybody else Addison spent time with off campus. Townies, right? Anyhow, Tyler got pretty jumpy pretty quick. He seemed rattled. Started stumbling over his words, cutting himself off, backing up. It was clear enough there was something he wasn't saying. So I asked him what it was. And then do you know what he told us?"

He was toying with me, a cat batting a mouse. But he was waiting, so I answered.

"No, I don't."

"Any idea?"

"No."

"Tyler said we aren't going to find Addison because Addison is
dead." I held my body still, keeping my eyes on his. "Does that surprise you?"

"What kind of question is that?"

"It's the question I'm asking. But never mind—wait until you
hear this next part. Tyler said you had gotten stressed because
Addison knew what was going on between you two. You and him
sleeping together or whatever. And you started worrying Addison
was going to rat you out. That's what the fight in Columbus was
about, not how much you did or didn't have to drink. And that
during spring break the three of you had been in the dorms
together and you got in another fight with Addison. Things escalated. You pushed him, not really meaning to hurt him, but he fell
and hit his head. Some kind of bad luck fall and he died on the spot."

Tyler had done exactly what I'd taught him: bring your lies as
close to the truth as possible.

"That isn't true."

"I'm not finished," Laurence said. "So Tyler says that he wanted
to come to us, but you made him swear not to. Pressured him to
help dump the body. But he was having second thoughts, feeling guilty."

"He seemed really upset," Hoffer said.

Tyler was scared and I wasn't there to reassure him. The cops
had shaken him, freaked him out. He was unraveling, grasping at
straws. He didn't mean any of this.

"And he says this Thursday," Laurence continued, "he tried to get you to turn yourselves in. You told him to keep his mouth shut. You threatened him. And smacked him around to make the point. He was looking pretty banged up."

"Definitely," Hoffer said. "The side of his face was going purple."

"And a swollen bottom lip. You roughed him up pretty good."

"I didn't—"

"That wasn't you?"

"It wasn't like that."

Laurence considered this, tipping his head side to side. "Regardless, it's not very nice to hear, is it?"

"It's not."

"I'll be honest. I'm not sure that's how it all went down. It was too pat, all of a sudden this convenient story. A handsome professor taking advantage of an impressionable kid. I don't think Tyler's telling us the truth. Or not all of it."

"Okay," I said.

"But you know, I thought—it's kind of interesting, isn't it, that Tyler ended up with you? Maybe he's into professors. I think that's a thing."

"I think so," Hoffer said. "It's probably exciting for them."

"But of all the professors, strange that he found you."

"How do you mean?" I asked.

Laurence took his time opening a thick brown folder. He slid a sheet across the table. A printout of my faculty bio page from the English Department.

"Well, just looking you up. It seems like you're doing a book about gay killers and—what does it say?" He squinted at the page and read. "*Cultural discourses of sexuality and crime.* Interesting topic."

"We didn't have any classes like that when I was in college," Hoffer said.

Laurence looked over at him. "I'll never stop being surprised at the fact that some poor college let you in."

"Shut up," Hoffer said, but smiled.

"You know I'm just messing with you." Laurence turned back to me. "Anyway, you have to admit it's pretty interesting. A guy who devotes his time to studying gay murder cases ends up in a situation like this."

"Just because I'm working on that book doesn't mean I've killed anybody."

"I didn't say you had." He grinned. "Tyler did." He was enjoying this. And I almost admired it, the way he was stringing me along. He had me in the grip of his story; even I wanted to know what I had done. "But the thing about Tyler, there's something sort of odd about him. Off-kilter? I don't know how to say it. A wild kind of look in his eyes. Anyone could see it, I'm sure you did. And there was obviously something intense between him and Addison. I don't know if it was sexual or what—" he waited for a reaction, but I offered none "—and so it made me think. Maybe Tyler's done this. Killed off his roommate, for whatever reason."

"Or no reason at all," said Hoffer.

"Sure, that's possible. But I wondered, if Tyler did kill Addison, maybe it wasn't an accident. Maybe he planned the whole thing. So he's had time to think about how to pull it off and get away with it. And in that case, who better to go to than you?"

"I'm not sure I understand."

"I think maybe you do understand. Maybe Tyler's been planning this all year. And that's why he came to you in the first place. Because he thought, lonely prof stuck in this shit town, I'll strike up a relationship. Who wouldn't like the attention of a cute kid like Tyler? Weird, sure, but endearing. And Tyler's thinking, he's an expert on murder. I'll have his help when I need it."

Tyler after that first class, asking about my book. Me, flattered he was interested.

Laurence went on. "I wondered even about this fight the other night. I don't know you well but you don't really strike me as a violent man. So I thought, maybe Tyler picked this fight because he was planning to turn on you. Getting himself beat up so he can prove you're dangerous. Frame you for what he had done."

Tyler refusing to leave, goading me on.

"That's not true," I said.

"None of this ever occurred to you?"

"Tyler wouldn't do that."

"Which part?"

Laurence was trying to rattle me, get us to contradict each other. Already, against the force of his story, I could feel my memories of these months breaking apart, getting confused.

"Tyler cares about me."

"I don't doubt that. You know what they say—we always hurt the ones we love."

I looked down at the table. Without realizing it, I'd laid my hands across it. I saw my fists clench and open. I saw the edge of the folder, the recording device. My chest rising and falling beneath me.

"Now is there anything you want to say?" asked Laurence.

He reached toward me and tapped a finger, two short, quick punctuations.

"Yes," I said. "I want to speak with a lawyer."

* * *

It was as if I had flipped a switch, ending the charade this was just a conversation among friends gone sour. Laurence clicked off the recorder, slammed shut the folder, and leapt to his feet. He motioned at Hoffer and they strode to the door. "We'll be back. Don't go anywhere."

I was alone in the room. I closed my eyes. I inhaled and held my breath—trying to slow the fast, hard punching of my heart in its cage. After some minutes it started to work and I could think about what had just happened, what might happen next.

I wish I could say I remained silent from some instinct of self-preservation. If I'd ever had that instinct, certainly it had left me by now. No, it was for Tyler. I wouldn't betray him with the truth. In all honesty, I had wanted to confess everything. And not because I sought absolution. If that were to come, it would not be like this and not from them; they knew nothing about me and had nothing to offer. I wanted to talk because the desire to unburden myself of the past seven months, of everything I had seen and felt and done, burned within me, ferocious, unbearable. Waiting for them to return, I felt dizzy at the thought of finally speaking aloud my longing for Tyler and what it had done to me. I wanted someone else to know.

And as I sat there playing through the story of Tyler and me, what I would say if I could speak, I thought about this: that, in fact, everything Laurence said had already occurred to me. Some version of it at least. In the dorm room, looking at Addison's inert body on the bed, I wondered if it wasn't an accident, if Tyler had planned it. Was that why he waited, why he didn't call 911? And in my apartment, I am not sure the exact moment, sometime after I knocked Tyler to the floor but certainly before I dragged him to my bedroom—I thought, *Am I being set up?* By the time I had him facedown on the bed I didn't care if it was a setup, or if the entire thing had been one. What is love, after all, if not life's greatest setup?

But in the end, I wasn't sure Tyler could mastermind something so big—he was making impulsive decisions with no real sense of consequence; he was too young to understand how life is a series of choices best understood as self-limiting constraints. He certainly wasn't smart enough to plan the cover-up. That was all me. It was my idea to hide the body, after all, and to scatter a trail of false leads to make Addison's last hours difficult to retrace. When I found Tyler in my apartment that night, soaking wet, crying, terrified, what had he said? *I know I have to go to the police, but I'm too scared. I can't go alone.* And then he asked me to take him to the station, that was it. That was all the help he wanted. I was the one who convinced him it wasn't worth it. I told him he'd be throwing his life away. I promised I would protect him. When I finally got what I wanted—to know that Tyler needed me—it wasn't enough; greedy men and our insatiable wants. Maybe if I had listened, if I'd just given the help he asked for, only my company, if I had let that be enough—everything would have been fine. Maybe it was me who had set us up.

I was thinking about all this and then a strange thing happened. The door swung open. Someone stood there. Plainclothes, a stack of file folders clutched to her chest.

"Am I in the wrong room?" She looked down the hallway then back at the door.

Some noise came from beyond view. A throaty voice called out, "Coming through," and she stepped back, leaving the door open. Two uniformed officers appeared in the hallway. They had someone between them, pulling him forward. It was Tyler. His hands were cuffed behind him. The violet of his bruised cheek shone garish and beautiful. His hair was wild and frantic and his mouth hung open, like an injured animal. He turned his head and looked into the room where I sat. For an instant, our eyes met. My entire body seized; I was held in suspension. Tyler's mouth opened as if to speak, it seemed to form itself around some words—*Help me? I'm sorry? I love you?*—and then he was pulled away, hoisted really, down the corridor and out of sight.

I stared at the empty hallway. I did not think to flee. Where would I go? I had no life to which I could return. A moment later someone must have realized the door had been left open. I heard a muttered "Jesus Christ," and then it clanged shut, sealing me in.

PART III

wake abruptly from sleep. The HVAC system has gone out again. The heat presses on me like a block, thick and unyielding. The air is gamy, saturated with the breath and sweat of too many bodies in too little space. A strained muscle in my neck sings. I dig fingers into it, press and release. I shift to my side. The bunk creaks. Rough snores rattle beneath me.

I have no sense of the hour, if it is the middle of night or almost morning. Time here does not pass, it accumulates. I cannot shed it. Artificial light, acid white, cuts through the murky black of the cell.

I try to recall a dream but nothing comes. I have stopped dreaming in this place. All I do is wait—for the trial, for my fate. I let my mind wander; at least that's allowed. The day before, someone at lunch told a story about a carnival and it makes me think of that night with Cassie, at the fair. And I realize—my mother was right. It wasn't Cassie who had taken me on that roller coaster as I insisted. It was some friend. Of course it was. I don't know how I got the memory so scrambled, Cassie wouldn't do that to me. I cannot see the friend's face, it's blanked out, a blur. But now I am with Cassie. She's yelling at the friend. Cassie holds me to her, soothes her hand across the top of my head. She sends the rest of her friends on. We'll find you later, she tells them.

She leads me to a concession stand. My face is tight with dried tears. Cassie passes me a giant soda. Never have I seen a soda this big, the unexpected heft of it in my hands. The soda fizzes in my mouth, burns pleasantly in my throat as I suck down long, deep gulps. The icy coldness hurts my teeth, but I like it.

Cassie scans, looking for something. Come on, Marky, she says. Another stand. The bright sweet smell of oil and sugar. A sign announces ELEPHANT EARS. What is this? I ask, apprehensive. I've had enough surprises tonight. Just wait, she says. Cassie passes some cash to the guy. He says something I can't hear, but it makes Cassie smile. He hands her a paper plate piled with an enormous disk of fried dough doused in powdered sugar. It's too big for the plate and flops over the edges—and I get it. Elephant ears. The plate blooms spots of oil. We stand right there and eat. Cassie balances the plate in her palm. She tears a piece and offers it to me. I need both hands for the soda, I'm nervous I'll drop it, the waxed cardboard growing slick with condensation. I open my mouth and she places it in and pulls another bite for herself. We cannot believe how delicious it is, the dough hot and chewy against our tongues.

I ask if we should find her friends and Cassie says, *Let's just walk a while*. She has a hand on me, where my neck and shoulder meet, her fingers soft against my skin. Powdered sugar dusts the front of my T-shirt. The crowds stream by, currents of people effusive and loud. The lights of the rides and games sizzle, an explosion of blossoms or flames. The noise of everything mixes together, delirious shrieks from overhead, the tinny pop of music, the loud, playful calls of teenage boys rousing up customers at the arcade. The air is warm and sticks to us although it's late. The evening has held its warmth, saved it for us. We don't speak. We are together and that is enough. The world, lit up, swirls around us. We wander with no direction in mind. We are in no rush. We have all night.

THE END

ACKNOWLEDGMENTS

I wrote the first draft of *Providence* on Amtrak trains between New York and Washington, DC. This was just one leg of an absurd six-hour commute I made once a week for four years so I could keep my teaching job in Northern Virginia and my life in Brooklyn. I had no idea that the fall in which I started writing would be my final one at that job. A lot of things led to me quitting, but one of them was finishing that first unreadable (but complete) draft, which set in motion a tidal wave of desire. That job gave me the financial security and time (much of it on trains) to realize something wasn't working; I feel so lucky I got the opportunity to take a leap—what a terrifying, overwhelming joy.

I am truly humbled by the support this project has been given. Thank you to Claire Wachtel, whose generous and demanding questions pushed me to remain dissatisfied until we got this story where it wanted to go; Barbara Berger, for the care and editorial rigor and for shepherding this from a Word doc to a real thing; Melissa Farris for the sexy stunner of a cover—you really went for it, thank you! And everybody at Union Square for your labor and talents. To Robert Guinsler, whose unwavering faith and clarity of vision made all this possible—thank you so much—and everyone else at Sterling Lord.

Many people read drafts and gave feedback that essentially taught me how to write. This book would not exist without Svetlana Kitto, who put her foot down with me at key moments (when I didn't want to pick this project back up, and when I tried to put it down again). Thank you for your company and making me a better writer. To the world's greatest workshop group: Megan Milks, Rebecca Novack, Ayeh Bandeh-Ahmadi, Raechel Anne Jolie, Casey Plett, and Svetlana—I cannot believe I got to hang with such a brilliant crew. Bernadine Mellis for your perfect notes and Lawen Mohtadi for your confidence. Andrea Lawlor for your guidance, for making me feel this could really happen, for your incredible heart and generosity.

Thank you to Soniya Munshi for co-forging this path, what a gift; KayCee Wimbish, my number one favorite person to read books with; Dean Spade, I am blown away and carried by your belief in me; Matt Hooley, for taking my early attempts seriously and giving me the best advice (use fewer words); Every Ocean Hughes, our studio visits have changed everything; Matt Savitsky for showing me what a life of art and self-discovery can be; Patricia Clough for mentoring me in how to stay living; all my writer-friends for making Los Angeles home, but especially Cyrus Dunham, Rosie Stockton, Emma Ayers, Hannah Rubin, and Alisa Bierria; everyone at Lambda Literary, the 2021 Fiction Fellows, and Nicole Dennis-Benn; the editors at *Joyland*, *HAD*, and *Fence* for making me feel like a real writer; Alejandro Varela for the intro and camaraderie; Morgan Bassichis for your curiosity and commitment, you are an inspiration; Greg Goldberg, my sister; David Suarez, my Rachel; Allison Palmer for cheering me on for so many years. I am so grateful for all the friendships I found at CUNY and George Mason (especially Students Against Israeli Apartheid for giving me purpose) and the College of Wooster (which gifted me with a year back in my most conflicted, beloved state); and honestly, I'm grateful for the enemies I made along the way as well—thanks, that was the push I needed!

Thank you to my parents, Dave and Jeri, for everything, but in particular for nurturing my rebellious spirit and providing examples of how to change your whole life in your forties. To my siblings, Keith, Matthew, and Katie, and your gorgeous families, for putting up with my shenanigans; I love you all so much. Thank you to my chosen family: Rania, Katrina, Riley, and Kale Spade, Calvin Burnap, Colby Lenz, Liz Goldschmidt, and Dean—wow, how did I get so lucky? And to all the queer and trans writers and artists and activists and organizers (past, present, and future) who are making something beautiful out of this total shit-show of a world: we are everywhere, thank you.